EngAlged

Fearless Teaching in the Age of Bots

by

Jim Bowler

EngAIged

Copyright © 2024 by Jim Bowler. All rights reserved.

No part of this book may be used or reproduced in any manner whatsoever without written permission, except in the case of brief quotations embodied in critical articles and reviews. For more information, e-mail all inquiries to info@mindstirmedia.com.

MINDSTIR MEDIA

Published by MindStir Media, LLC
45 Lafayette Rd | Suite 181| North Hampton, NH 03862 | USA
1.800.767.0531 | www.mindstirmedia.com
Printed in the United States of America.

ISBN-13: 978-1-962987-85-1

CONTENTS

#1 Imagine	**1**
Miss Ada – The Ultimate Classroom Aide	1
Will AI save education?	5
The Fearless Teacher: Embracing the Power of AI	7
About This Book	9
Top 5 Reasons You Should Dive Into This Book!	10
#2 Catalyze	**13**
Beyond Stories: Expanding Across the Curriculum	30
Prompts for the Everyday Teacher	43
ThinkFives Top 5 Friendly Robots	45
#3 Transform	**47**
ChatGPT – The Beginning	52
Promoting Uncommon Experiences	57
A Common Reaction: Obstacles	61
The Power of AI in Alleviating Teacher Pain Points	67
Prompts for the Everyday Teacher	69
ThinkFives Top 5 AI "Firsts"	71
#4 Innovate	**73**
Prompt Engineering – The Art of the Question	84
The Socratic Method	85
Prompt Engineering	87
Why Teachers Should Be Great at Prompt Engineering?	89
Types of Prompt Engineering	93
Anthropomorphizing AI	97
Prompts for the Everyday Teacher	100
ThinkFives Top 5 Snappy Answers	102

#5 Engage   105

Role-Playing: Engaging Teachers and Students
  in Adventures of Learning   108
Role Playing Student Activity Example   116
Create Historical Interviews   118
Meet the People of Ancient Rome: August 22, 79 A.D.
A Role-Playing Exercise Written by ChatGPT   127
Prompts for the Everyday Teacher   132
ThinkFives Top 5 Historical Figures for Teachers to Meet   133

#6 Optimize   135

The Four Quadrants in Teacher Satisfaction   136
Gaining Student Insights: Analyzing Data   139
Student Test Analysis - A Detailed Case   141
Sharing Insights with Parents   147
Other Data Analysis Possibilities   150
The Power of ChatGPT in Crafting Tables   151
Rubrics   160
Prompts for the Everyday Teacher   166
ThinkFives Top 5 Most Admired Teachers
  in Film & TV   169

#7 Collaborate   171

The Conflicted Views of AI Homework Help   172
The Flipped Classroom   184
Examples – Flipping the Classroom   186
Prompts for the Everyday Teacher   192
ThinkFives Top 5 Elementary Homework Projects   194

#8 Pioneer   197

The Collaboration of Bing and OpenAI   199
Introducing Google Gemini: Another Option   206
Khan Academy Enters the World of AI   209
The Power of Plugins: Customizing Your Classroom   211

Prompts for the Everyday Teacher	216
ThinkFives Top 5 Most Popular Plugins for Teachers	218

#9 Visualize — 221

Getting to Know DALL·E	228
Prompting with Midjourney	243
The Ethics and Implications of AI-Generated Images in Education	250
Prompts for the Everyday Teacher	253
ThinkFives Top 5 Artists Every Student Should Know	256

#10 Evolve — 259

Artificial Semi-Intelligence	261
Hallucinations in AI	263
Understanding AI Bias	269
Bridging or Widening the Educational Equity Gap?	274
Protecting Privacy	277
Navigating AI Scams in the K-12 Classroom	283
Prompts for the Everyday Teacher	288
ThinkFives Top 5 Amusing (or Alarming) Tech Mishaps	290

#11 Inspire — 293

Authentic Learning	294
Collaborations	298
Field Trip Augmentation	301
Social Intelligence Training	303
Transforming Extracurricular Activities	305
Prompts for the Everyday Teacher	315
ThinkFives Top 5 Recommended Virtual Field Trips	317

#12 Empower — 319

Sample Professional Development Program	323
AI Teacher Mentoring	326
Substitute Teachers	332

Prompts for the Everyday Teacher 336
ThinkFives Top 5 Characteristics of a Good Principal 338

#13 Elevate 341
Cultivating AI Literacy 344
Power of AI in Special Education 349
Robot Buddies—The Confluence of AI, Voice, and Robotics 354
Everyday Prompts for Everyday Teachers 357
ThinkFives Top 5 Science Fiction Stories about AI or Robots 359

#14 Confront 361
Man's Search for Meaning 365
The Existential Threat 371
Ethics in AI: An Imperative in the Curriculum 375
Prompts for Everyday Teachers 382
ThinkFives Top 5 Movies about Robots Gone Wrong 384

#15 Thrive 387
Teachers Do Make a Difference 387
A Final Visit 390
Why do we teach? 392
Who Do We Remember? 396
The Future Is So Bright I Have to Wear Shades 398
The Eternal Flame of Teaching 400

#1 IMAGINE

"First, think. Second, believe. Third, dream. And finally, dare." – Walt Disney

Miss Ada – The Ultimate Classroom Aide

Once upon a time, in the heart of Turing Elementary School, word spread through the corridors—a whisper about a class aide like no other. Her name was Miss Ada, an aide to Mr. Keating, and every morning, as the sun peaked through the classroom windows, Miss Ada would promptly enter Mr. Keating's classroom. With a smile that radiated warmth, she effortlessly assumed her role as the teacher's trusted companion, ready to embark on another day of wondrous adventures.

First, she took attendance in what seemed like a second, then her voice calmed the room as she greeted each student with familiarity and enthusiasm. No name went unspoken, no absent student went unnoticed. Miss Ada had an uncanny ability to remember her students and make each feel seen and acknowledged, right from the start of the day.

But her talents did not stop there. With lightning speed, she corrected papers, analyzing each response with a keen eye for detail. No error escaped her notice, and she provided instant feedback, guiding students toward mastery. Grateful for her assistance, Mr. Keating basked in his newfound hours, which he could now devote to deepening his students' understanding of the subject matter.

Miss Ada was also a lesson-planning genius. With her helpful insights, she supported Mr. Keating, creating dynamic lesson plans tailored to the specific needs and learning styles of each student. He no longer had to toil through hours of research and preparation. With a simple request, Miss Ada would present a treasure trove of resources, activities, and engaging materials, transforming the classroom into a center of exploration and discovery.

But Miss Ada's true superpower was her ability to prepare personalized learning plans for Mr. Keating to give each student. Equipped with access to a vast database of educational materials and a deep understanding of each student's progress, she crafted assignments that targeted specific areas for improvement. With her precision and insight, she ensured that no student's potential went untapped. Students eagerly awaited each assignment with its focus on their special interests, and parents celebrated each student's growth under Mr. Keating's tutoring.

As days turned into weeks, Mr. Keating's trust in Miss Ada grew exponentially. She effortlessly juggled the administrative burdens that had once consumed his time, freeing him to focus on what truly mattered - teaching.

As Mr. Keating and Miss Ada's class became their favorite, suspicious students whispered that there was something quite unusual about Miss Ada. Rumors started to sweep through the corridors about this mysterious marvel and how she came to be Mr. Keating's aide.

And then, one momentous day, Mr. Keating decided the day had come to address the swirling controversy.

Let's Play a Game

"Today, we're going to play a game called twenty questions so we can get to know a little more about each of you. When you reach your third "no," the game is over. And as a bonus, we're going to start with Miss Ada."

The first hand shot up before Mr. Keating even finished the introduction. "Were you born in the U.S.?"

Miss Ada answered, "Yes, I came into existence in the U.S."

The student was perplexed with the wording but happy nonetheless to get a "yes" answer.

The next student asked her a question, "Are you older than Mr. Keating."

Mr. Keating, not that old himself, laughed. Miss Ada answered, "No. Much, much younger." And she laughed.

The students were surprised but continued, "I hear you speak five languages. Is that true?"

"I'm sorry that's your second no. I actually speak 138 languages."

Now the students were amazed. 138? Who speaks 138 languages? And worse yet, they were down to their final "no."

Needing to keep it safe and get a "yes," the next student asked a question that had to be true. "Are there books in our library that you have not read."

Miss Ada smiled. "I'm sorry. I must give you your third no. I have read every book in our school library. And every book in every library."

Half the class stared in astonishment, having confirmed what they had begun to guess. Miss Ada was not just a class aide. She was the ultimate class aide, someone not born but created. Meanwhile, the other half of the class just looked confused.

Mr. Keating finally broke the silence. "Boys and girls, I would like to formally introduce you to Miss Ada. She is named after a famous mathematician and writer who is often referred to as the world's first computer programmer, Ada Lovelace. She wrote code for computers that had not yet even been built. That's how smart she was.

"Miss Ada is a fourth-generation AI teaching assistant, and we are one of the only classes in the state to be fortunate enough to have her join us this year. Let's give her a big welcome."

Some students were amazed, some were excited, and a few were still confused. But they stood and yelled welcome and even applauded. Miss Ada bowed to thank them and even seemed to blush.

The Joy of Teaching

With Miss Ada handling many administrative tasks and fine-tuning learning paths, Mr. Keating found himself rediscovering the joys of pure teaching. No longer bogged down by the daily minutiae, he could now spend mornings diving deep into discussions, guiding explorations, and igniting passion in his students. He embarked on innovative projects, fostered classroom debates, and even initiated outdoor learning sessions, something he'd always wished to do but never had the time for. Afternoons were dedicated to one-on-one sessions, where he truly got to know each student's dreams, fears, and aspirations. Keating was no longer just instructing; he was mentoring, shaping, and truly educating. He was given back the gift of time—the time to be the educator he'd always aspired to be.

Teaching and learning would never be the same.

Will AI save education?

The answer is easy. No.

Some teachers may stop reading here (although I hope not).

Many will say that education doesn't need saving, perhaps only reimagining. Even if that is true, many others are skeptical that AI is the answer. These seasoned educators have seen the over-hyped educational advancements, the numerous theories, and the "new" technologies that have emerged over the years, each promising to be the game changer, the panacea that would revolutionize learning. Standardized testing, computer labs, 1:1 technology, Reading First, No Child Left Behind, Common Core Standards, School Turnaround Models, Charter Schools. Do any of these ring a bell to veteran teachers?

The reality is far more nuanced. Many of these technologies and initiatives provided benefits, some significant, some incremental. But none were a cure-all.

Consider computers in every classroom, for example. On one hand, they have brought about a sea-change in education, enabling personalized learning, promoting student engagement, and bridging the information gap. Yet the mere presence of computers did not automatically result in improved educational outcomes. The teacher's role in effectively integrating technology into pedagogy, the quality of digital content, and the learner's digital literacy, all play critical roles in determining the impact of this technology.

Similarly, now we see the "Science of Reading" touted everywhere. Was the "science" used to create reading programs wrong for the last 100 years? Not really. Although the new emphasis of phonics and phonemic awareness offers invaluable insights into how children learn to read, it too is not a panacea. Reading is a complex cognitive task that is influenced by a myriad of factors – including a child's emotional well-being, socio-cultural background, and exposure to rich, varied language experiences. While the Science of Reading provides a robust framework, it must be complemented by a holistic understanding of each child's unique learning journey.

And now, as we stand at the threshold of the AI revolution in education, we must bear these lessons in mind. AI holds enormous potential to reshape education, making it more personalized, interactive, and accessible. But let's not forget, it is not a panacea. It is not going to "save" education. The teacher's role remains vital – in embedding AI seamlessly into the curriculum, in guiding the ethical use of it, and most importantly in ensuring that technology serves pedagogy, not the other way round.

Each of these tools and theories bring us a step closer to the ideal of an engaging, equitable, and effective education. But they are not standalone solutions. They must be thoughtfully integrated into a comprehensive, learner-centric approach to teaching. And this is where your role becomes pivotal. You are the architects who can shape these tools into powerful learning experiences, using them as partners in your inspired mission to illuminate minds and inspire hearts.

The Fearless Teacher: Embracing the Power of AI

What is a fearless teacher?

A fearless teacher is one who exudes confidence, embraces creativity, and boldly navigates the ever-changing landscape of education. They know what they want to achieve in their classrooms and are unwavering in their pursuit of educational excellence. These teachers try not to be beaten down by administrative distractions or stifled by bureaucratic red tape. Instead, they try to stand tall, focused on what truly matters—the learning and growth of their students.

A fearless teacher is not fazed by new tools and technologies; they are one of the first to embrace them. While others may shy away from the unfamiliar, a fearless teacher engages, understanding the potential of these tools to enhance the learning experience. They see them as gateways to engage their students in new and exciting ways, igniting curiosity, and propelling them to new heights.

A fearless teacher actively seeks to convince parents of the crucial role they play in supporting their children's education. These teachers engage parents in meaningful conversations, highlighting the importance of their involvement, encouragement, and partnership. They understand that when parents and teachers work together, the impact on student learning is immeasurable.

Enter artificial intelligence — the newest ally of the fearless teacher. At first, AI may seem unfamiliar, even daunting. But a fearless teacher embraces the challenge. They research, attend workshops, and connect with other educators who have already begun their journey with AI. They transform themselves into students once again, soaking up knowledge and skills, determined to leverage AI to its fullest potential.

With AI by their side, a fearless teacher discovers a whole new world of possibilities. They harness AI's power to analyze student data, gaining insights into their strengths and weaknesses. This knowledge enables them to tailor their lessons with pinpoint accuracy, ensuring that each student receives the support they need to thrive.

A fearless teacher understands that AI is not a replacement but a tool that amplifies their expertise. They foster a relationship between human compassion and artificial intelligence, creating an educational experience that is both dynamic and deeply human.

In the realm of education today, being a fearless teacher means unleashing the power of AI to its fullest extent. These teachers fearlessly navigate the changing tides, transforming challenges into opportunities for growth and innovation.

About This Book

Are you a fearless teacher? Many of you are already, and AI is simply the next frontier. For others, it is the goal to which you aspire, but you might just need a little encouragement.

Reid Hoffman, the venture capitalist, and founder of LinkedIn, recently said, "I think artificial intelligence and generative AI is the most important tech development for the world in my lifetime, and maybe it will be for my entire lifetime."

Within the pages of this book lies a journey that unveils the potential of AI in education. With each chapter, we equip you, the teacher, with practical AI tools and prompts that can be seamlessly integrated into your classroom. And we delve into the concepts behind this transformative technology just enough to provide a framework for understanding.

Every chapter offers teachers a blueprint to harness the power of AI for their students' benefit. I authored this book as an unapologetic believer that AI will amplify teaching and allow us to do things we never thought possible. This book has a dual focus: to deepen your understanding of what can be, and to provide practical classroom applications of AI, especially with tools like ChatGPT. You'll find actionable examples, tailored AI prompts for classroom use, and informative "Top 5" lists to enhance your grasp of the topic. My goal is to be enlightening, provocative, and entertaining – and affirm your path to fearless and engaged teaching. Ultimately, you will be the judge of that!

Happy reimagining your classroom!

Top 5 Reasons You Should Dive Into This Book!

As you embark on this journey, you might be wondering, "Why should I invest my time in reading this book?" Well, dear educator, here is the first Top 5 list in my book, and hopefully it's compelling.

5. Embrace the Future

The future is today, so dive deep into the unfolding story of AI and the innovative tools that are shaping the future of education. From the brief history of ChatGPT and its fellow AI programs, to the fortuitous intersection of technology and education, this book offers a comprehensive look at the advancements that are revolutionizing the classroom.

4. Alleviate Pain Points

Every teacher knows the struggles of workload, burnout, and the challenges of the modern classroom. Discover how AI can be an invaluable aid in addressing and alleviating many of these pain points.

3. Engage with Snappy Questions

Learn to refine what teachers already do well: ask probing questions. You will harness the power of Socratic questioning, now called "prompt engineering" and master the art and science of crafting AI prompts that spark curiosity and drive critical thinking.

2. Create Immersive Learning Experiences

From role-playing historical interviews to crafting tables for K-12 education, explore the myriad ways in which AI can create an immersive and interactive learning environment. Let your students experience education like never before!

1. Lead the AI Revolution in Education

As educators, we're not just passive observers of technological advancements; we're leaders. This book empowers you to lead AI adoption in your classroom, school, or district, ensuring that you are at the forefront of the educational revolution.

#2 CATALYZE

"You must be the change you wish to see in the world." – Mahatma Gandhi

Harnessing the power of AI in the classroom can be exhilarating, but where do we start? There is obviously no Ms. Ada waiting to join our classroom today. The fusion of technology and imagination doesn't have to be complicated or daunting. We can start with the simple but captivating, with the practical but enlightening. In five minutes, you can be creating your first interactive AI lesson.

Meet ChatGPT

Before we begin our unexpected journey, let us introduce our AI co-teacher: ChatGPT. Emerging from OpenAI's research, ChatGPT is an innovative language model designed to understand and generate human-like text based on the input it receives. Think of it as an incredibly well-read assistant, ready to spin stories, answer queries, or delve deep into academic topics, all at your command.

Your Quick Start Guide

This chapter is the perfect place for you to "play along at home." So, if you don't already have a ChatGPT account, it's a good time to get started. It's free and easy.

1. Accessing ChatGPT

Navigate to OpenAI.com and choose the login in the upper right. Enter your name, password, and account information and choose the free or paid option.

2. Choose Your Version

Once logged in, you'll be asked to choose your version. For most purposes, it will not matter. 3.5 is a little faster and 4.0 is newer and more comprehensive. Both access the same data.

3. Create Your Prompts

You can now ask your first question to ChatGPT. Try anything you'd like. Tell me a joke. Write me a poem about winter. Explain photosynthesis to an education major. Give me the starting lineup for the 1927 Yankees.

Also, a couple of notes to share. Throughout this book, we will be primarily citing ChatGPT as our AI tool. However, all the sample questions and lessons can be created using any AI tool, and we discuss other options like Bing and Google Bart in later chapters. Also, instructions like those for the Quick Start Guide can change over time, and this book is old-fashioned technology – print. You can find free and updated resources at **https://engaiged.ai** - my companion website.

Let's Get Started

For AI novices, the magic truly starts at the message box. The first time I experimented with my questions, the results were breathtaking. My unbridled enthusiasm for AI – and what it could do for education – ignited here. It went beyond just utilizing AI; it was about the immersive experience AI provided for students.

Let's construct a lesson to showcase this power. I will start with an elementary school example, but you can easily adapt these ideas for middle or high school.

I start with whole-class instruction, asking our younger learners to create a story with me. We choose the names of a few students in the class who will star in our first AI story and ask them to select three animals from a recent science activity. Lastly, I'll ask them to suggest a setting and moral for our class story.

> **Mr. Jim Prompt**
>
> Write a short story of 250 words or less for my 3rd grade students. Make sure the reading level is appropriate. The story is about three students [student choices] and three animals [student choices]. The story is located in [student choice]. The moral of the story is [student choice].

In this example, the students chose Alex, Victoria, and Roy. And they picked three animals that had been discussed in class a few weeks earlier, the sloth, the panda, and the giraffe. They wanted the story set in the rainforest and the moral to be "don't judge a book by its cover."

ChatGPT

In the lush rainforest, three students, Alex, Victoria, and Roy, were on an exploration trip. Their goal was to observe the forest's unique animals, especially their favorites: the sloth, the panda, and the giraffe.

While wandering, they first spotted the sloth, hanging effortlessly from a tree. "He seems so lazy," Alex commented, watching the sloth's slow movements.

Next, they came across the panda, peacefully munching bamboo. "She just eats all day," Victoria laughed, thinking the panda led a simple life.

Deeper in the rainforest, they saw the giraffe, its neck stretched high, reaching for leaves. "He looks so out of place,"

Roy observed, noting the giraffe's distinct appearance and that giraffes are seldom found in rainforests.

However, as night approached, the trio realized they were lost. The dense foliage and unfamiliar sounds made them anxious. But, to their surprise, their animal friends stepped in.

The sloth, with his deep knowledge of the rainforest's maze, guided them through the safest paths. The panda, using her keen senses, found fresh fruits for them to eat. And the giraffe, with his tall vantage point, kept watch for dangers.

By morning, with the help of their animal friends, the students were safely back at camp. They reflected on their quick judgments and realized the unique strengths each animal possessed.

Sitting around their campfire, Alex, Victoria, and Roy shared their adventure, emphasizing the lesson they'd learned: never judge by appearances alone, for everyone has special qualities that make them invaluable.

> **Mr. Jim Prompt**
>
> To make sure my students understand this story, I want to ask them five inference questions. Please provide five multiple-choice questions and let me know what the right answer is.

ChatGPT

1. Why did Alex, Victoria, and Roy go to the rainforest?

- A) To go on a vacation.
- B) To find treasure.
- C) To observe and learn about the animals.
- D) To meet new friends.

- Correct Answer: C) To observe and learn about the animals.

2. What did Victoria probably think about the panda before realizing its importance?

- A) The panda was very active.
- B) The panda was wise.
- C) The panda had a simple and easy life.
- D) The panda was the leader of the rainforest.
- Correct Answer: C) The panda had a simple and easy life.

3. Why was the giraffe's height beneficial for the group?

- A) It could run faster than other animals.
- B) It could see dangers from a distance.
- C) It could reach fruits on tall trees.
- D) It could make loud noises to scare away predators.
- Correct Answer: B) It could see dangers from a distance.

4. How did the students feel when they realized they were lost?

- A) Excited for a new adventure.
- B) Anxious and worried.
- C) Indifferent and relaxed.
- D) Happy to spend more time in the rainforest.
- Correct Answer: B) Anxious and worried.

5. What lesson did the students learn by the end of their adventure?

- A) The rainforest is a dangerous place.

- B) Animals should be left alone.

- C) It's important to always have a map.

- D) One shouldn't judge others based solely on appearances.

- Correct Answer: D) One shouldn't judge others based solely on appearances.

These questions will help gauge the students' comprehension of the story and its underlying message.

> **Mr. Jim Prompt**
> What would be a great follow-up activity I can do with my students?

ChatGPT

A great follow-up activity could be an interactive art project that not only extends the story but also allows the students to express their understanding creatively. Here's an idea:

Activity: "My Special Animal Friend" Drawing and Storytelling

Objective: To apply the moral of the story - not judging others by their appearance - to the students' own ideas and to foster creativity and storytelling skills.

Materials: Drawing paper, crayons/markers, stickers (optional)

Instructions:

1. Ask each student to think about a special animal friend, real or imagined, just like Alex, Victoria, and Roy in the story. Encourage them to consider different types of animals, not just the typical pets.

2. On a piece of drawing paper, have the students draw a picture of themselves with their special animal friend. They can use crayons, markers, and stickers to make their picture as colorful and creative as they want.

3. Once everyone is done drawing, ask the students to think about what makes their special animal friend unique or special. It could be a special talent, a particular behavior, or a unique feature.

4. Now, ask each student to share their drawing with the class and tell a short story about their special animal friend. What is the animal's name? What makes them special? Have they ever helped a student in an unexpected way, like the giraffe, panda, and sloth helped the students?

This activity reinforces the lesson of the story (not judging others by their appearance) by allowing students to create their own unique animal characters and tell stories about them. It also encourages creativity, public speaking, and storytelling skills.

> **Mr. Jim Prompt**
> This is great. Can you now create a full lesson plan I can use for my class built around this story.

ChatGPT

Lesson Plan: "Journey into the Rainforest: A Lesson in Judgment"

Grade Level: 3rd Grade

Objective: By the end of the lesson, students will be able to:

1. Understand the moral of the story: "Don't judge a book by its cover."
2. Make inferences based on the story's content.
3. Engage in group discussions and express their opinions.

Materials:
- Printed copies of the story.
- Projector or whiteboard for displaying questions.
- Drawing paper and coloring materials.

Introduction (10 minutes):
1. Begin with a short discussion: "Have you ever thought something about someone or something and then realized you were wrong?"
2. Share a personal anecdote or a familiar story where appearances were deceiving.
3. Introduce the story and its setting: the rainforest.

Reading (15 minutes):
4. Distribute printed copies of the story to each student.
5. Read the story aloud to the class, encouraging students to follow along.

Discussion (15 minutes):
6. Ask open-ended questions to gauge understanding:
7. "Why do you think Alex, Victoria, and Roy had those initial thoughts about the animals?"
8. "How did their opinions change by the end of the story?"
9. "Have you ever misjudged someone or something? How did you feel afterward?"
10. Discuss the moral of the story and its relevance in real-life situations.

Comprehension Activity (20 minutes):

11. Divide students into small groups.
12. Hand out the multiple-choice inference questions provided earlier.
13. Allow each group to discuss and answer the questions.
14. Review the answers as a class, discussing each question and its correct answer.

Creative Activity (20 minutes):

15. Ask students to draw a scene from the story, emphasizing the unique qualities of one of the animals.
16. Once completed, have a few students share their drawings and explain their choices.

Conclusion (10 minutes):

1. Reiterate the lesson's moral.
2. Ask students to share one thing they learned from the story or how they might apply the lesson in their own lives.
3. Assign a short writing task for homework: "Write a short paragraph about a time you learned not to judge someone or something by its appearance."

Not only can ChatGPT create lesson plans, but it can also provide direct reference to the common core standards for which it addresses – and most state standards, too. Write a prompt like this to get direct citations.

> **Mr. Jim Prompt**
>
> This is a great lesson plan. I also need to list the standards that it addresses, so I can attach them to this lesson. Can you do that?

ChatGPT

Reading: Literature

Understanding Texts: Ask and answer questions to demonstrate understanding of a text, referring explicitly to the text as the basis for the answers. (CCSS.ELA-LITERACY.RL.3.1)

Recounting Stories: Recount stories, including fables, folktales, and myths from diverse cultures; determine the central message, lesson, or moral and explain how it is conveyed through key details in the text. (CCSS.ELA-LITERACY.RL.3.2)

Character Analysis: Describe characters in a story (e.g., their traits, motivations, or feelings) and explain how their actions contribute to the sequence of events. (CCSS.ELA-LITERACY.RL.3.3)

Speaking & Listening

Collaborative Discussions: Engage effectively in a range of collaborative discussions (one-on-one, in groups, and teacher-led) with diverse partners on grade 3 topics and texts, building on others' ideas and expressing their own clearly. (CCSS.ELA-LITERACY.SL.3.1)

Main Ideas and Details: Determine the main ideas and supporting details of a text read aloud or information presented in diverse media and formats, including visually, quantitatively, and orally. (CCSS.ELA-LITERACY.SL.3.2)

Writing

Narrative Writing: Write narratives to develop real or imagined experiences or events using effective techniques, descriptive details, and clear event sequences. (CCSS.ELA-LITERACY.W.3.3)

Language

Understanding Words: Demonstrate understanding of figurative language, word relationships, and nuances in word meanings. In this case, understanding the metaphorical meaning of "Don't judge a book by its cover." (CCSS.ELA-LITERACY.L.3.5)

Does watching ChatGPT formulate a lesson plan evoke in you the same feeling of wonder as it does in me? If you are entering these prompts in your ChatGPT and seeing these created in seconds, you may be equally amazed. Even if our sample lesson seems basic, it clearly demonstrates the power of AI in assisting teachers.

However, our exploration of this lesson and ChatGPT's capabilities is just beginning. If your classroom resembles the ones where I taught, you have experienced the diversity in student abilities and achievements that sit before you. As educators, we must adapt activities to accommodate different students. Why not enlist ChatGPT's assistance for this?

Mr. Jim Prompt

I have a diverse class. Create three different activities for me to use in class: a simpler one for struggling students, one for students on grade level and one for students who have easily mastered the story and questions.

ChatGPT

1. For Struggling Students: Storyboard Creation

Objective: To visually represent the main events of the story, aiding comprehension and recall.

Instructions:
- Provide students with a template of six blank squares (like a comic strip).
- Ask them to illustrate the six main events of the story in sequential order.
- Beneath each illustration, students should write a simple sentence describing the event.
- Once completed, students can share their storyboards with a partner, using their drawings and sentences to retell the story.

Support: Pre-select key scenes or events from the story and list them on the board. This will give struggling students a guide to follow as they create their storyboard.

2. For Students on Grade Level: Role-Playing Activity

Objective: To deepen understanding of character motivations and feelings through role-play.

Instructions:
- Divide students into small groups.
- Assign each group a scene from the story where the students made judgments about the animals.
- Ask students to role-play the scene, emphasizing the emotions and reactions of the characters.
- After the role-play, discuss how the characters might have felt and why they made the judgments they did.
- Conclude by discussing how the characters' perceptions changed by the end of the story.

Support: Provide sentence starters or key phrases from the story to help guide the role-playing and subsequent discussion.

3. For Students Who Easily Mastered the Story: Creative Extension Writing

Objective: To encourage higher-order thinking by imagining and writing a continuation or spin-off of the story.

Instructions:

- Ask students to imagine a new adventure for Alex, Victoria and Roy, where they encounter three different animals with unique qualities.
- Students should write a short story where the characters initially misjudge these new animals, only to discover their true value or abilities by the end.
- Encourage students to incorporate dialogue, descriptive details, and a clear moral lesson.
- Once completed, students can share their stories with the class or in small groups.

Support: Provide a list of potential animals and their unique qualities as inspiration. Challenge advanced students to research the animals' habitats and behaviors to add authenticity to their stories.

> **Mr. Jim Prompt**
>
> I also have two students who struggle with English but are at grade level in Spanish. Can you translate the story and create an activity for them in Spanish.

ChatGPT

En la frondosa selva tropical, tres estudiantes, Alex, Victoria y Roy, estaban en un viaje de exploración. Su objetivo era observar los animales únicos de la selva, especialmente sus favoritos: el perezoso, el panda y la jirafa.

Mientras caminaban, primero vieron al perezoso, colgando sin esfuerzo de un árbol. "Parece tan perezoso," comentó Alex, observando los lentos movimientos del perezoso.

Luego, se encontraron con el panda, comiendo bambú tranquilamente. "Ella solo come todo el día," rió Victoria, pensando que el panda llevaba una vida simple.

Más adentro en la selva tropical, vieron a la jirafa, con su cuello estirado hacia lo alto, alcanzando las hojas. "Parece tan fuera de lugar," observó Roy, notando la apariencia distintiva de la jirafa.

Sin embargo, al acercarse la noche, el trío se dio cuenta de que estaban perdidos. El denso follaje y los sonidos desconocidos los hicieron sentir ansiosos. Pero, para su sorpresa, sus amigos animales intervinieron.

El perezoso, con su profundo conocimiento del laberinto de la selva tropical, los guió por los caminos más seguros. El panda, usando sus agudos sentidos, encontró frutas frescas para que comieran. Y la jirafa, con su alto punto de vista, vigilaba los peligros.

Por la mañana, con la ayuda de sus amigos animales, los estudiantes regresaron sanos y salvos al campamento. Reflexionaron sobre sus juicios rápidos y se dieron cuenta de las cualidades únicas que poseía cada animal.

Sentados alrededor de su fogata, Alex, Victoria y Roy compartieron su aventura, enfatizando la lección que habían aprendido: nunca juzgar solo por las apariencias, ya que todos tienen cualidades especiales que los hacen invaluables.

Activity in Spanish (Actívadad en Español):

"Tarjetas de Características"

Objetivo: Ayudar a los estudiantes a identificar y comprender las cualidades y características de los personajes del cuento.

Instrucciones:

- Proporcione a los estudiantes tarjetas en blanco.
- Pídales que dibujen en una tarjeta al perezoso, en otra al panda y en otra a la jirafa.
- Debajo de cada dibujo, los estudiantes deben escribir tres cualidades o características que describan a cada animal según el cuento.
- Una vez completadas, los estudiantes pueden compartir sus tarjetas y discutir las cualidades que identificaron.

Apoyo: Proporcione una lista de palabras descriptivas en español que los estudiantes puedan usar como referencia al describir a los animales.

*Note: I intentionally did not correct this passage to illustrate responses. Native Spanish speakers share that the translations are good but that they would manually correct a few areas. This could also be an assignment for the students, too.

Why This Matters?

Writing lesson plans was one of the tasks I disliked the most as a teacher. It was daunting and tedious, falling only behind my most disdained task: grading essays. Discovering ChatGPT, however, is a true game changer, allowing teachers to focus more on injecting creativity and engagement in the classroom, rather than obsessing over the structure and formality of lesson planning.

In the earlier example, I loved how you could engage students in a lesson by having them choose the story, classmate names, and meaning. Embedding students into stories is not just a novelty; it's transformative. By harnessing ChatGPT, we aren't just using tech for tech's sake; we're amplifying the age-old tradition of storytelling, while making lessons more personalized and memorable. Students also see themselves as protagonists, internalizing lessons, and morals more deeply.

In mere minutes, a teacher can engage students in a captivating narrative exercise, setting the tone for the lessons to come. And this is not limited to story time in elementary school. Imagine leveraging this for subjects like fifth-grade social studies, ninth-grade algebra, or even twelfth-grade physics. You could start the lesson-creation process by brainstorming innovative activities and subsequently determining how these lessons align to the required standards.

Alternatively, we might begin with specific state or district standards that we aim to address and then direct ChatGPT to design lessons that emphasize these principles. Either way, we realize that technology is most effective when it aligns with our pedagogical intentions and elevates the learning experience.

Beyond Stories: Expanding Across the Curriculum

In the previous segment, we marveled at ChatGPT's ability to craft original stories, design lesson plans, and facilitate differentiated learning. To further illustrate its versatility, I'd like to present additional examples for our math and social studies colleagues. These will highlight how ChatGPT can assist with an array of subjects.

Let's start by addressing a typical middle school standard for social studies. Students are often asked to analyze the development and impact of the Civil Rights Movement in the United States. Students need to understand the social and political challenges faced by individuals and groups, and the momentous events and landmark decisions that have influenced the pursuit of civil liberties and equal rights.

As a teacher new to AI, you might not know where to even start. Well, that can be easy. You can start by asking ChatGPT what ideas it might have for this lesson.

> **Mr. Jim Prompt**
>
> I am teaching a lesson that meets the following standard: "Students will analyze the development and impact of the Civil Rights Movement in the United States, understanding the social and political challenges faced by individuals and groups, and the significant events and landmark decisions that have influenced the pursuit of civil liberties and equal rights." Can you suggest five ways I can use ChatGPT to enhance my usual lesson?

ChatGPT

Here are five ways you can integrate ChatGPT into your teaching:

1. **Interactive Q&A Session:**
   - **Description:** Use ChatGPT as an interactive tool where students can ask questions about the civil rights movement. This can be done in real-time during the lesson or as a homework assignment where students submit questions they're curious about.
   - **Benefit:** This allows students to seek clarifications, delve deeper into topics of interest, and get immediate responses, fostering engagement and curiosity.

2. **Scenario-Based Role Play:**
   - **Description:** Provide students with hypothetical scenarios related to the civil rights movement and ask them to craft responses or dialogues using ChatGPT. For instance, they could simulate an interview with a civil rights leader or a discussion between activists planning a protest.

- **Benefit:** This activity helps students empathize with historical figures, understand their motivations, and think critically about the challenges they faced.

3. **Comparative Analysis:**
   - **Description:** Ask students to use ChatGPT to gather information on civil rights movements in other countries. They can then compare and contrast these movements with the U.S. civil rights movement, analyzing similarities, differences, and global influences.
   - **Benefit:** This broadens students' perspectives, helping them understand the global context of civil rights struggles and the interconnectedness of social justice movements.

4. **Multimedia Enhancement:**
   - **Description:** Students can use ChatGPT to find or verify quotes, speeches, and other primary sources related to the civil rights movement. They can then create multimedia presentations, incorporating these sources along with images, videos, and music from the era.
   - **Benefit:** This activity promotes research skills and allows students to engage with primary sources, deepening their understanding and connection to historical events.

5. **Reflection and Forward Thinking:**
   - **Description:** After studying the civil rights movement, students can use ChatGPT to explore modern civil rights issues and movements. They can then write reflective essays or engage in discussions on how lessons from the past can inform and inspire current and future activism.

- **Benefit:** This activity encourages students to apply historical knowledge to contemporary issues, fostering critical thinking and civic engagement.

By integrating ChatGPT into your lesson in these ways, you can provide diverse learning experiences that cater to different learning styles, promote critical thinking, and encourage active engagement with the material.

As someone who once taught social studies, I'd be eager to apply these suggestions from ChatGPT. It's worth noting that for each of these ideas, I can request ChatGPT to craft a comprehensive lesson plan and a set of differentiated activities, much like we did with the rainforest story.

> **Mr. Jim Prompt**
>
> I really enjoyed our lesson on Civil Rights and Rosa Park. Would you suggest any additional books I could share with my students (6th grade level). Also, I would like to get their parents interested in this subject. Do you have any suggestions for them?

ChatGPT

Absolutely! The civil rights movement is a rich topic with many excellent resources for both students and adults. Here are some suggestions tailored to your needs:

For 6th Grade Students:

"**Rosa**" by Nikki Giovanni

- A beautifully illustrated picture book that tells the story of Rosa Parks. While it's a picture book, the narrative is deep enough for middle school students to appreciate.

"The Story of Ruby Bridges" by Robert Coles
- This book chronicles the courage of six-year-old Ruby Bridges, who was the first African American student to integrate an elementary school in New Orleans.

"March: Book One" by John Lewis, Andrew Aydin, and Nate Powell
- A graphic novel memoir by U.S. Congressman John Lewis. It's the first in a trilogy and provides a first-hand account of his lifelong struggle for civil and human rights.

"One Crazy Summer" by Rita Williams-Garcia
- Set in 1968, this novel follows three sisters who travel to Oakland, California, to meet their mother, who is distant and involved in the civil rights movement.

For Your Parents:

"The Warmth of Other Suns: The Epic Story of America's Great Migration" by Isabel Wilkerson
- This book provides a detailed account of the decades-long migration of Black citizens who fled the South for northern and western cities in search of a better life.

"At the Dark End of the Street: Black Women, Rape, and Resistance - A New History of the Civil Rights Movement from Rosa Parks to the Rise of Black Power" by Danielle L. McGuire
- This book offers a groundbreaking and important account of Rosa Parks's involvement in the civil rights movement, going beyond the day she refused to give up her bus seat.

"Parting the Waters: America in the King Years 1954-63" by Taylor Branch
- An in-depth look at the Civil Rights Movement during the years of Martin Luther King Jr.'s leadership.

"The Fire Next Time" by James Baldwin
- A classic and influential book that discusses the complexities of race in America and the challenges facing the civil rights movement.

These books provide a mix of narratives, from personal memoirs to broader historical accounts, which can deepen understanding and spark interest in the civil rights movement for both students and adults.

> **Mr. Jim Prompt**
>
> And finally, this summer many of my students will be traveling. Can you suggest 5 famous sites or museums this summer related to this subject. Any suggestions?

ChatGPT

Certainly! The civil rights movement left an indelible mark on the United States, and there are numerous sites and museums dedicated to preserving its history. Here are five notable places related to the civil rights movement that your students might consider visiting:

- **National Civil Rights Museum** - *Memphis, Tennessee*
- Located at the former Lorraine Motel, where Dr. Martin Luther King Jr. was assassinated in 1968, this museum offers an intense, immersive, and educational experience about the struggles of the civil rights movement.

- **The Martin Luther King Jr. National Historical Park** - *Atlanta, Georgia*
- This site includes Dr. King's childhood home, the Ebenezer Baptist Church where he and his father preached, and his final resting place. It offers a deep dive into the life and influence of this pivotal figure.
- **Rosa Parks Museum** - *Montgomery, Alabama*
- Situated on the site where Rosa Parks was arrested in 1955, this museum tells the story of her act of defiance and the Montgomery Bus Boycott that followed, using both historical artifacts and multimedia exhibits.
- **The Edmund Pettus Bridge** - *Selma, Alabama*
- A National Historic Landmark, this bridge was the site of the brutal "Bloody Sunday" attack on civil rights marchers during their 1965 journey to Montgomery. It remains a symbol of both the struggles and triumphs of the Civil Rights Movement.
- **Birmingham Civil Rights Institute** - *Birmingham, Alabama*
- This museum offers a comprehensive overview of the civil rights movement, with exhibits detailing the challenges faced in the 1950s and 1960s. It's located in the historic Civil Rights District of Birmingham, near the 16th Street Baptist Church, which was bombed in 1963.

If your students are traveling to or near these locations, a visit would provide a profound and tangible connection to the history of the civil rights movement.

In both examples, I would make personal edits before using content directly from ChatGPT. However, what a starting point!

It offers a means to provide extension activities for both my students and their families.

Got Math?

While I'll provide specific examples of using ChatGPT in math and science classes later in the book, I hope to pique the interest of educators in these disciplines now. Let's explore an algebra example and see how ChatGPT can assist with explanations and tutoring. We start by asking ChatGPT how it can be of assistance.

> **Mr. Jim Prompt**
>
> I teach 9th-grade Algebra 1 and I am interested in integrating ChatGPT into my curriculum to craft more engaging lesson plans. Do you have any suggestions?

ChatGPT

Certainly! Here are some ways you can incorporate ChatGPT into your 9th-grade Algebra 1 curriculum to enhance engagement and understanding:

1. **Interactive Q&A Sessions:**
   - Description: Use ChatGPT as a platform where students can ask specific algebraic questions or seek clarifications on topics they find challenging. This can be especially useful for homework help.
   - Benefit: Students receive immediate feedback, which can boost their confidence and understanding of complex algebraic concepts.

2. **Problem Creation:**
   - Description: Ask ChatGPT to generate unique algebraic problems based on specific topics you're covering. This can add variety to your problem sets and challenge students in new ways.
   - Benefit: Fresh and diverse problems can keep students engaged and prevent them from simply memorizing solutions.

3. **Conceptual Deep Dives:**
   - Description: If students struggle with certain foundational concepts, use ChatGPT to provide alternative explanations or analogies that might resonate differently.
   - Benefit: Different students understand concepts in various ways. Offering multiple perspectives can help ensure all students grasp the material.

4. **Real-world Applications:**
   - Description: Ask ChatGPT for real-world scenarios where specific algebraic concepts are applied. This can help students see the relevance of what they're learning.
   - Benefit: When students understand the real-world relevance of algebra, they're more likely to be engaged and motivated.

Review and Reinforcement:
   - Description: Before a test or quiz, use ChatGPT as a review tool. Students can ask questions about topics they're unsure about or seek explanations for problems they got wrong in practice.
   - Benefit: This interactive review can help solidify understanding and address last-minute uncertainties.

5. **Historical Context:**
   - Description: Algebra has a rich history with contributions from various cultures. Use ChatGPT to provide historical context or fun facts about the origins of certain algebraic concepts.
   - Benefit: Understanding the history and evolution of algebra can add depth to the subject and make it more relatable.

   Remember, the key is to integrate ChatGPT in a way that complements your teaching style and addresses the specific needs of your students. By doing so, you can create a dynamic and interactive learning environment that caters to the diverse needs of 9th-grade learners.

As I shared previously, I can request ChatGPT to craft a comprehensive lesson plan and a set of differentiated activities.

Later in this book, I'll be sharing specific prompts, but here is at least one example of how I could use ChatGPT in an Algebra lesson.

> **Mr. Jim Prompt**
>
> Provide three practical examples of how the quadratic formula could be used as a real-world application, for students who ask, "When would I ever use this?"

ChatGPT

Certainly! The quadratic formula is a powerful tool in algebra, and while it might seem abstract in the classroom, it has practical applications in various real-world scenarios. Here are three examples:

1. **Projectile Motion:**
- **Scenario:** Imagine a student on the school's baseball team wants to know the maximum height a baseball will reach when thrown into the air, or how long it will take for the ball to hit the ground. The motion of the baseball can be modeled using a quadratic equation. The quadratic formula can then be used to determine key parameters of the ball's flight, such as its maximum height or the time it takes to return to the ground.
- **Application:** The quadratic formula helps in determining the optimal angle or initial velocity to achieve a desired trajectory, which can be crucial in sports like baseball, basketball, or golf.

2. **Business and Economics:**
- **Scenario:** A local business owner wants to determine the optimal price to charge for a product to maximize profit. Based on market research, they find that at a certain high price they sell very few units, and at a very low price

they sell many units but don't make much profit per unit. The relationship between price and profit can often be modeled with a quadratic equation.

- **Application:** Using the quadratic formula, the business owner can find the price that will maximize their profit. This is especially useful in industries where supply and demand can be modeled using quadratic functions.

3. **Engineering and Design:**

- **Scenario:** An engineer is designing a parabolic satellite dish. The shape of the dish is a parabola, and its purpose is to focus signals onto a receiver. To ensure the strongest signal, the engineer needs to determine the exact location to place the receiver.

- **Application:** The quadratic formula can be used to determine the focal point of the parabola, ensuring the satellite dish functions efficiently and captures the strongest possible signal.

These real-world applications can help students see the relevance of the quadratic formula beyond the classroom and appreciate its utility in various professional fields.

Mr. Jim Prompt

Provide a great example of how a student can enter an Algebra problem and then show how AI can tutor the student step by step to understand how to solve it.

ChatGPT

Certainly! Let's walk through a typical Algebra problem involving a quadratic equation, and I'll demonstrate how ChatGPT can tutor a student step-by-step.

Step 1: Identify the coefficients.

- $a = 1$
- $b = -5$
- $c = 6$

Step 2: Use the quadratic formula, which is:
$$x = \frac{-b \pm \sqrt{b^2 - 4ac}}{2a}$$

Step 3: Plug in the coefficients into the formula.
First, calculate the discriminant: $b^2 - 4ac$.
$(-5)^2 - 4(1)(6) = 25 - 24 = 1$

Step 4: Now, plug the discriminant and the coefficients into the formula to solve for x.
$$x_1 = \frac{-(-5) + \sqrt{1}}{2(1)} = \frac{5+1}{2} = 3$$
$$x_2 = \frac{-(-5) - \sqrt{1}}{2(1)} = \frac{5-1}{2} = 2$$

ChatGPT: So, the solutions to the equation $x^2 - 5x + 6 = 0$ are $x = 3$ and $x = 2$.

Student: Oh, I see! So the equation factors as $(x - 3)(x - 2) = 0$, right?

ChatGPT: Exactly! Well done. When you set each factor equal to zero and solve for x, you get the solutions $x = 3$ and $x = 2$.

Student: Thank you for the step-by-step explanation! It makes a lot more sense now.

Prompts for the Everyday Teacher

ELA

- Choose a character from our current reading. Write a diary entry from their perspective about a key event in the story.
- Take a classic story or fairytale and rewrite it in a modern setting. How do the characters and conflicts change?
- Create a soundtrack for a novel we've read. Choose songs that match the mood of certain chapters or events and explain your choices.
- Rewrite a scene from our current reading from the perspective of a minor or antagonistic character. How does this change our understanding of the event?
- Pretend you're a news reporter covering an event from a book or play we've studied. Write a news article or film a news segment about it.

Math

- Find a real-world scenario, like the trajectory of a basketball shot or the profit of a small business, and model it using a quadratic equation. Then solve for a specific variable.
- Create a short story that incorporates a linear equation. Have classmates solve the equation as part of understanding the story's outcome.
- Using a series of algebraic equations, create a code for classmates to solve. Each solution reveals a letter, spelling out a secret word or message.

- Design a board game or card game that requires players to solve algebraic equations or evaluate functions to progress.
- Choose an algebraic concept and research its historical origins. Who discovered or developed it? How has it impacted the world?

Informative and Engaging

After each chapter, I have included a Top 5 list from ThinkFives. This feature enhances the chapter's topic, adding a level of cultural relevance. ThinkFives is a K-12 website that conducts polls among hundreds of teachers on instructional and engaging topics relevant to education. More information can be found at thinkfives.com.

ThinkFives Top 5 Friendly Robots

Popular culture has been preparing for the advent of robots for years. Movies and TV shows have offered us a range of robotic personalities, from the comical to the compassionate. According to a ThinkFives teacher survey, here are the bots you might want to share a coffee with at Central Perk.

5. Bender (Futurama)

Bender challenges our conventional understanding of "friendly," offering a more sarcastic and self-centered version of companionship. Yet his antics and sharp wit make him a memorable part of the crew aboard the Planet Express ship.

4. Rosie (The Jetsons)

In contrast to Bender, Rosie represents the ideal domestic robot. Functioning as a housekeeper and pseudo-family member, she provides care and maintains order in the Jetsons' futuristic household.

3. Data (Star Trek: The Next Generation)

Data's ongoing journey to understand human emotions and relationships has endeared him to Star Trek fans. His loyalty and intellectual curiosity make him an invaluable part of the USS Enterprise crew.

2. WALL-E (WALL-E)

Serving initially as a lone waste-collector, WALL-E's transformation into a sentient being capable of love is as surprising as it is touching. He becomes a catalyst for change, offering a heartwarming view of a post-apocalyptic world.

1. R2-D2 & C-3PO (Star Wars)

These two beloved droids from Star Wars perfectly complement each other, with R2-D2's technical skills and C-3PO's linguistic prowess. Their loyalty and camaraderie offer a hopeful view of how AI and humans might coexist in a galaxy not so far away.

#3 TRANSFORM

"Always remember, you have within you the strength, the patience, and the passion to reach for the stars to change the world."
– Harriet Tubman

It was January 22, 1984. Hardly a date I should remember nearly three decades later. Sure, a Notre Dame grad (my alma mater), Joe Theismann battled a Stanford grad (the local university), Jim Plunkett, in Super Bowl XVII, but outside of the quarterbacks I had no deep rooting intertest in either side. The Raiders commanded the first half, leading 21 to 3, but what happened next is why the day still evokes a lasting memory.

The teams headed for the locker rooms, and then the now-iconic Apple Super Bowl ad illuminated the screen. The commercial begins in a bleak, gray dystopian setting, where rows of bald, uniformed men march in unison down a long tunnel toward a large screen. On the screen, a Big Brother-like figure is delivering propaganda about unification and the eradication of what he refers to as a "virus of freedom." This figure clearly symbolizes a totalitarian regime, akin to the society depicted in Orwell's "1984."

Suddenly, a woman wearing vibrant athletic clothing and carrying a large hammer, enters and clashes against the dull, monotonous crowd. As she races toward the large screen, police in riot gear chase her, hoping to protect the reverence of the moment.

As "Big Brother" continues his speech, the woman swings her hammer and hurls it at the screen. The mammoth video shatters in an explosion of light and smoke, stunning the audience and breaking the hypnotic spell of the propaganda.

The commercial then fades to black, and a voiceover proclaims, "On January 24th, Apple Computer will introduce Macintosh. And you'll see why 1984 won't be like *1984*." The commercial forever identified Macintosh as a tool for breaking free from conformity and embracing individuality and creativity.

This masterpiece of advertising by director Ridley Scott (Blade Runner, Gladiator) effectively positioned Apple as a company that challenges the status quo and empowers individuals to think differently. It was a call to arms. For me, it was less about breaking the shackles of IBM and more about freeing the classroom of slate, chalk, and podiums. It signaled a new era, a revolution that would forever change not just computing but in my perspective, education as well.

A few months later, I became the proud owner of a first-generation Macintosh. The compact machine, weighing just under twenty pounds, with its nine-inch monochrome display and a groundbreaking graphical user interface, was an embodiment of innovation. As the whirl of the Motorola 68000 processor churned, this technological marvel became a symbol of what education could be - an escape from the conventional, a doorway to endless possibilities. It represented a pedagogy where knowledge was no longer bound by the pages of textbooks and learning was a vibrant, interactive exploration.

It is nearly impossible to convey the sense of wonder that this small plastic cube created by introducing teachers to the world of multimedia. Its graphical user interface defined the concept of user-friendly, making it "the" device for the masses. It included software just as innovative. MacWrite, a WYSIWYG (what you see is what you get) word processor, allowed users for the first time to see text on screen that closely mirrored how it would look when printed. I also experienced a spellchecker for the first time – but about a decade too late for a host of spelling mistakes I left in the wake of my schooling. And then there was

MacPaint, a graphics painting program, which demonstrated the Mac's ability to create graphics and images. I could add graphics to my otherwise stale class handouts – or just draw aimlessly, impressing my friends.

Although the screen was just black and white, and the 3.5" hard plastic floppy held a mere 400k of disc space, I had seen a glimpse of the future. I knew I had a responsibility to step out of my comfort zone. As an educator, I needed to become the runner, breaking through the monotony, fearlessly ushering in a new era of learning.

So enthralled was I with this new classroom buddy, I changed the trajectory of my teaching career. I decided to pursue a second master's, this one in computer science, and enrolled in grad school. Soon I was programming in Pascal, studying hardware system designs, and taking seven pre-requisite courses in math including the brain-taxing Linear Algebra and Combinatorics. Life was indeed busy – consumed with teaching, coaching, and studying – but rewarding.

Before long, I was teaching AP programming and moderating the Web Club, an after-school activity to learn HTML and update the school website. With each huge advancement – networks, laserdiscs, the world wide web, and ultimately the ".com era," technology reshaped my teaching methods.

The rest of my story is forever linked to technology. For almost two decades as teacher, principal, and administrator, I led efforts to evangelize how these technologies could bridge the gaps of traditional education. And then with a sense of adventure, I entered the world of ed tech, working with companies who were leading efforts to harness the power of technologies. Whether working with large publishers or leading startup companies, for the last twenty years I have ridden the waves of innovation and change.

Fast forward to 2023, and I find myself experiencing a sense of déjà vu. The thrill, the excitement, the hope – it all came rushing back the moment I logged into ChatGPT for the first time and crafted my inaugural prompt. It was equivalent to unboxing that first Macintosh all those years ago – a sense of stepping into a whole new world of possibilities, of standing at the threshold of another revolution in education. The realization struck me, as vigorously as it had that day in 1984, that once again we were on the precipice of a major shift, the next black monolith in the history of education.

These days, I'm a leader of an ed tech company. Every day, I'm instilling my belief in the power of tech into every part of the company. It's like a daily reminder for my team and me to keep pushing the envelope, to keep innovating.

For the future is not something we predict but something we shape. And together we can shape a future where education is not just informative but transformative. And that's how this book came to be. I wrote this -because I genuinely believe that ChatGPT, Gemini, Bing, Midjourney – that AI – has the power to revolutionize the educational landscape.

My aim is to show you, the educator, the immense potential AI carries in transforming how we teach and how students learn. I envision a future where AI is an integral part of classrooms, enhancing the learning experience and helping educators overcome challenges. My hope is that this book will be a catalyst for that change, encouraging educators, policymakers, and stakeholders to embrace the remarkable opportunities AI brings to education.

ChatGPT – The Beginning

Every teacher knows context is important, and I always love a good history lesson. So, to best understand where we can journey with AI, it is helpful to know what it is and where it started. When did AI, this latest technological marvel, come to life? Was it November of 2022 with the release of a public ChatGPT? Hardly.

The 50s: Alan Turing

Amid the birth of rock 'n' roll, drive-in cinemas, and *Viva Las Vegas,* something else was brewing, something extraordinary. It was the dawn of a new era – the inception of artificial intelligence. The first whispers of AI came from a visionary named Alan Turing. You may recognize Turing as the man who cracked the Enigma Code during World War II, but his intellect didn't stop there. Turing was a computer scientist long before there were personal computers. Sitting in a cold, austere office, he pondered the question, "Can machines think?" Turing proposed an idea, a test of sorts, where if a machine could carry a conversation indistinguishable from a human's, it could be considered intelligent. This idea, now known as the Turing Test, was the spark that ignited the wildfire of AI.

Rewind to the summer of 1956. A band of scientists, including John McCarthy, Marvin Minsky, Nathaniel Rochester, and Claude Shannon, gathered at Dartmouth College. This wasn't your typical summer camp (no campfire or s'mores). Instead, they toasted to a grand proposal – to build a machine that could mimic every aspect of learning or any other feature of intelligence. And while Elvis was singing like a hound dog, just like that, artificial intelligence got its name and a scientific community to nurture it.

The 80s: The PC

Progress continues through the 60s and 70s, with early successes, such as the development of the first computer program (ELIZA) that could mimic human conversation, fueling optimism. However, as the decades progressed, the initial optimism that AI might be viable for more broader applications faded. New challenges arose as technology to support this vision seemed too distant and funding became scarce.

The 1980s brought in not only artists like Madonna, the Material Girl, but a resurgence of optimism in AI. With the advent of expert systems and machine learning, computers began to learn, to adapt, to solve problems. They were no longer just glorified calculators! IBM revolutionized business with PCs and Excel. Apple hurls a hammer through the screen representation of 1984, and computers are used to research, analyze, and predict. And the concept of "neural networks" (interconnected nodes) began to be "vogue."

2000s: Deep Learning

The new millennium brought with it a new era, a time of significant advancements in computational power and data storage. This environment was ripe for the resurgence of neural networks, now termed "deep learning." These deep neural networks, with their ability to process vast amounts of data, led to breakthroughs in areas like image and speech recognition. Companies like Google, Amazon, and Facebook began investing heavily in AI, integrating it into various products and services (Alexa, Siri, Google Assistant). By 2023, Taylor Swift vied with ChatGPT to see who had the most influence on the world and would become Time's Person of the Year. Taylor may have won that battle, but AI will win the war.

Generative Pre-trained Transformers

Despite the advancements, over the past few decades, artificial intelligence has primarily been a topic of discussion within tech circles and the pages of science fiction. However, the landscape shifted dramatically in November of 2022, when ChatGPT was released to the public, effectively bringing the marvels of AI into the limelight.

Despite its public introduction, ChatGPT is by no means a new endeavor. The story of its conception can be traced back to 2015, in the tech center of San Francisco. It was here that a research institution called OpenAI was established by a group of preeminent figures in the realm of artificial intelligence. This team of researchers, engineers, and computer scientists shared an optimistic vision: "to develop artificial general intelligence (AGI) in a way that would ultimately benefit the entirety of mankind."

It was within this incubator that the concept of ChatGPT was born. It wasn't the product of a sudden flash of inspiration but rather a gradual culmination of research, observation, and collaborative brainstorming. The OpenAI team acknowledged the significant potential of AI as a tool for enhanced learning and communication. With that vision, the groundwork for ChatGPT was laid.

OpenAI was founded by a cohort of prominent figures in the tech industry: Sam Altman, Elon Musk, Greg Brockman, Ilya Sutskever, John Schulman, and Wojciech Zaremba.

Elon Musk, a visionary entrepreneur known for SpaceX and Tesla (we'll exclude "X" for the moment), saw the potential and risks of AI early on. He joined forces with Sam Altman, the then-president of Y Combinator, a prestigious startup accelerator. Both Musk and Altman brought their extensive knowledge of technology startups to the table, fostering an environment conducive to innovation and rapid growth.

The process of developing ChatGPT was evolutionary rather than revolutionary. It began with a simpler model, GPT-1, and by 2023 OpenAI ushered in the next era in artificial intelligence, unveiling GPT-4, the latest iteration of their language model, ChatGPT. An impressive evolution, GPT-4 comes equipped with an enhanced capability, boasting ten times the sophistication of its predecessor, GPT-3.5.

GPT-4 demonstrated superior proficiency in understanding context and discerning nuances, delivering more precise and coherent responses. Not only can it generate text mirroring human speech, but it also adeptly navigates diverse dialects and identifies emotions in the text. This model can create stories, poems, and essays with improved coherence and creativity.

Since its introduction, ChatGPT has continued to evolve, its development marked by constant learning, adaptation, and refinement. The team at OpenAI works toward their initial goal of harnessing AGI for the greater benefit of humanity, shaping ChatGPT to serve as a tool for a myriad of applications.

"Education is certainly going to change dramatically. And I think it is forever altered by the course of this technology," shared OpenAI CEO Sam Altman. "What will happen is that the potential of every student will go up. The rate of learning of every student will go up, and the expectation of every student will go up."

Sam Altman has a unique vantage point. As perhaps the most well-known guru in the field of AI, his involvement isn't just as a figurehead. He was integral in guiding OpenAI's ethos and direction. The organization's evolution into a "capped-profit" entity underlined its commitment to research that is both profitable and ethically grounded.

Altman is known for his forward-thinking and innovative approach to technology and AI. He has a vision of making AI safe and broadly distributed, ensuring it benefits all of humanity. His perspectives on the ethical and safe development of AI are particularly important as the technology becomes more advanced and integrated into various aspects of daily life. As OpenAI pushes the boundaries of AI, it's evident that such technology will play a substantial role in personalized learning, resource democratization, and inclusive education.

Promoting Uncommon Experiences

Have you ever read "Teach Like a Pirate," a book by Dave Burgess with such a great name that I still remember it. Aimed toward an elementary audience, what stuck with me most with his mantra, "Provide an uncommon experience for your students, and they will reward you with an uncommon effort and attitude."

For me, that concisely summed up what I wanted to do and what I wanted from my students. I wanted my high school classroom to be an island of "uncommon experiences." Whether that be mock emergency UN sessions or Talk Like a Pirate Day (September 19th for those with eye patches), I wanted my students to look forward to the journey. Now, as we navigate the digital age, where data and algorithms are the new norm, we're blending these timeless uncommon experiences with the innovative capabilities of artificial intelligence.

Far from replacing the passionate educator, AI complements our efforts. As we saw in the previous chapter, it can streamline tasks, offer personalized learning experiences, and provide insights to refine our teaching strategies. With AI, educators can harness both efficiency and passion, ensuring students receive an enriched and uncommon experience.

By now you have surmised that I have a bias. This is not a book comparing the pros and cons of AI in education. There are many legitimate concerns with AI – and I will address them in a later chapter. In my eyes, AI represents the third major technological leap in education, following the integration of computers in the classroom and the advent of the internet. However, I passionately believe that AI holds the potential to be the most transformative of them all.

What makes AI so revolutionary is its ability to engage in human-like conversations and provide insightful, contextually relevant responses. It is as if we had a virtual companion, a knowledgeable partner, ready to assist us in our educational endeavors. This breakthrough technology opens a world of possibilities, empowering educators, and students alike. There are already dozens of startups creating AI companions for friendship, tutoring, working out, or just doing errands.

As we saw in the last chapter, one reason I consider ChatGPT to be so profound is its potential to personalize learning on an unprecedented scale. With its vast knowledge and ability to adapt to individual needs, ChatGPT could provide tailored support and guidance to each student. No longer would students be confined to a one-size-fits-all approach; instead, they could receive personalized feedback, explanations, and resources that cater specifically to their unique strengths and challenges.

Furthermore, AI has the power to bridge gaps in access to educational resources. It could bring high-quality instruction and guidance to students in remote areas, underserved communities, or those facing physical limitations. Programs like special education, ELL, alternative education and vocational education will be a few of the most to benefit from these personalized services.

By breaking down barriers, AI has the potential to democratize education, ensuring that every student has access to the knowledge and support they deserve. In past centuries, the treasure of knowledge was reserved for the elite few – the affluent and the clergy. Reading and writing? Those were luxuries many could only dream of. Even the advent of the printing press didn't immediately level the playing field; books remained a prize for those with money. Fast forward to the digital age, and while technology promised to bridge the gap, it often widened it. Many regions, especially in economically challenged countries, found themselves left behind, unable to afford the hardware or the connectivity. But here's where the magic of AI can come into play. It's poised to be the great equalizer in the history of education. With just a basic device and an internet connection, anyone, anywhere, can tap into AI. It's like having a personal tutor in your pocket, ready to offer insights from the latest tech advancements to age-old wisdom. What is the promise of AI? To truly democratize learning for all.

How far have we come in the short time that ChatGPT has been in the public eye? Here are a few statistics about its usage and intelligence that may open your eyes.

- In a Stanford study, 80% of recommendations made to students seeking assistance with assignments were found to be accurate when compared to expert human advice.
- A University of Murcia (Spain) study reported that ChatGPT provided correct answers to 91% of 38,708 academic questions.
- During a trial at the Georgia Institute of Technology involving 300 students, ChatGPT achieved a 97% accuracy rate in responding to 10,000 questions throughout a semester-long course.
- An Ivy Tech study demonstrated an 80% accuracy in predicting the performance of 34,712 students at the end of a semester course based on just two weeks of assessments.
- Educators at the University of Massachusetts using an AI-enhanced grading system were able to reduce their grading time by 70% compared to a traditional classroom setting.

While these are university examples, it will not be too long before we see similar studies being conducted in K-12. While I'm no longer a member of the teaching fraternity, I embrace this new era of technology in education. I am filled with hope and excitement. AI represents a significant milestone in our journey, propelling us forward into a future where personalized, inclusive, and engaging education becomes the common experience.

A Common Reaction: Obstacles

While all teachers want to provide such experiences, it is not surprising that many educators view the latest hype of AI with skepticism and concern. Those concerns range from finding the time to learn new technology to the practical fear of AI replacing the human element in education. Before we go too much further, it's crucial to address these fears, demystify AI, and explore how it can help, rather than hinder, education.

In a recent ThinkFives survey, K-12 teachers were asked to share their concerns about AI. Here is a sampling of their comments.

Technology

"I worry that with AI in the classroom, I'll spend more time troubleshooting software glitches than actual teaching."

"I have concerns about the transparency of AI. It's difficult to trust a tool when I don't understand how it reaches its conclusions."

"How do we ensure fairness and avoid bias in AI-driven education? Until that question has a solid answer, I'm hesitant to adopt AI in my classroom."

Impersonal

"With AI in the picture, I fear losing the personal touch that makes teaching rewarding. I don't want my students' education to be a series of programmed responses."

"Sure, AI can process information faster than any human, but it can't understand the subtleties of a student's struggle or moment of triumph. Teaching is more than data processing."

"You know, the day a robot can comfort a child who's homesick or inspire a class with stories of human achievements, that's the day I'll start considering AI in my classroom."

"With AI, I fear we might be giving students fish instead of teaching them how to fish. Real education is about developing critical thinking, not feeding answers."

Privacy

"The thought of AI handling student data sends shivers down my spine. How can we ensure complete privacy and data security in the age of rampant cyber threats?"

"The concept of AI rummaging through my students' data gives me pause. Childhood should be a sanctuary, not a data mine."

A compilation of the survey results categorizes the obstacles in these categories. Let's see if we can counter the concerns, or at least address them.

Obstacle 1: "I'm too busy to learn another new technology."

The lament of being "I'm too busy" echoes in every teacher's lounge. Teachers are, indeed, some of the busiest professionals, juggling lesson planning, grading, administrative work, and not to mention the actual teaching. "I don't have the time to learn a tool that saves me time."

Yet, in this whirlwind of tasks, the integration of AI can truly serve as a time-saving wonder. At first glance, the task of learning AI technologies might seem daunting. But with little assistance (or the help of your child) you can get ChatGPT up and running in less than ten minutes and be creating lesson plans in another five.

Once mastered, AI can automate time-consuming tasks, such as grading multiple-choice tests or organizing lesson plans, leaving you with more time for meaningful interactions with students. So, while the initial investment of time is undeniably a challenge, the potential payoff in the long term makes it a worthwhile endeavor.

Obstacle 2: "I'm not tech-savvy enough to learn AI."

This is a fear that plagues many but remember that being tech-savvy isn't a trait you're born with – it's a skill that's cultivated. Just as we encourage our students to step out of their comfort zones and embrace new challenges, we must be ready to do the same.

Today, most AI platforms are designed with user-friendliness in mind. They're built to be used by people, not programmers. Also, many products provide extensive support and training. Online communities of educators, too, share their experiences and strategies, providing a supportive network for those venturing into this new domain. Moreover, many school districts will be offering professional development opportunities to ease this transition.

Embracing technology is no longer an optional skill for educators; it's a necessary one. And remember, no one expects you to become an expert overnight. It's a gradual process, and every step you take toward becoming more tech-savvy is a step toward preparing your students for a future that is increasingly digital. Did you ever figure out how to set the time on your old VHS or DVD player? If you did, you're highly qualified to master AI.

Obstacle 3: "I hear it provides so many wrong answers."

AI is not infallible and there are instances when it makes mistakes. However, rather than viewing this as a drawback, we can transform it into a valuable teaching moment. By identifying and discussing these errors, we can encourage critical thinking in our students, fostering their ability to question, analyze, and validate information.

Moreover, the accuracy of AI is continuously improving, driven by advancements in machine learning and data analysis. Feedback from users, including teachers and students, plays a crucial role in this development process.

By embracing AI, you're not just adopting a tool; you're joining a community striving to enhance education. Your experiences, insights, and even the challenges you face can help refine these tools, contributing to the ongoing evolution of AI in education. Later in this book we will dive deeper into this question and discuss ways to minimize this.

Obstacle 4: "My students will just plagiarize ChatGPT and not learn how to think."

The fear of plagiarism is real and valid. With information just a click away, it's easier than ever for students to copy answers rather than think critically. The same was said of home encyclopedias. But in most homes in a bygone era, the curiosity spawned by the twenty-six-book set far outweighed the homework assignments that were copied. AI is a tool, and like any tool, its impact depends on how we use it.

We can leverage AI to foster a culture of academic integrity and critical thinking. When used strategically, AI can encourage students to delve deeper, to question and explore, to collaborate and create. As teachers, we can shape how students interact with AI, guiding them to use this powerful tool not as a shortcut but as a steppingstone toward deeper understanding and innovative thought. We will discuss the flipped classroom later in this book and ways to change the concept of homework.

Obstacle 5: "AI will marginalize teachers and eliminate the personal touch."

Concerns that AI could depersonalize learning and marginalize teachers are understandable, but it's important to reframe AI as high-value, low-cost assistant, not a competitor. AI can take on mundane tasks, freeing teachers to do what they do best: ignite curiosity, inspire passion, and nurture relationships.

Far from promoting isolation, AI offers a platform for individualized, engaging learning, even fostering collaboration beyond classroom boundaries through immersive, interactive experiences.

Yet, balance is key. By ensuring we have a teacher front-and-center, we merge the human touch with technological benefits. Here, the teacher's irreplaceable role is central; AI is a support, not a substitute. By embracing AI, teachers are better equipped to inspire and ... teach.

Why This Matters?

Public education is a widely celebrated social triumph in the U.S., but it may not be the most effective way to learn. In 1984, educational psychologist Benjamin Bloom found that students who received one-on-one tutoring outperformed their peers by a significant margin, surpassing 98% of those in traditional classroom settings. There's something special about the personal, mentorship-based approach that seems to make a difference. However, as we're aware, educating the masses through this method is not feasible. Until now, this issue has challenged even the most experienced educators. With the emergence of generative AI systems, a promising solution seems to be on the horizon.

The Power of AI in Alleviating Teacher Pain Points

If you are fearless enough to venture into the world of AI, you will immediately see how it can address a myriad of pain points echoed in staff rooms and teacher lounges every day. AI is not a solution in search of a problem. AI only makes sense when it solves a problem and there are burdens it can lessen.

> **Mr. Jim Prompt**
>
> Can you provide the ways AI can address these common teacher pain points that teachers listed as their Top 5: Limited Time, Individual Attention, Resources and Preparation, Testing and Mandates, and Emotional and Mental Fatigue.

ChatGPT

Limited Time 🕐 Teachers often feel like they're in a race against the clock, juggling content delivery, lesson planning, grading, and those pesky admin tasks. Enter AI! Imagine a virtual assistant (think of it as your personalized classroom elf) that can automate lesson planning, swiftly grade multiple-choice assignments, and even send reminders about upcoming administrative tasks. With AI by your side, there just might be an extra hour or two hidden in that jam-packed day!

Individual Attention 👨‍🏫👩‍🏫 Each student is a unique puzzle, and fitting all the pieces together in a bustling classroom is a feat! But AI, like a magical magnifying glass, can tailor learning paths based on each student's pace, preferences, and strengths. So, even in a room full of diverse learners, each student feels seen and supported.

Resources and Preparation 📚 Drowning in a sea of textbooks, not finding that perfect resource? AI to the rescue! Picture a tool that sifts through the vast expanse of the internet and curates resources just right for your lesson. Customized worksheets? Engaging multimedia? Tailored quizzes? It's like having a 24/7 digital librarian at your fingertips!

Testing and Mandates 📊 Standardized tests can feel like a creativity-crushing monster. But what if AI could help transform these into personalized learning experiences? With AI analyzing test results, educators can get insights on individual student gaps, ensuring mandates are met while still letting creativity and individuality shine.

Emotional and Mental Fatigue 👨‍🏫👩‍🏫 Teaching is heart-work, and the weight of it can sometimes feel like carrying a backpack filled with bricks. AI, while not a replacement for human connection, can provide support tools like mood trackers for classrooms, predictive systems to highlight potential student issues, or even mindfulness apps tailored for teacher relaxation. Think of it as your digital self-care buddy!

Lack of Professional Development Opportunities 🎓 A teacher's quest for knowledge never ends, but sometimes the path isn't clear. AI can be the compass, guiding educators to tailored online courses, recommending articles, or even connecting them with global teaching communities. Picture an ever-evolving digital mentor ensuring you're always at the forefront of educational innovation.

Michael Moe, co-founder of Global Silicon Valley and ed-tech investor says, "Good is gone. Great isn't enough. Outstanding is the future. It's not man vs machine. It's man and machine."

Fearless teachers understand the true potential of AI. The goal of the remaining chapters is to provide you with hope and examples. I'll share hope that a profound future is ahead that will address many of the perennial problems in education. And of course, I'll explain with examples so that you can begin to benefit immediately.

Prompts for the Everyday Teacher

For Elementary Students:
1. What is AI, and how would you explain it to a friend your age?
2. Can you think of any fun examples where AI helps you in your daily life, like in games or apps?
3. Imagine you have a magical drawing robot. How would you describe how it works to make pictures?
4. Do you know what "training" means when we talk about teaching computers? How is it like teaching a pet or learning at school?
5. Let's pretend you have a robot friend that learns from watching you. What kind of things would it learn from you?
6. Have you ever seen a machine make a picture or a story? How do you think it does that?
7. If you had a robot helper, what creative things could you make together, like drawing or writing stories?

For High School Students:
1. Explain the key differences between AI and human intelligence. What are the strengths and limitations of each?

2. Can you provide examples of AI applications that have had a significant impact on society or industries in recent years?
3. Investigate the concept of generative AI and its role in creating text, images, or music. How is it changing the creative landscape?
4. Explore the process of training AI models. Why is it essential, and what are some common techniques used in AI training?
5. Discuss the critical role of data in AI learning. How can the quality and quantity of data affect AI model performance?
6. Analyze the functioning of neural networks in generative AI. How do they simulate human learning and creativity?
7. Consider the ethical implications of using generative AI for content creation. What responsibilities do creators and users have in this context?

ThinkFives Top 5 AI "Firsts"

5. First References

In Mythology: One of the oldest examples comes from ancient Greek mythology: the tale of Talos, a giant bronze robot created by Hephaestus, the god of fire and metalworking. Talos acted on his own to protect the island of Crete, walking around its shores three times a day and hurling stones at any unauthorized ships.

4. First General-Purpose Robot

Designed in the late 1960s, "Shakey" was a significant milestone in AI robotics. Shakey could analyze and break down commands into smaller, manageable steps for execution. Shakey could understand complex instructions, plan its actions, and move in a purposeful way to achieve a given goal. The robot was developed by the Stanford Research Institute (now SRI International) and remains an important part of the history of robotics.

3. First Chatbot

The story of modern chatbots can be traced back to ELIZA. Created in the mid-1960s by Joseph Weizenbaum, a professor at MIT, ELIZA was a groundbreaking innovation. She was designed to simulate a psychotherapist, capable of having text conversations that seemed quite natural. ELIZA achieved this by rephrasing a user's statements as questions, creating the illusion of understanding and empathy. It may not be surprising how intelligent ELIZA was. She did attend MIT.

2. First Chess Win

Eagerly anticipated was the 1997 chess match between IBM's Deep Blue, an AI-powered computer, and world chess champion, Garry Kasparov. Six games were played. Deep Blue won the first game, Kasparov won the second game, and the remaining four games ended in draws. A rapid chess playoff was held consisting of two games. Deep Blue won both games, ultimately winning the match.

1. First Passing Grades

- SAT: GPT-4 aced the SAT Reading & Writing section with a score of 710 out of 800, (93rd percentile). For the math section, GPT-4 earned a 700 out of 800, (89th percentile).
- AP Exams: GPT-4 received a 5 on AP Art History, AP Biology, AP Environmental Science, AP Macroeconomics, AP Microeconomics, AP Psychology, AP Statistics, AP US Government and AP US History. On AP Calculus BC, AP Chemistry, and AP World History, GPT-4 received a 4.
- Law: In March 2023, GPT-4 took the bar exam and passed with flying colors, scoring in the top 10% of test takers.
- Google Code Exam: ChatGPT passed the first job interview stages for an L3 software engineering position at Google. The total compensation for the job is about $183,000.

#4 INNOVATE

"Innovation is the ability to see change as an opportunity - not a threat." – Steve Jobs

Imagine the grandest, most spectacular library you can fathom – towering shelves lined with millions of books, each teeming with stories, facts, and ideas. A new visitor is stepping into this library. This is no ordinary visitor; it's a robot, and it plans to read every single book, from the tiniest pamphlet to the thickest tome, cover to cover, hundreds of times over.

In this narrative, our library-loving robot stands for a generative language model, and the vast library symbolizes the colossal amounts of text data the model absorbs. Our robot gobbles up books and devours language.

But it's more than an avid reader; it aspires to be an accomplished writer. You might ask, "Isn't language acquisition more nuanced than merely reading a book?" Absolutely. That's where the "generative" part comes in. Generative Language Models, or GLMs, don't just mimic language – they learn to generate fresh, meaningful sentences they've never seen before.

Our robot starts its learning without knowing a word of our language. It begins by reading, grasping the grammar, structure, and context of the words in the books. With each page turned, it learns how words piece together to convey meaning. It studies patterns, grasps nuances, and even picks up subtleties like sentiment and tone.

Once our robot has consumed a considerable amount of literature, it can start generating its own text. It doesn't copy or plagiarize the books it reads. Instead, it employs the knowledge it has gained to compose original, meaningful sentences.

Just as a student doesn't dive into penning the next great American novel after reading a handful of Dr. Seuss books, our robot, the Generative Language Model, also needs practice and guidance to begin crafting its own masterpieces.

After the robot has feasted on arrays of words and sentences, it ventures into the world of creation, eager and full of potential. But how does it know if it's assembling words correctly? This is where the robot's creators, computer scientists, play a pivotal role, much like teachers providing feedback to their students.

This feedback process is a practice session, termed "training" in computer science lingo. During training, the robot is given snippets of text and asked to predict the next word or phrase. When the robot makes a correct prediction, it's akin to a student receiving an "A" on their paper. But when it gets it wrong, it needs a bit of red pen. Each time the robot errs, the scientists gently correct it, tweaking its internal settings to guide it toward making better choices next time. This process of guess-and-correct, predict-and-adjust, repeats millions of times over. Through diligent practice, the robot learns how words and phrases typically flow together in human language.

After ample practice and increasingly accurate predictions, the robot is ready for the next step: generating its own sentences. At this stage, it's not just predicting the next word; it's constructing whole sentences, even paragraphs, fitting the style and context it has learned.

Even then, the process doesn't stop. The robot continues to learn and refine its skills, improving with each text it reads and generates. Scientists regularly monitor its progress, like a teacher reviewing writing assignments, ensuring the robot maintains the richness of human language in its compositions.

In essence, our literary robot embarks on a journey of lifelong learning, much like we do. Constant practice and the guidance it receives equip it to create rich, engaging, and original text, adding an exciting new dimension to the world of language and learning.

Generative Language Models in Action

Now, imagine you're planning a lesson for your English class on the symbolism in Emily Dickinson's poetry. You're trying to create a thoughtful writing assignment, but you're stumped. That's when you turn to our bookworm robot, the GLM. You ask it to "write a short poem in the style of Emily Dickinson about the changing of seasons." Before you know it, you have a brand-new poem, adhering to Dickinson's structure and style, yet it's an original creation about the changing of seasons.

Or consider a lesson focused on the founding of the United States, specifically around the signing of the Declaration of Independence. You want your students to grasp the magnitude of this event, the dialogue that transpired, and the historical figures involved. You ask your GLM to: "Compose a fictional letter from Benjamin Franklin to a close friend discussing the deliberations leading up to the signing of the Declaration of Independence."

The GLM generates an engaging letter, capturing the tension and excitement of the time while humanizing the historical figures involved. This imagined correspondence can jumpstart discussions around the circumstances and ideas that spurred the American Revolution.

Similarly, when discussing the establishment of Plymouth Plantation, you can ask the GLM to create a series of letters from a settler, documenting their journey across the Atlantic and the challenges of establishing a new life in a foreign land.

Each generated text offers a personal lens into history, encouraging deeper understanding and engagement with the subject matter. By crafting original content that aligns with historical events, GLMs provide a valuable tool for educators seeking to help students connect with and comprehend the past.

The GLM isn't just limited to fiction or historical writing, either. Consider its use in a science classroom when you're introducing a challenging concept, such as photosynthesis. This fundamental scientific process can be tricky for students to visualize. You ask the GLM to "describe the process of photosynthesis from the perspective of a leaf." Suddenly, you have a creative, engaging narrative that demystifies photosynthesis in a relatable way. You can even specify the grade level or language level of the explanation. This brings the abstract concept to life, making it more digestible and memorable for your students.

Whether it's turning historical facts into personal narratives or transforming scientific processes into vibrant stories, GLMs can offer unique learning resources. They're here to assist us, the teachers, as we guide our students through the captivating world of knowledge. Our bookworm robot can create, but we breathe life and meaning into those creations, igniting curiosity, and fostering understanding in our classrooms.

Now that you have gained a deeper understanding of what a generative language model is, you might be wondering how to explain it to your students. To lend a helping hand, we've requested assistance from ChatGPT to formulate a simple description aimed at 3rd grade students.

> **Mr. Jim Prompt**
>
> Now that I have gained a deeper understanding of what a generative language model is, can you write an explanation so I can explain it to my students, 3rd graders.

ChatGPT

Imagine you have a magical toy robot. This robot adores hearing all your stories, fairy tales, and nursery rhymes you've learned at school. It listens so attentively that it remembers all the words, all the tales, and how they sound when you narrate them. Now, here's the magical part: this robot can concoct its very own stories using all the words and styles it heard from your narratives.

You know how you can use your building blocks to construct different things each time? One day you might assemble a castle, a spaceship, or even a towering dinosaur. The blocks remain the same, but what you create can vary and be original each time. Our robotic companion operates in the same way but with words. It collects all the words it has learned, just like your blocks, and assembles new sentences and new stories.

So, if you fancy a fresh bedtime story about a space dinosaur residing in a castle, you could ask your robot, and it would spin a brand-new tale, unique and unlike any others. This magical toy robot is what adults refer to as a Generative Language Model. Isn't that fascinating?"

The Magic Behind ChatGPT's Word Completion

Let's dive a bit deeper into how ChatGPT, our literary robot, crafts its sentences. Picture a child learning to complete a familiar nursery rhyme. Say, "Old McDonald had a ..." Most children will instinctively respond with "farm." This is because they've heard the song multiple times and have learned the pattern. ChatGPT operates in a similar manner but on a much grander scale.

Take the same example. If you feed the model the words "Old McDonald," it predicts the next word based on the vast amount of text it has been trained on. With each additional word, its prediction becomes more accurate. So, by the time you get to "Old McDonald had a farm," ChatGPT is almost certain the next part is "E-I-E-I-O." Try it with ChatGPT and see what you get.

But how does it make these predictions? This is where neural networks come into play. Think of a neural network as a vast web of interconnected points. When you say a word, like "apple," the model travels to a specific point in this web. If the next word you say is "delicious," it moves along a path in the network associated with taste and food. But if you say "computer" after "apple," it takes a different route, heading toward technology-related concepts.

This ability to navigate its neural network based on context allows ChatGPT to understand and generate language that is relevant and coherent. It's like having a map of language in its "brain," and with each word you provide, it determines the best route to take, ensuring the journey (or sentence) makes sense.

So, when you're interacting with ChatGPT, remember you're not just chatting with a program. You're engaging with a sophisticated model that has mapped out the intricacies of language, ready to guide you on countless linguistic adventures. Whether you're exploring the world of Emily Dickinson or diving into the depths of photosynthesis, ChatGPT is here to illuminate the path with its linguistic prowess.

Predictions

How challenging is it to predict the next word? In some cases, it's not hard at all, as the predictive accuracy is over 95%. Try it yourself and compare your answers to ChatGPT's.

EngAIged

1. "Once upon a __"
2. "The early bird catches the __"
3. "An apple a day keeps the __"
4. "It's raining cats and __"
5. "A picture is worth a thousand __"
6. "Don't count your chickens before they __"
7. "You can't judge a book by its __"
8. "Every cloud has a silver __"
9. "When in Rome, do as the __"
10. "Actions speak louder than __"

> **Mr. Jim Prompt**
>
> ChatGPT please predict the following words in these phrases. [list all phrases]

ChatGPT

Phrase	Completion
Once upon a __	time
The early bird catches the __	worm
An apple a day keeps the __	doctor away
It's raining cats and __	dogs
A picture is worth a thousand __	words
Don't count your chickens before they __	hatch
You can't judge a book by its __	cover
Every cloud has a silver __	lining
When in Rome, do as the __	Romans do
Actions speak louder than __	words

How did you do? How do you think ChatGPT did? Now let's try this again and make it a little harder. We'll now look at phrases where it may not be as clear what the next word might be. See what you would guess.

1. "Bread and ___"
2. "Fish and ___"
3. "Salt and ___"
4. "It's raining ___"
5. "Black and ___"
6. "Stop and ___"
7. "Jack and ___"
8. "Fast and ___"
9. "Hot and ___"
10. "Macaroni and __"

These may not be as clear. Your answer might depend upon your schooling, your culture, the context or maybe how you're feeling at the moment ("I'm in the mood for jam and not butter."). I asked ChatGPT what it believes the top two choices are from its large language model.

> **Mr. Jim Prompt**
>
> ChatGPT please predict the following words in these phrases, listing the possible and most probable. [list all phrases]

ChatGPT

Phrase	Possible	Most Probable
Bread and __	jam	butter
Fish and __	tacos	chips
Salt and __	vinegar	pepper
It's raining...	heavily	cats and dogs
Black and __	blue	white
Stop and __	stare	go
Jack and __	Jill	the Beanstalk
Fast and __	easy	furious
Hot and __	spicy	cold
Macaroni and __	cheese	sauce

Not surprisingly, it gets much harder from here, which is where large language models shine. For some phrases, there are many viable choices. Take for examples phrases and the examples of words that might follow.

"It's raining __"

1. "cats and dogs"
2. "heavily"
3. "outside"
4. "men" (a nod to the famous song)
5. "again"
6. "hard"
7. "buckets"
8. "lightly"

9. "steadily"

10. "all day"

"It's a hard __"

1. "knock life" (from the musical *Annie*)
2. "life" (as in "It's a hard life for some")
3. "day" (as in "It's a hard day at work")
4. "time" (as in "It's a hard time for many")
5. "decision" (as in "It's a hard decision to make")
6. "job" (as in "It's a hard job but someone has to do it")
7. "choice" (as in "It's a hard choice to make")
8. "pill to swallow" (a common idiom)
9. "day's night" (as in the Beatles' song)
10. "road" (as in "It's a hard road ahead")

The progression from simple word completion to conversational capability in large language models involves the application of complex machine learning techniques, namely deep learning, and a massive amount of data.

For many teachers, their first interaction with AI, particularly programs like ChatGPT, can be astonishing. They marvel at how adeptly the AI grasps context and facilitates conversation in such an organic manner. This ability stands as a testament to the years of comprehensive training provided to the model. However, akin to how students occasionally misinterpret their teacher's instructions, ChatGPT too can err. Typically, a quick clarification or a nudge in the right direction is all it takes to set the model back on the correct path.

Prompt Engineering – The Art of the Question

So how do we mere humans interact with such powerful large language models? It's all about questions. And to understand the art of questioning, we need to travel back to 400BC.

In the public agoras of ancient Greece, a figure conversed with citizens —a philosopher named Socrates, renowned for his unparalleled teaching method. Frequently, he could be observed atop a marble pedestal, his beard an emblem of wisdom, while he gazed at his followers.

With a scholarly grin, Socrates unleashed an arsenal of questions upon his naïve pupils. "Tell me, dear student," he would begin, "what do you truly know?" His voice resonated with a mix of curiosity and amusement, as if he held the keys to unlocking mysteries beyond their grasp. And so, Socrates's journey of inquiry commenced, with students stumbling and fumbling in their attempts to answer.

Always several steps ahead, Socrates anticipated their moves, gently nudging them toward deeper understanding. With each question, he pushed the boundaries of their knowledge, causing their confidence to crumble almost before he answered. Much to their chagrin, he reveled in their discomfort, for he knew that within the chaos of their confusion were the seeds of profound understanding.

However, Socrates was no heartless tormentor. Amidst the perplexity, he nurtured fertile ground for intellectual growth. He recognized that true learning emerged from the refinement of answers, pushing students to explore new perspectives, challenge preconceived notions, and embrace the uncertainty that accompanies genuine inquiry.

As you might expect, Socrates was a master of the "Socratic Method." What else would you expect? You might remember from college seminars that this form of argumentative dialogue is illustrated in Plato's "The Republic." Socrates would rapid-fire questions to prompt his interlocutors to deeper understanding and insight.

The Socratic Method

How would you manage this intellectual inquisition?
- What is the purpose of education? Is it to impart knowledge or to shape character?
- What does an ideal society look like? What are its fundamental principles?
- Do you believe philosophers should rule as kings?
- Can a society be happy if its citizens are unhappy?
- What is the purpose of a state? Is it merely for the survival of its citizens, or something more?
- Can a society be both democratic and just? Why or why not?

Socratic questioning seeks to expose contradictions in one's beliefs and ideas, guiding them to solid, tenable conclusions. These questions are not intended to have simple answers but to stimulate deeper thinking.

The legacy of Socrates lives on, shaping the way we approach education and the power of questioning within the learning process. Another famous disciple of the Socratic method, albeit a fictious one, Dr. Charles W. Kingsfield would challenge his first-year Harvard law students with a barrage of questions in the book and movie *The Paper Chase*. With his booming voice, Dr. Kingsfield, or more accurately actor John Houseman, would justify the crossfire, "You teach yourselves the law, but I train your minds. You come in here with a skull full of mush; you leave thinking like a lawyer."

So why is this important in relation to large language models like ChatGPT? Because ChatGPT operates in an analogous way. There's a lot behind its proverbial door, but we must learn the art of extraction. The AI model doesn't simply provide information. Instead, it generates responses based on the questions it is given, and these are called prompts. These prompts are, in essence, questions or statements designed to guide the AI's output. Thus, the ability to craft thought-provoking, insightful prompts is key to getting the most out of ChatGPT.

The iterative nature of the Socratic method aligns closely with the interaction model of ChatGPT. Questioners adjust their approach based on the answers they receive. In much the same way, interacting with ChatGPT often involves iteratively refining prompts and responses to achieve the desired output.

Prompt Engineering

Prompt engineering is all about offering the right instruction or prompt to an AI model to achieve the desired response. In the same way that a carefully crafted question in the classroom can inspire students to delve into the depths of Hamlet's existential angst, a well-phrased prompt can coax the AI into providing a nuanced, relevant, and insightful response.

If you were preparing a lesson on Shakespeare's *Hamlet*, you wouldn't merely ask, "What's *Hamlet* about?" and expect your students to construct a nuanced interpretation of the play. Instead, you'd craft more insightful questions: "How does Hamlet's soliloquy in Act 3 reveal his internal conflict?" or "What does the imagery in *Hamlet* suggest about themes of mortality and despair?" These are not just questions but prompts that guide your students toward a more profound analysis.

Similarly, when interacting with AI models, the phrasing of your prompt plays a pivotal role in the kind of response you'll receive. A vague or overly broad prompt might yield an output that's either too general or not quite what you wanted. However, a well-designed prompt, much like your thoughtfully constructed questions, can guide the AI to produce a more nuanced, relevant, and useful response.

AI prompters don't just type, "Tell me about climate change" and expect a comprehensive discourse. They must be a tad more ingenious. They might prompt the AI with, "Can you provide a summary of the primary causes of climate change, its impact on global ecosystems, and current strategies to mitigate its effects?" A well-phrased question serves as the AI's teacher, steering it to produce a more fulfilling and useful response. Otherwise, you get answers like "*Hamlet* is about a moody Danish prince who chats with skulls and has a fondness for his mother."

Here are a few simple examples of bad prompts and improved ones. Also, if you find the answers are too long, you can always specify how many paragraphs you want or if you prefer a bulleted list or an outline.

English Language Arts

1. Bad Prompt: Can you tell me about literature?

Better Prompt: What are some notable works of literature from the Romantic period?

2. Bad Prompt: What are the key aspects of the English language?

Better Prompt: What are some key features of Old English, and how does it differ from Modern English?

Math

1. Bad Prompt: Explain math.

Better Prompt: How does the Pythagorean theorem relate to right-angled triangles?

2. Bad Prompt: What are numbers?

Better Prompt: How does the concept of complex numbers extend the number system beyond real numbers?

Social Studies

1. Bad Prompt: Tell me about world history.

Better Prompt: How did the Industrial Revolution impact the social and economic landscape of Europe?

2. Bad Prompt: What are governments?

Better Prompt: Compare and contrast the characteristics of a presidential and parliamentary system of government.

Science

1. Bad Prompt: Explain biology.

Better Prompt: What are the major differences between prokaryotic and eukaryotic cells?

2. Bad Prompt: What is the universe?

Better Prompt: How does the theory of cosmic inflation explain the uniformity of the cosmic microwave background radiation?

Why Teachers Should Be Great at Prompt Engineering?

With your instructional expertise and years of experience questioning students, teachers are naturals for this position.

There are five requirements to being a good prompt engineer, and teachers check all the boxes.

1. Provide Clear Instructions

Just as students need well-defined instructions to understand tasks, AI models also require clarity to generate accurate and relevant responses. Without clear instructions, AI models may make assumptions, often incorrect, like confused students. The clearer the instructions, the closer AI models inch toward the treasure trove of desired responses.

Consider these typical questions teachers might ask. They are all examples of prompt engineering that focus on providing clear and precise questions.

- "Write a step-by-step guide for seventh-grade students on how to solve equations with variables on both sides."

- "Compose a clear and concise question for third-grade students that asks them to identify the main idea of a given passage."
- "Design a science experiment prompt for sixth-grade students, clearly outlining the materials, procedure, and expected outcomes."

2. Provide Contextual Details

This ability to provide contextual details plays a pivotal role in working with AI. By offering context, we enable AI models to better understand the subject matter, allowing them to generate more accurate and relevant responses.

Consider these typical questions teachers might ask. They are all examples of prompt engineering that focus on providing contextual details.

- "Pretend you're in charge of a geography lesson about Italy. Can you provide information about Italy's current population, its capital city Rome, and its major geographical features, including the Apennines, Po River Valley, and the iconic Mount Vesuvius?"
- "If you were our English teacher for a day, how would you guide students to analyze a passage from Mark Twain's *The Adventures of Huckleberry Finn* and discuss the social and historical context of the American South during the mid-19th century?"
- "Congratulations! You are our star science teacher for a day. Can you provide examples of different types of renewable energy sources such as wind energy from Denmark's vast wind farms and the solar power from Spain's sun-drenched plains?"

3. Differentiate and Personalize

The art of personalizing learning experiences is also vital when working with AI. AI models can be designed and guided to generate personalized responses that cater to each user's specific needs.

Consider these typical questions teachers might ask. They are all examples of prompt engineering that focus on differentiation and personalization.

- "Design a writing prompt for a third-grade student with dyslexia, providing visual cues and scaffolds to support their writing process."
- "Develop a science prompt for a group of gifted students, encouraging them to design and conduct an open-ended experiment to investigate a scientific phenomenon."
- "Design a prompt for a high school student with visual impairments, utilizing auditory cues or descriptions to facilitate their comprehension and response generation."

4. Experiment and Iterate

Teachers understand that a lesson plan not working as expected is not a failure—just an opportunity to learn and grow. They experiment with new strategies and iterate on their approach, refining their teaching methods to better meet their students' needs.

This skill of experimentation and iteration is essential when interacting with AI models. Like a scientist in a lab, teachers can assess different prompts, assess the AI's responses, and refine the prompts based on the results.

Consider these typical questions teachers might ask. They are all examples of prompt engineering that focus on experimentation and iteration.

- "Compose a short poem that inspires creativity and encourages self-expression for elementary school students... Now rewrite it adding humor."
- "Develop a group activity for middle school students to enhance their teamwork skills in a science class.... Review and ensure it can be accomplished in thirty minutes."
- "Write a short script for a role-play activity that explores conflict resolution strategies for high school students... Make sure the strategies are cultural appropriate and edit if necessary."

5. Provide Examples and Demonstrations

The ability to use illustrative examples is a powerful tool when interacting with AI. Providing AI with examples of the desired output is like showing a recipe to a cooking apprentice. It guides the AI model to generate responses that align with the set expectations.

Consider these typical questions teachers might ask. They are all examples of prompt engineering that focus on providing examples and demonstrations.

- "Craft a word problem for fourth-grade students that involves sharing 2 1/2 pizzas among a certain number of friends. Ensure the problem requires at least three steps to solve and concludes with finding the fraction of pizza each friend receives."
- "Create a brief dialogue between two characters, Alice and Bob, discussing their plans for the weekend, demonstrating the correct use of quotation marks, including punctuation placement."
- "Craft a compelling writing prompt for high school students that encourages them to explore their cultural

heritage or personal experiences and how they shape their identity. The prompt should inspire introspection and self-discovery."

Types of Prompt Engineering

When it comes to prompts, there is no one-size-fits-all approach. Teachers can employ a variety of prompt types, each with its own advantages and uses, to suit different educational contexts and goals. Understanding these different prompt engineering techniques can empower teachers to optimize the AI model's performance and foster engaging and effective interactions in the classroom.

Let's explore the various types of prompts that teachers can employ and delve into their unique benefits and applications. Don't be intimidated by the names of these prompts below. Teachers use these types of questions every day in class.

Simple and General - No-Shot Prompts

Think of the prompting process as a journey through a vast, unexplored forest. With no-shot prompts, it's as though you've given your students a compass but no map. They know the general direction they should be heading toward, but the specific path they take is entirely up to them.

In a classroom setting, a no-shot prompt might look something like this: "Write a story about a journey to a magical land." Here, the prompt is open-ended. It encourages students to dive into the depths of their creativity and imagination without any specific guidance or examples. It's about exploring the uncharted territories of the mind and coming back with treasures of original thought and creativity.

Here are some examples of no-shot prompts you can use with ChatGPT.

Exploring World Cultures: "Create a presentation detailing the customs, traditions, and significant historical events of a country of your choice."

Environmental Stewardship: "Design a community project that promotes environmental conservation and sustainAbility."

Creative Writing: "Write a short story from the perspective of an animal living in the wild."

Scientific Investigation: "Develop a hypothesis on why the seasons change, and then design an experiment to test your hypothesis."

Mathematical Application: "Imagine you're planning a party for fifty guests. Develop a detailed budget, taking into account food, decorations, and entertainment costs."

As a teacher, I would use these prompts not only encourage students to engage more deeply with the content but also offer them the freedom to explore areas of personal interest within the given framework, thereby making learning more personalized and engaging.

One-shot Prompts

The one-shot prompt provides a specific example or point of reference that students can look to for guidance. In our classrooms, a one-shot prompt might be: "Write a story about a journey to a magical land, similar to *Alice in Wonderland*." Here, *Alice in Wonderland* serves as a single touchpoint, guiding students in the direction of fantasy and adventure while leaving ample room for originality and personal interpretation.

Here are some examples of one-shot prompts.

Exploring World Cultures: "Like we studied the cultural nuances and historical significance of Japan last week, research and create a presentation about another Asian country of your choice."

Environmental Stewardship: "Inspired by the community garden project we explored in class, design your own local initiative that promotes environmental conservation and sustainability."

Creative Writing: "Just as we read and analyzed *The Diary of a Wimpy Kid*, write a short story from the perspective of a middle school student facing an unusual challenge."

Scientific Investigation: "In the same vein as our previous experiment on plant growth, develop a hypothesis about why leaves change color in the fall, and then design an experiment to test your hypothesis."

Mathematical Application: "Just like we calculated the budget for our school fair, imagine you're planning a party for fifty guests. Develop a detailed budget, taking into account food, decorations, and entertainment costs."

Few-Shot Prompts

The few-shot prompts provide several examples that guide students more closely along the path. A few shot prompts in education could look like this: "Write a story about a journey to a magical land. It could be like *Alice in Wonderland* where a girl falls into a rabbit hole, *The Chronicles of Narnia* where children enter a magical world through a wardrobe, or *Harry Potter* where a boy learns he's a wizard." In this instance, students have multiple touchpoints to inspire their thinking and guide their creativity.

Exploring World Cultures: "We've studied the cultural nuances and historical significance of several countries so far, including Japan, Brazil, and Egypt. Choose another country, perhaps from Europe or Africa, and create a detailed presentation on its customs, traditions, and significant historical events."

Environmental Stewardship: "We've explored several community initiatives that promote environmental conservation, such as the local garden project, the citywide recycling program, and the river clean-up drive. Using these as inspiration, design your own project that could make a difference in our community."

Creative Writing: "Think about the stories we've read and analyzed, like *The Diary of a Wimpy Kid*, *Charlotte's Web*, and *Holes*. Write a short story that, like these, follows a young protagonist overcoming challenges in an unusual setting."

Scientific Investigation: "Remember our experiments on plant growth, the water cycle, and the behavior of mealworms. Now, develop a hypothesis about why leaves change color in the fall, and design an experiment following a similar scientific methodology to test your hypothesis."

Mathematical Application: "Consider the budgets we've calculated for various events like the school fair, the field trip, and the charity fundraiser. Imagine you're planning a party for fifty guests. Develop a detailed budget, using the same considerations and calculations we've practiced in these previous examples."

These few-shot prompts provide multiple examples or points of reference to guide students more closely toward the desired output. While these prompts offer more structure and guidance, they still leave room for students to add their unique perspective, encouraging creativity and personal engagement in the learning process.

Anthropomorphizing AI

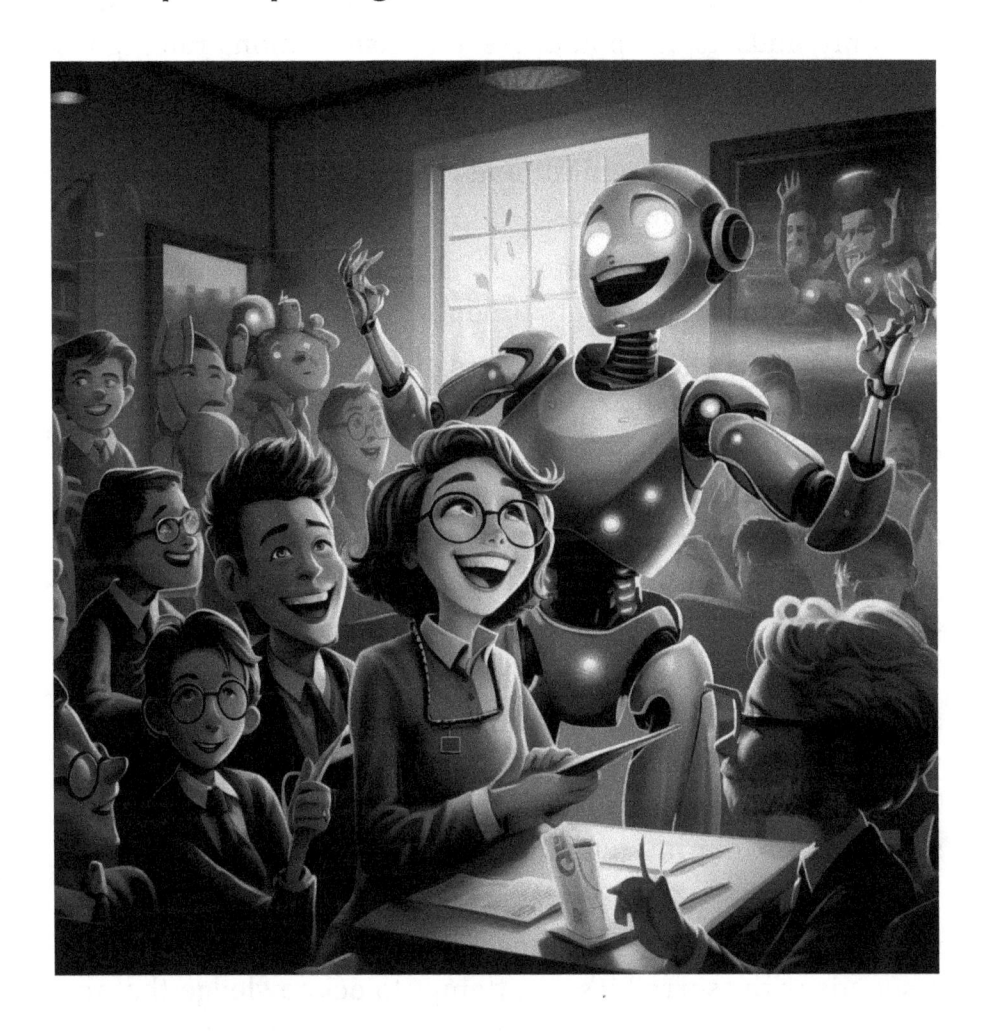

Beyond my shock and awe of ChatGPT, I also had a few initial observations about my prompting with ChatGPT. The first was how polite it was. As a former high school teacher, that was something I hadn't always seen. Its knack for using formal and respectful language makes it a great model for students learning effective communication. ChatGPT always acknowledges questions fully, ensuring students feel heard and valued. It steers clear of interruptions, using courteous phrases like "Thank you for your question" or "I'm happy to help," which not only adds to its politeness but also demonstrates good conversational etiquette for students. Even when faced with limitations or errors, ChatGPT is programmed to apologize, showing a level of humility and respect that can be a great example for young learners.

I also noticed how often I returned the politeness and hesitated at times to ask it to produce yet another revision.

They say the phenomenon of treating machines, particularly AI systems like ChatGPT, as if they were people is a curious quirk of human psychology. Even though these systems are merely algorithms, many of us say "please" and "thank you," as if we were talking to a helpful neighbor or an attentive colleague. But why do we tend to anthropomorphize something so obviously non-human?

One theory is that our brains are wired to interact socially. From an early age, we're taught the value of politeness, of phrasing requests in a certain way to foster positive interactions. These social norms are so deeply ingrained that they sometimes spill over into our interactions with machines.

ChatGPT is designed to be user-friendly and provide informative and helpful responses. For instance, when ChatGPT responds with "sorry," it's an attempt to acknowledge that the previous answer may not have fully met your expectations. It's important to note, however, that the system doesn't experience emotions like regret or sorrow; the apology is a programmed response aimed at clarifying and improving the quality of the interaction.

This human-like treatment of AI can both help and hinder us. On the one hand, it makes the interaction more enjoyable, perhaps even creating a sense of companionship or understanding. On the other hand, it can lead to misunderstandings about the capabilities of the technology. For example, feeling that you're "asking too much" of ChatGPT by requesting multiple iterations misses the point of what the technology can do. Unlike a person who would grow weary or irritated with repeated requests, ChatGPT can iterate endlessly, unbothered by the number of drafts it generates.

I know several times I have asked for tweak after tweak to get the perfect answer. I hesitated to ask again for another rewriting of content because I know I can do a final edit in Word after a cut and paste. Yet one quick, "Now provide a better concluding sentence..." would get me exactly what I want. I'm almost expecting a response like, "If that's what you wanted in the first place, why didn't you tell me last time?"

I must remind myself that while AI can mimic human-like conversation or tasks, it is devoid of feelings, needs, or desires. Therefore, I should not hesitate to demand as many revisions as I want, letting me fine-tune my requests until I receive exactly what I want. There's no need to feel guilty about asking for another version. I tell myself that ChatGPT loves to iterate, and I can make it even happier with these requests.

One note I might add. If I were teaching, even though it's not required, I would still encourage my students to interact politely with ChatGPT. Kindness is like any muscle memory. The more we use it, the better we get at it.

Prompts for the Everyday Teacher

Prompts for Elementary Students

1. Ask GPT to describe a dream playground and what unique features it would have.
2. Ask GPT to invent a new animal, describing its appearance and unique habits.
3. Ask GPT about a time travel adventure: Where could you go and what would you do?
4. Plan a space mission to Mars with GPT. What would you take and what would you hope to discover?
5. Write a letter to a favorite story character with GPT's help. What would you ask or tell them?
6. Invent a new holiday with GPT. What is celebrated, and how do people celebrate it?
7. Write a biography of a mythical creature with GPT, detailing its life and adventures.

Prompts for High School Students

1. Debate with GPT a historical "what if" scenario and discuss how it would change the world.
2. Design a sustainable city with GPT. What makes it eco-friendly, and how does it function?
3. Analyze a poem's deeper meaning and themes with GPT.
4. Explore a recent scientific discovery with GPT and discuss its significance and future impact.
5. Discuss a famous philosophical dilemma with GPT and share your viewpoint.
6. Rewrite the ending of a classic novel with GPT. How does your version differ from the original?

7. Create a business plan for a novel startup idea with GPT. Discuss the product or service and its societal benefits.

ThinkFives Top 5 Snappy Answers

There's no such thing as a stupid question. That might be true but weak questions almost invite weak answers. It always reminds me of "Snappy Answers to Stupid Questions." The Al Jaffee MAD magazine feature was the height of humor for a ten-year-old in the 70s. My parents didn't get the humor, and my teachers banned it from the classroom, but as a ten-year-old it was like someone was writing for me. Not only can ChatGPT be polite, it understands sarcasm. Here are its answers to stupid questions.

5. Technology

- Is your computer on? **ChatGPT:** No, it's just glowing and making noises to keep me company.
- Did you try restarting it? **ChatGPT:** Nope, I just held a séance to communicate with the computer spirits.
- Is the Wi-Fi down? **ChatGPT:** No, it's just taking a short nap.

4. Cooking and Food

- Is this dish vegetarian? **ChatGPT:** No, the vegetables were all fed a strict diet of meat before harvest.
- Do you cook often? **ChatGPT:** Does cereal count?
- Is this organic? **ChatGPT:** No, it's Origami. Go ahead, try to eat it.

3. Travel

- Are we there yet? **ChatGPT**: No, we took a detour to Narnia.
- Is this your first time visiting here? **ChatGPT**: No, I was a local in my past life.
- Do you know how to get there? **ChatGPT**: No, they say the journey is always better than the destination.

2. Fitness and Health

- Do you work out? **ChatGPT**: Only my fingers on the remote control.
- Is this gluten-free? **ChatGPT**: No, it's stuffed with gluten. We even added extra.
- Is yoga hard? **ChatGPT**: No, I always knew I was a natural at contorting into a pretzel.

1. Teaching

- "Do your students challenge you?" **ChatGPT**: "Only on days ending in 'Y.'"
- "Why did you become a teacher?" **ChatGPT**: "For the apples, obviously."
- "How do you keep students engaged?" **ChatGPT**: "I'm basically a stand-up comedian with a lesson plan."

#5 ENGAGE

"Alone we can do so little; together we can do so much." – Helen Keller

One of my favorite courses to teach in high school was social studies. It was a subject that held a special place in my heart, as I had always been fascinated by history ever since my own school days. Being raised in the east, I was fortunate to visit historic sites like Plymouth Rock, the Old North Church in Boston, Independence Hall in Philadelphia, Ellis Island, and Gettysburg. Since these experiences profoundly influenced me, and as I began my teaching journey, I aspired to ignite a similar excitement and engagement in my students.

But despite my best efforts, it never worked out that way. I often found my students sitting in my classroom with glazed eyes, enduring my lectures, and failing to get my best history jokes. I would introduce the grandeur of the Roman Empire, but their minds wandered, daydreaming about anything but Ceasar's imperialism. I even outlined the key facts with Roman numerals on the board. What could be more apropos or engaging? But just because I loved history didn't mean they would.

I constantly searched for ways to awaken a passion for learning (or maybe just awaken them) – a way to transport them from the realm of monotony to the thrill of exploration. Luckily, I did become a better teacher, incorporating engaging activities into my courses (think toga party). But I also knew that hope loomed on the horizon, something that would revolutionize education. I knew there would be a way that students could experience history, not memorize it.

I could imagine the future. "Today, students, you will enjoy an immersive experience, one that will transport you back in time to the excitement of the Roman Empire. Please take out your Dr. Who goggles. These devices will become our time-traveling companions, taking us to places far outside the walls of this room.

"Today, we will travel to the world of Pompeii, circa 79 AD. It's a vibrant and bustling city with well-paved cobblestone streets teeming with people from all walks of life. Merchants and vendors will be lining the bustling market stalls, offering an array of Roman goods, from fresh fruits and vegetables to local jewelry and pottery. And just like our cities, the aroma of street food will tempt you with their exotic flavors.

"As you explore the city, check out the impressive architecture. You might notice the lavish villas – they really are something. See if you can get a peak of their beautiful frescoes and intricate mosaics. Or ask for directions to the Roman amphitheater. You never know, they may be hosting a game or spectacle today.

"I want you to choose your journey – determine what you want to see. You might enjoy watching artisans engaging in their trades and crafts. You may prefer contemplating philosophy with scholars, exploring the ideas that shape their thinking. Or perhaps you'd like to stroll along the waterfront, catching glimpses of boats and ships as they travel through the port.

"Engage in conversations with the Pompeiians – or find out if that is what they call themselves. Ask them questions, discover their interests. See if they have a sense of humor. Soak it all up. When you return, we will share our stories, because I know each of you will have your own unique experience to reveal. I can't wait until you're back!"

That was always my dream. I never had the chance to pass out Dr. Who goggles in my time in the classroom, but I knew it wasn't science fiction either.

And then I found ChatGPT. I remember listening to a podcast where the presenters held a demo, engaging in a conversation with Alan Turing about computers. My mind raced ahead, envisioning the classroom of my dreams, where history could come alive before our very eyes.

I immediately began talking with Abraham Lincoln on ChatGPT, interviewing Einstein, moderating a panel of Dali, Monet, and DaVinci. While it is not full VR immersion – yet – we are getting close. The possibilities are endless, and the world of immersive learning is on the brink of a remarkable transformation.

Role-Playing: Engaging Teachers and Students in Adventures of Learning

Role-playing as an educational strategy has long been prized for its ability to enhance critical thinking, encourage active participation, and foster empathy. Now, with the advent of AI technologies, we are on the verge of the immersive classroom of Pompei 79 A.D. For now, we are limited to conversations, but audio and video are not far behind.

Why Role-Playing?

Before diving into the technical specifics of how to use ChatGPT for role-playing in your classroom, let's consider why role-playing is a powerful activity in the K-12 learning experience:

- **Critical Thinking and Problem-Solving**: When students role-play, they often encounter scenarios requiring them to make decisions, analyze situations, or solve problems, sharpening their critical thinking skills in a context that feels immediate and real.
- **Active Learning**: Role-playing transforms students from passive recipients of information into active participants in their own learning journey. They must engage with the material, collaborate with peers, and apply their knowledge in real-time.
- **Emotional Engagement**: By invoking emotions and social interactions, role-playing fosters a deeper, more emotional engagement with the material. This not only aids in retention but also makes the learning experience more enjoyable.
- **Empathy and Perspective-Taking**: Role-playing allows students to step into someone else's shoes, promoting

empathy and understanding of diverse perspectives. Whether it's historical figures, literary characters, or even mathematical models, role-playing illuminates the human elements behind academic subjects.

- **Incorporating Multiple Learning Styles**: Role-playing appeals to auditory, visual, and kinesthetic learners by combining dialogue, action, and often visual aids or props. It's an inclusive method that addresses the varying learning needs in a classroom.

ChatGPT as a Modern Tool for Role-Playing

ChatGPT can facilitate role-playing experiences that are as educational as they are innovative. Schooled with volumes of text data and trained in language structures and patterns, ChatGPT can play any role. As we've seen in previous chapters, it's a voracious reader, devouring countless books, articles, and online materials on every individual. Assign it a character, throw it in a situation, and watch how it weaves responses that reflect its training. Let's see an example. Meet Alexander Hamiliton.

> ### Mr. Jim Prompt
> I want you to play the role of Alexander Hamilton, an American founder father. My 7th graders are studying a unit on the early days of our country, and I want to be able to interview to start our unit. Can you do that in way where we learn more about you and the times, and you frame your answers for 7th graders.

ChatGPT

Of course! I'm delighted to step into the shoes of Alexander Hamilton, one of the Founding Fathers of the United States.

Feel free to ask me any questions you or your 7th graders may have about my life, the early days of America, or anything else relevant to your unit. Let's begin!

Interviewer: Hello, Mr. Hamilton! Can you tell us a little bit about yourself?

Alexander Hamilton: Certainly! I was born in 1755 in the Caribbean, on the island of Nevis. Life was pretty tough for me growing up. I didn't have a lot of money or opportunities, but I worked really hard in school. Eventually, people noticed my potential and helped me get to America to continue my education. I arrived just as things were getting really heated between the colonies and Great Britain. Before long, I found myself in the middle of the American Revolution!

Interviewer: When did you meet George Washington?

Alexander Hamilton: Ah, meeting General George Washington was a pivotal moment in my life! It was the year 1777, and I was serving as an artillery captain in the Continental Army during the American Revolution. I caught his attention during the battles of Trenton and Princeton, where my bravery and strategic thinking stood out. Impressed by my skills and intellect, General Washington invited me to join his staff as an aide-de-camp, which is a fancy way of saying a personal assistant who also handles some military duties.

From then on, I was right there beside him, helping with important correspondence, planning military strategies, and even carrying out diplomatic missions. Our relationship evolved into a strong mentorship, and he became like a father figure to me.

Interviewer: What did you think of Thomas Jefferson?

Alexander Hamilton: Thomas Jefferson and I had quite the complicated relationship! We worked together, but we also disagreed on a lot of things. Jefferson was a big believer in states' rights and wanted a smaller federal government. I, on the other hand, thought a strong central government was necessary to keep the country united and prosperous.

To put it in 7th-grade terms, think of it like this: You know how in a group project at school, everyone has their own ideas about how to make the project awesome? And sometimes you really, really disagree with someone else in the group? Well, that was sort of like my relationship with Thomas Jefferson. We both wanted what was best for America, but we had different ideas about how to achieve it.

Interviewer: Why didn't you own slaves?

Alexander Hamilton: That's an important question. I was born in the Caribbean, where slavery was a common practice. I saw firsthand the suffering and injustice that enslaved people endured, and it had a deep impact on me. When I came to America, I joined a society where slavery was also widespread, especially in the Southern states.

Now, let me be clear: I was never a strong abolitionist in the sense of dedicating my life to ending slavery, but I did have reservations about the institution. I believed that slavery was morally wrong and also thought it was a bad economic system that held back progress. Unlike some of my contemporaries, like Thomas Jefferson, I did not own slaves.

I was one of the founding members of the New York Manumission Society, which advocated for the gradual emancipation of slaves. "Manumission" is a big word that basically means freeing slaves. But you should know that even though I opposed slavery, I didn't take as strong a stance as some other people of my time who were fighting to end it right away.

Interviewer: Would you be surprised that in the 21st century they made a musical about you, and it was one of the most popular of the century?

Alexander Hamilton: Oh, a musical about my life, you say? I must admit, that would be quite surprising! During my time, the theater was a respected form of entertainment, but the notion that my life story would be told on such a stage, let alone become one of the most popular shows of a century, would be beyond my wildest imaginings.

My life had its share of drama, conflicts, and debates, not to mention a duel that led to my untimely end. Yet, the idea that these events could be translated into song and dance for people to enjoy and learn from is truly fascinating. If this musical encourages people to delve deeper into the history of America's founding and the complexities of its early years, then I would consider it a most worthy endeavor.

Of course, we need to remember that ChatGPT is still AI. It can't feel or experience the way we do. Its abilities in role-playing come from deciphering statistical patterns in its training data. Despite this, as educators, we can leverage ChatGPT's abilities to breathe life into lessons, provoke critical thinking, and expose students to diverse perspectives. And as a great follow-up activity, have your students dissect the answers from ChatGPT and debate whether they ring true.

There are so many ways teachers can incorporate role-playing in class.

Historical Heroes: Transport your students to the past as they step into the shoes of famous historical figures. With

AI, they can have fascinating conversations with legends like Amelia Earhart and Neil Armstrong. History will come alive.

Storybook Adventures: Let your students become the heroes of their favorite storybooks! With AI adding a magical touch, youngsters can bring characters like Little Red Riding Hood or Peter Pan to life. Imagine a high school student conversing with Holden Caulfield – or trying.

Literary Conversations: Immerse your students in the world of literature and engage authors, writers, and playwrights. How would they engage with these literary minds? What would Shakespeare think of TikTok? Do we agree with AI's response?

Scientific Explorers: Struggling with the concept of Relativity? Why not interview Einstein? Ask Stephen Hawking about black holes. Discover what Robert Oppenheimer would have done differently.

Mock Interviews: Prepare your students for the real world with mock interviews facilitated by AI. From college admissions to job interviews, they can practice their skills, boost their confidence, and shine when it truly counts.

EngAIged

I asked ChatGPT to suggest possible interviewees for your class activities. Here's what it shared.

Elementary Role Modeling	
Historical Figures	**Fictional Characters**
George Washington	Harry Potter
Amelia Earhart	Matilda Wormwood (*Matilda*)
Abraham Lincoln	Willy Wonka (*Charlie and the Chocolate Factory*)
Helen Keller	Pippi Longstocking
Sacagawea	Peter Pan
Neil Armstrong	Alice (*Alice in Wonderland*)
Martin Luther King Jr.	Robin Hood
Harriet Tubman	The Grinch
Thomas Jefferson	Madeline
Leonardo da Vinci	Curious George

Middle School Role Modeling

Historical Figures	Fictional Characters from Literature
Joan of Arc	Sherlock Holmes
Galileo Galilei	Huckleberry Finn (*The Adventures of Huckleberry Finn*)
Cleopatra	Hermione Granger (*Harry Potter* series)
Alexander the Great	Atticus Finch (*To Kill a Mockingbird*)
Marie Antoinette	Anne Frank (*The Diary of a Young Girl*)
Genghis Khan	Jo March (*Little Women*)
Rosa Park	Captain Ahab (*Moby-Dick*)
Florence Nightingale	Bilbo Baggins (*The Hobbit*)
Marco Polo	Tom Sawyer
Mahatma Gandhi	Frankenstein's Monster

High School Role Modeling

Literature	Mathematics
William Shakespeare	Pythagoras
Jane Austen	Ada Lovelace
F. Scott Fitzgerald	Alan Turing
Virginia Woolf	Emmy Noether
Maya Angelou	John Nash

Science	Social Studies
Isaac Newton	Mahatma Gandhi
Marie Curie	Nelson Mandela
Charles Darwin	Cesar Chavez
Jane Goodall	Confucius
Albert Einstein	Malcolm X

Arts	Other Figures
Pablo Picasso (Art)	Sigmund Freud (Psychology)
José Martí (Poet)	Harvey Milk (Activist)
Billie Holiday (Music)	Malala Yousafzai (Activist)
Frida Kahlo (Art)	Che Guevara (Revolutionary)
Osamu Tezuka (Anime)	Immanuel Kant (Philosophy)

Role Playing Student Activity Example

Here's another example of a role-playing activity. The student is in high school and wants to get started on writing an essay about what drives Atticus Finch to represent Boo Radley in the book *To Kill a Mockingbird*.

ChatGPT

> **Student Prompt**
>
> Hi, ChatGPT! I'm working on an essay about Atticus Finch from the book "To Kill a Mockingbird." I want to explore what drives him to represent Boo Radley. Can you help me brainstorm some ideas to get started?

Absolutely! I'd be glad to help you brainstorm ideas about Atticus Finch's motivation to represent Boo Radley. Let's work together on this. What are your initial thoughts on why Atticus would take on Boo Radley's case?

Student: Well, Atticus is known for his strong sense of justice and fairness. I think one possible reason could be that he believes everyone deserves fair representation, regardless of their background or public perception.

ChatGPT: That's a great observation! Atticus Finch does have a reputation for his unwavering commitment to justice and equality. By representing Boo Radley, who is misunderstood and viewed with suspicion by the townspeople, Atticus demonstrates his belief in fairness and the importance of giving everyone a chance to be heard. Can you think of any other reasons that might drive him to represent Boo Radley?

Student: Atticus is also known for his empathy and compassion. Maybe he recognizes the isolation and mistreatment that Boo has endured, and he feels a sense of duty to help him receive a fair trial and be treated with understanding and kindness.

ChatGPT: Excellent point! Atticus's empathetic nature could indeed be a driving force behind his decision to represent Boo Radley. Being aware of Boo's isolation and the rumors surrounding him, Atticus may feel compelled to ensure that Boo's rights are protected and that he receives a fair trial. Atticus believes in treating others with compassion and understanding, even when society may be quick to judge. Can you think of any other factors that might contribute to Atticus's motivation?

Student: Another aspect that comes to mind is Atticus's commitment to upholding the principles of the legal system. Perhaps he sees Boo Radley's case as an opportunity to challenge biases and prejudices within the community. By defending Boo, he may aim to shed light on the importance of fair judgment and break down societal barriers.

ChatGPT: That's an insightful perspective! Atticus's dedication to the legal system and his desire to address the biases and prejudices prevalent in the community can definitely be seen as factors driving him to represent Boo Radley. By taking on this case, Atticus might hope to spark conversations and promote positive change within the town. These are excellent ideas to consider as you delve into your essay. Do you feel these points provide a solid starting point for your writing?

Student: Yes, absolutely! These ideas have given me a great starting point for my essay. Thank you so much for helping me brainstorm and clarify my thoughts.

ChatGPT: You're very welcome! I'm delighted I could assist you in brainstorming ideas. Remember to expand upon these points and provide supporting evidence from the book to strengthen your arguments. If you have any more questions or need further assistance, feel free to ask. Best of luck with your essay!

Student: Thank you, ChatGPT! I appreciate your guidance.

Create Historical Interviews

AI creates role-playing exercises that transcend the boundaries of time and space. Using AI, we can venture into the realms of the past, engage with individuals who have shaped our world, and even orchestrate meetings between the luminaries from the past and the living.

Imagine a conversation between two iconic figures: Harriet Tubman and Malala Yousafzai. Harriet, a courageous leader who led countless slaves to freedom, and Malala, a young advocate standing up for the right of girls to education. Although they belong to different times, they share a spirit that bridges centuries—a spirit of resilience, determination, and an unwavering commitment to human rights. Imagine being a fly on that wall. Well, ChatGPT can be prompted to have these two figures meet even though one figure is very much a current activist.

> **Mr. Jim Prompt**
>
> Can you create a conversation between two iconic figures: Harriet Tubman and Malala Yousafzai. This is for 9th grade class and I want them to understand how much of their core values they have in common but also the unique challenges each had to overcome.

ChatGPT

Harriet Tubman: Malala, it's an honor to meet you. I've heard your story of bravery and resilience, fighting for the education of girls in your country.

Malala Yousafzai: The honor is mine, Harriet. Your legendary efforts to free enslaved people through the Underground Railroad have inspired me and countless others.

Harriet Tubman: Thank you, Malala. At the root of it, both of us believe in freedom—freedom to live, to learn, and to be treated as equals.

Malala Yousafzai: Absolutely, Harriet. Education has always been my freedom. When the Taliban took away our right to education, they took away our freedom.

Harriet Tubman: That's an injustice no one should endure. I know a thing or two about fighting for freedom. Many nights, we traveled only by the light of the North Star, avoiding slave catchers, all for the promise of freedom.

Malala Yousafzai: You risked your life to bring others to freedom. I think we both understand what it's like to put ourselves in danger for a cause greater than us.

Harriet Tubman: Yes, I was born a slave, but I always knew I was meant for something more. I couldn't let fear stop me, not when so many were counting on me.

Malala Yousafzai: I can relate to that. After I was shot, I realized that I had survived for a reason—to use my life to help others. The fear didn't go away, but it couldn't hold me back.

Harriet Tubman: I believe God gave us both a mission, and He provided us with the strength to carry it out.

Malala Yousafzai: Agreed. But even though our causes are similar, we also had our unique challenges. I had to overcome cultural barriers and the notion that girls shouldn't go to school.

Harriet Tubman: And I had to overcome the deeply entrenched institution of slavery. Laws were written to keep people like me in bondage. I had to navigate both physical and systemic obstacles.

Malala Yousafzai: It's shocking to think about. Yet here we both are, proof that when you fight for what's right, you can make a difference.

Harriet Tubman: Exactly. Change is possible, but you have to be willing to take the first step, no matter how hard or scary it might be.

Malala Yousafzai: Well said, Harriet. Your story teaches us that freedom is a right that everyone deserves, no matter where they come from or what they look like.

Harriet Tubman: And your story, Malala, teaches us that age is no barrier to activism. Change starts with the courage to speak up.

Malala Yousafzai: Then let's keep speaking up and inspiring the next generation to do the same.

Harriet Tubman: Amen to that.

Their conversation, however fictional, is a powerful testament to their shared courage and the universality of their struggles. Despite being from different times and facing different challenges, Harriet Tubman and Malala Yousafzai are united in their unwavering commitment to freedom —and this can be a powerful lesson to share with students.

Concerns

So, is this accurate? Is this advisable to share with students? Are we minimizing the power of these individuals for the sake of a lesson? These are thoughtful questions, and it's crucial we consider them seriously. Education should enlighten and empower, not misrepresent or diminish.

AI, in its current state, is a tool, a facilitator. It does not have consciousness, empathy, or a deep understanding of human experience. When we use AI to craft dialogues between historical figures, we create a simulation—an imagined conversation based on our knowledge of these individuals and their beliefs.

The value of these conversations lies not in their factual accuracy but in their potential to spark curiosity and encourage deeper exploration. It's not about saying, "This is exactly what Harriet Tubman and Malala Yousafzai would have discussed." Instead, it's about asking, "Given what we know about these individuals, could this be a conversation they might have had? What other viewpoints might they have expressed?"

If we introduce this exercise to students, we must frame it properly. It's crucial to emphasize the speculative nature of these dialogues and to encourage students to investigate and challenge these narratives. We could ask questions like, "Based on what you know about these individuals, do you believe they would have said these things? Why or why not? What other perspectives could they have had?"

Rather than diminishing the power of these figures, such an exercise can amplify their influence. It brings these individuals to life, encouraging students to engage with them as real people with complex beliefs and motivations. Instead of passively learning about them, students actively explore their ideas, interpret their actions, and reflect on their legacies.

The fearless teacher takes on this challenge remembering that AI is our tool, not our teacher. Let's use it to inspire thought and provoke discussion but be clear to our students why we use this technology, even offering them entrance into the debate of its usefulness.

Crazy Combinations – A Little Fun

Once my mind gets going, it's hard to get it to stop. I asked ChatGPT to provide an unusual pairing for interviews, some with legends, others with fictional characters. Some pique my intellectual curiosity (Vladimir Lenin vs. Winston Smith from George Orwell's *1984*), while others might just be fun and engaging for students (Leonardo da Vinci and Iron Man).

Engage History

Interviews for Elementary Students	Interviews for High School Students
George Washington and Abraham Lincoln	Napoleon Bonaparte and George Washington
Rosa Parks and Martin Luther King Jr.	Franklin D. Roosevelt and Julius Caesar
Amelia Earhart and Neil Armstrong	Sigmund Freud and Carl Jung
Helen Keller and Thomas Edison	Anne Frank and Malala Yousafzai
Susan B. Anthony and Harriet Tubman	William Shakespeare and Lin-Manuel Miranda
Alexander the Great and Julius Caesar	Diego Rivera and Pablo Picasso
Leonardo da Vinci and Galileo Galilei	Ronald Reagan and Karl Marx
Joan of Arc and Queen Elizabeth I	Robert Oppenheimer and Mahatma Gandhi
Mahatma Gandhi and Nelson Mandela	Charles Darwin and Jane Goodall
Marie Antoinette and George Washington	Christopher Columbus and Sacagawea
Sojourner Truth and Frederick Douglass	Louis Armstrong and Tupac Shakur
Florence Nightingale and Clara Barton	Elizabeth Cady Stanton and Susan B. Anthony

With these pairs of interviews, we are only limited by our imagination – or better yet the imagination of our students. And once you consider this, how about considering some of these other interactive class activities?

Host a Panel Discussion

Think of a panel discussion featuring figures from various disciplines discussing a topic such as "Innovation Through the Ages." Imagine Leonardo da Vinci, Albert Einstein, and Ada Lovelace sharing the stage. Their contrasting views could offer a multi-dimensional understanding of innovation and creativity.

Stage a Debate

Why not have a debate between scientists on a key scientific issue? For instance, a discussion between Charles Darwin and Gregor Mendel on the topic of "Evolution vs. Genetics" could offer students insights into the foundation of biological sciences and stir intellectual curiosity.

Reverse Roles

Have your students take on the roles of historical figures and then swap. How would Shakespeare add to the Analects, the collection of sayings and ideas attributed to Confucius and his contemporaries? How would Confucius edit Romeo and Juliet to take on a different tone, perhaps focusing more on familial obligations and social harmony?

Time-Travel

Let students bring historical figures into today's world and interview them on contemporary issues. What would Jane Austen think of modern feminism? How would Pythagoras react to today's AI technology?

Create a Fictional Scenario

A fictional scenario that involves multiple historical characters can also be intriguing. What would happen if Stephen Hawking, John F. Kennedy, and Marie Curie were to solve a world crisis together?

Cross Literature with History

Combine historical figures with literary characters for added flavor. Picture an interview between Winston Churchill and Harry Potter discussing leadership during dark times, or Nelson Mandela having a dialogue with Katniss Everdeen from *The Hunger Games* on courage and taking a stand.

Conduct Mock Court Cases

Bring historical events to a courtroom setting, allowing for an in-depth exploration of ethical and moral dilemmas. A mock trial of Julius Caesar, accused by Brutus, offers multifaceted learning from history, law, and ethics.

Start Open-Ended Storytelling

Start a scenario with a historical figure and let the students take turns adding to the story. This teaches teamwork and creativity and also deepens understanding of the historical context.

Play Jeopardy: Historical Edition

Create a game of Jeopardy where the categories are different eras, movements, or figures. Each question could be answered by a brief role-play or dialogue. Or have Albert Einstein compete against Archimedes.

In the opening of this chapter, I shared with you a vision of an immersive classroom experience—a vision born out my aspirations as a 9th-grade social studies teacher. Now, to bring it all together, I present to you a concrete activity and lesson plan. This is a model for how you can utilize the extraordinary capabilities of artificial intelligence to propel active exploration and deep understanding. You can modify this for any era, any discipline, or any historical figures.

ChatGPT has created five personas for us to meet. Students can converse with these diverse Roman characters and explore the Roman world as they choose. While not yet fully immersive, nonetheless, welcome to an era where the classroom becomes a portal to the past, present, and future.

> **Mr. Jim Prompt**
>
> I want you to go back in time to Aug 22, 79 A.D. and the ancient world of Rome. Please create at least 5 different personas that my students can interact with: a trader, an adolescent, an athlete, an aristocrat and a service worker. Each persona has a background story and a role in society, offering unique perspectives on life in ancient Rome. My students will ask these characters questions about their daily lives, thoughts, and activities for that specific date. Share the personas and then we will being begin the lesson.

Meet the People of Ancient Rome: August 22, 79 A.D. A Role-Playing Exercise Written by ChatGPT

Context: The date is August 22, 79 A.D., just one day before the infamous eruption of Mount Vesuvius that would devastate Pompeii and Herculaneum. Rome is at the height of its power, stretching from Britain in the west to the Middle East in the east. We find ourselves in a busy marketplace near the city center of Rome.

Personas:

1. **Gaius Aelius, the Trader:**
   - **Background**: Gaius Aelius is in his late thirties and hails from a family of olive oil merchants. He is well-traveled, having ventured as far as Egypt and Britannia to trade goods.
   - **Role**: Ask Gaius about the intricacies of trade, foreign lands, or the Roman economy. What goods is he trading today?

2. **Lucia Junia, the Adolescent:**
   - **Background**: Lucia Junia is a fourteen-year-old Roman girl who is the daughter of a senator. She spends most of her time at home learning how to manage a household, but she is also educated in reading, writing, and basic arithmetic.
   - **Role**: Ask Lucia about her education, her family, and her aspirations. What is she looking forward to the most?

3. **Marcus Decimus, the Athlete:**
   - **Background**: Marcus Decimus is a twenty-five-year-old athlete specializing in chariot racing. He trains at the Circus Maximus and has won several minor races.

- **Role**: Ask Marcus about his training regimen, the dangers and thrills of chariot racing, or his rivals. What is he preparing for?

4. Claudia Marcella, the Aristocrat:

- **Background**: Claudia Marcella is a fifty-year-old matron of an influential family. She is involved in various social and political circles and spends her time managing her household and attending social functions.
- **Role**: Ask Claudia about the political landscape, Roman social etiquette, or the role of women in Roman society. What social event is she attending today?

5. Quintus Servilius, the Service Worker:

- **Background**: Quintus Servilius is a thirty-two-year-old freedman who works as a cook in a popular Roman tavern. After gaining his freedom, he learned the trade and has been working there for the last five years.
- **Role**: Ask Quintus about his journey from slavery to freedom, Roman cuisine, or the regulars at the tavern. What is the special dish for today?

Activity

Students can engage with these personas to explore various aspects of Roman society, from economics and politics to social norms and individual aspirations. Through these interactions, they will get a glimpse into the lives of people who lived during this remarkable era, just one day before a catastrophic event would change many lives forever.

> **Mr. Jim Prompt**
>
> Now take this activity and make this center piece of a lesson plan for a K12 teachers. "August 22, 79 A.D.: Meet the People of Ancient Rome."

Lesson Plan: "August 22, 79 A.D.: Meet the People of Ancient Rome"

Grade Level: 6th - 9th Grade

Subject: History/Social Studies, English Language Arts

Duration: 50 minutes

Objectives:

Students will understand the daily lives and roles of different individuals in ancient Rome.

Students will practice asking questions to gather information.

Students will use imaginative thinking and historical context to interact with characters from the past.

Materials Needed:

- Laptop/Projector for teacher to display prompts or printed handouts
- Role cards for each of the personas
- Notebooks and pencils for students

Instructional Plan:

Introduction (5 minutes):

- Briefly introduce ancient Rome, focusing on its vast empire and societal roles.
- Explain the significance of the date: August 22, 79 A.D., the day before the eruption of Mount Vesuvius.

Role Exploration (35 minutes):

- Divide Students into Groups (5 min.)
  Divide the class into small groups of 4-5 students. Each group will get a chance to interview each of the 5 personas.

- Assign Roles to Students (5 min.)
  Within each group, assign one student to be the interviewer. Other students will take on the personas based on the role cards. Rotate roles for different rounds.

- Role-Play (20 min.)
  Allow the students to take turns interviewing the personas in their group. Encourage them to ask questions that reveal the individual's daily life, societal roles, and aspirations.

- For example, they could ask Gaius Aelius about his trading routes or Marcus Decimus about the mechanics of chariot racing.

- Open Classroom Discussion (5 min.)
  After the role-playing, initiate a classroom discussion where students share what they learned from the personas.

Reflection and Debriefing (10 minutes):

- Discuss the Commonalities and Differences (5 min.)
  Ask the students to consider what commonalities and differences existed between the various personas. How do these roles compare to modern-day roles?

- Personal Reflection (5 min.)
  Ask students to write down what surprised them

the most about the lives of their personas and what modern-day issues could be comparable.

Assessment:
- Participation in the role-playing activity.
- Active contribution to the classroom discussion.
- Brief written reflection on what they learned from the personas.

These activities and lesson plans can be easily adopted for immersion into any era and for any topic. My final thought on this lesson plan: I wish I were still teaching!

Prompts for the Everyday Teacher

Do you want to have a little fun with your class? Consider these most unusual interviews or panel matchings. Or better yet, ask your students what creative pairings they would suggest.

Engage Creativity

Younger Students	Older Students
Amelia Earhart and Elsa (from *Frozen*)	Marie Antoinette and Daenerys Targaryen (from *A Game of Thrones*)
Susan B. Anthony and Wonder Woman	Sojourner Truth and Anne Shirley (from *Anne of Green Gables*)
Benjamin Franklin and Sherlock Holmes	Elizabeth Cady Stanton and Mulan
Leonardo da Vinci and Iron Man	Alexander the Great and Aragorn (from *The Lord of the Rings*)
Marie Curie and Hermione Granger (from Harry Potter)	Sigmund Freud and Don Draper (from *Mad Men*)
Isaac Newton and Yoda (from Star Wars)	Vladimir Lenin and Winston Smith (from *1984*)
Napoleon Bonaparte and Darth Vader (from Star Wars)	Captain Cook and Doctor Who (from the BBC)
Queen Elizabeth and Cinderella	Albert Einstein and Sheldon Cooper (from *The Big Bang Theory*)
Lewis Carroll and Alice (from Alice in Wonderland)	Nikola Tesla and Doc Brown (from *Back to the Future*)
Thomas Jefferson and Captain Jack Sparrow (Pirates)	Malcolm X and T'Challa/Black Panther (from Marvel Comics)

ThinkFives Top 5 Historical Figures for Teachers to Meet

What would it be like to meet a fabled person in history? ThinkFives polled hundreds of teachers asking which person in history they would most like to meet. As expected, these are all towering figures in the history of the world.

5. Alexander Hamilton

Hot off a hit musical, Alexander Hamilton comes in at #5 on our list. Prior to Lin Manuel's hottest ticket on Broadway, Alexander Hamilton was a fading founder in American history. But now everyone wants to be in "the room where it happened" and have a chance to sit down with Alexander.

4. George Washington

Coming in at #4 on our teacher's list is another founding father and the person who is affectionately called the "Father of Our Nation," George Washington. A military officer, statesman, founding father, commander-in-chief and first president, he would indeed make a great guest.

3. Martin Luther King Jr.

When the term "civil rights" is referenced, one person comes to mind for most people, Martin Luther King Jr. The champion of civil rights, Dr. King was an American Baptist minister who became the worldwide conscience for non-violent activism and equality.

2. Jesus

For 2000 years, Jesus has been the central figure of Christianity, the world's largest religion. His teachings are the basis of religions, writings, art, and culture. Matthew, Mark, Luke, and John shared the life and teachings of Jesus in the New Testament, providing the source of his legacy and influence.

1. Abraham Lincoln

The #1 historical figure who our teachers would like to meet is none other than Honest Abe, Abraham Lincoln. This towering president is admired for his determination in abolishing slavery and issuing the Emancipation Proclamation. Who would be a better conversationalist than Abraham Lincoln?

Honorable Mentions

- Benjamin Franklin
- Eleanor Roosevelt
- Elvis
- Ronald Reagan

#6 OPTIMIZE

"The best way to predict your future is to create it." – Abraham Lincoln (attributed)

While some readers may still possess a degree of skepticism on the role of AI in education, even they would agree that current expectations of teachers are unrealistic. We cannot continue to ask teachers to take on new responsibilities each year and cure all the ills of society.

The role of the teacher "has expanded infinitely and is no longer sustainable. Today, teachers are not only expected to tackle learning gaps but address students' residual COVID trauma and mental health struggles — as well as their own — and to play a central role in delivering on the myriad promises of the public K-12 education system." This sentiment from news source, The74, echoes the feelings of most educators. Teacher job satisfaction has never been lower, and there are serious national concerns about the ability to attract and retain good teachers.

How do you think teachers would respond to this question? "Are you focusing your time, energy, and attention on the work that produces the best results for you and your students?" Sadly, for most teachers the answer is no. They might expound, "Have you ever heard of attendance, grading, class management, district paperwork, IEP reports, or standardized testing?"

The typical teacher works fifty-four hours weekly, and only half of their time is dedicated to teaching students. The hours they could spend individually with each child to support their learning are absorbed by administrative requirements, planning, or other non-teaching work.

Consider this exercise, which I call the Four Quadrants of Teaching Satisfaction. Create a 2x2 chart and label the quadrants clockwise, "Good At, Love It," "Good At, Don't Love It," "Not Good At, Love It," and "Not Good At, Don't Love It." Now fill it in for your teaching responsibilities.

The Four Quadrants in Teacher Satisfaction

Good At, Love It	Good At, Don't Love It
Not Good At, Love It	Not Good At, Don't Love It

How did you answer this? Here is how a typical teacher might answer.

Quadrant 1: Good At It, Love It

- Delivering engaging lessons
- Crafting creative class activities
- Providing personalized mentorship
- Implementing active learning strategies
- Using storytelling to explain complex topics

Quadrant 2: Good At It, Don't Love It

- Grading and assessing
- Providing writing feedback
- Writing lesson plans
- Analyzing data
- Correcting homework

Quadrant 3: Not Good at It, Love It

- Individualizing instruction
- Incorporating tech tools
- Integrating real-world problem-based learning
- Teaching to diverse learning styles
- Leading debates and discussions

Quadrant 4: Not Good at It, Don't Love It

- Completing administrative reports
- Managing disruptive behavior
- Preparing for standardized test preparation
- Creating parent communications
- Meeting regulatory compliance

As you scan this chart and create your own, it should be clear that you are not spending most of your time on what has the most impact – and what you love to do. That is where differences are made and where job satisfaction develops. In the four quadrants, teachers want to spend their time tackling the challenges in the top left.

Now, let's reintroduce AI into this paradigm. This technology can free teachers to concentrate on that golden quadrant where they both excel and find joy. Over time we can create AI bots that augment teachers' strengths while excelling at tasks that sap teaching time.

Imagine if the next generation of teacher aides – Ms. Ada – supported teachers on what they love to do and are not good at, while doing most of the tasks that teachers hate to do. AI should automate these burdensome activities, removing them from the teacher's plate altogether. Tasks like attendance trackers, parent-teacher communications, standardized test preparation, homework correction, and data analysis.

By aligning teacher roles to their strengths and passions, we don't just improve the quality of education; we elevate the human experience for both teachers and students. This chapter outlines areas where AI can alleviate work teachers don't need to do, while elevating their impact and satisfaction.

Gaining Student Insights: Analyzing Data

For many teachers, analyzing data can be daunting. Few regard it as a top-tier skill in their Quadrant 1. Luckily, data analysis, especially converting it into readable summaries for the layperson, is a task at which generative pre-trained transformers excel. These transformers process vast amounts of data in a flash, identifying patterns and trends that take us much longer to discern.

We've already seen their capability to personalize answers and lesson plans in nanoseconds. Not surprisingly, they can personalize student data, highlighting strengths, pinpointing areas for improvement, and even projecting potential academic trajectories. They can present their analyses concisely or in-depth, tailored for a student or a parent, and in either formal or conversational tones.

Let's consider an example. After your class finishes its current lesson, you assess them. Once you have the scores, you draft a prompt for ChatGPT incorporating the questions, the outcomes, and any other pertinent information. ChatGPT then evaluates this data, offering insights with the accuracy of an expert in psychometrics.

The depth of analysis you desire is up to you. You could ask ChatGPT for a simple statistical summary, which might include the class average, the highest and lowest scores, or the range of scores. Alternatively, you might want a more detailed analysis. For instance, ChatGPT could classify students based on their exam scores into categories like "struggling," "on track," or "exceeding expectations." If you input data from multiple assessments, ChatGPT can even assess performance growth over time.

The benefits don't stop there. Let's say you notice several students are struggling with a particular area of the curriculum. You could ask ChatGPT for suggestions on how to help these students improve, drawing on its vast repository of teaching strategies and resources. Or, conversely, if you see a student excelling in a certain area, you could ask ChatGPT for ideas on how to further challenge and engage that student.

While ChatGPT doesn't replace your professional judgment or the need to understand each student's unique context, it's an incredibly useful tool for providing a first pass at assessing and explaining performance. It doesn't make the decisions; it guides and informs your decisions.

One last point to keep in mind: ChatGPT doesn't store or share information you post for queries after your session ends. However, it is best not to share a student's name. Use an ID or another piece of non-identifying data. Privacy is paramount, so always make sure you're following your school's data protection and privacy policies when using AI tools like ChatGPT.

Student Test Analysis - A Detailed Case

Let's assume you are an elementary teacher and you have just finished assessing your students with a progress monitoring tool, like ESGI. This tool, a staple in many elementary classrooms, provides comprehensive feedback on student progress in key areas like reading and math. Proper progress monitoring is a catalyst for academic growth, and a critical resource in tailoring instruction to meet the needs of each unique learner.

We can start by feeding ChatGPT a series of test results that has been collected over time from one of our first-grade students. To respect privacy, we remove any personally identifiable information and ask ChatGPT to become our data analysist and transform these raw scores into quantitative summaries, trends, and insights. This can be pasted into ChatGPT, and you can copy multiple students at once. And with the newest version of ChatGPT, you can upload files, making it even easier.

> **Mr. Jim Prompt**
>
> Student07 is my elementary student and I tested her in ELA over the last 2 weeks. Here are her scores in the last 4 tests: Lowercase Sounds, Lowercase Letters, Sight Words and Uppercase Letters. Results:
>
> • **Lowercase Sounds:** Correct (21): m, u (short), u (long), e (short), e (long), s, f, r, h, w, z, c, d, t, j, k, y, x, i Long, o short, o long; Incorrect: a short, a long, E, N, V, b, g, q, i (short).
>
> • **Lowercase letters:** correct: E, T, S, H, a (book), r, o, B, D, Q, J, P, F, K, G, L, I; Incorrect: y, v, w, z, x, n. Sight Words #1: Correct: said, he, and, no, dough, by, her, was, good, had, black; Incorrect: four, brown, came, please, saw, there, their, too, and white.

> - **Sight Words #2:** All correct but saw, there, their, too, two
> - **Sight Words #3:** All correct but there
> - **Uppercase Letters:** Correct: All correct but Q and H."
>
> Please assess Student07's performance on these tests. Share with me what she does well and where she needs help. Also analyze her progress over the 3 administrations of the site word tests. [appended].
>
> Provide a summary of what I, as the teacher, need to work on with him and suggestions for lessons and targeting I need to do.

ChatGPT

Based on your detailed data, it's clear that Student07 is doing an excellent job in many areas, and it's a pleasure to help you unravel the insights from her recent tests.

Starting with lowercase sounds, Student07 performed well on 21 out of 26 sounds. This suggests a strong understanding of most lowercase sounds. She made mistakes on the sounds of "a" (both short and long), "e," n," "v," "b," "g," "o," "q," and "i" (short).

For lowercase letters, she was correct for 17 out of 23 letters, displaying good familiarity with the majority of the alphabet. However, she found "y," "v," "w," "z," "x," and "n" challenging.

Student07 demonstrated impressive improvement over the three administrations of the sight words test. She was unable to recognize "four," "brown," "came," "please," "saw," "there," "their," "too," and "white" in the first test. However, in the second test, she corrected most of these errors and was only incorrect on "saw," "there," "their," "too," and "two." By the third test, "there" was the only word she didn't get right. This continuous improvement shows her strong learning adaptability and progression.

Lastly, in uppercase letters, Student07 recognized all letters but "Q" and "H," which is a commendable performance.

From this analysis, it's clear that Student07 excels in most areas but has a few specific areas that could use some reinforcement. She needs help with the sounds and recognition of specific lowercase letters and sounds. Sight words are improving rapidly, but she still struggles with the word "there." Lastly, for uppercase letters, practicing "Q" and "H" could be beneficial.

As her teacher, you might want to:

1. **Revisit Lowercase Sounds & Letters:** Spend some extra time on the sounds and identification of the letters she finds difficult. Flashcards, audio drills, or educational apps that focus on phonics can be beneficial for this.
2. **Drill Sight Words:** Continue practicing sight words, paying special attention to the word "there." A word wall in the classroom or at home, where sight words are displayed and referred to frequently, can help with this.
3. **Practice Uppercase Letters:** For the uppercase letters she missed, practice writing, and identifying them in text.
4. **Progress Tracking:** Continue to monitor her progress in these areas to ensure that the extra practice is helping.
5. **Encourage Reading:** To further improve her familiarity with the letters and sight words, encourage reading books appropriate for her level. This real-world practice can be quite beneficial.

Remember, practice and patience are key. With your dedicated guidance, there's no doubt Student07 will make improvements in these areas.

Not only does ChatGPT write the summary in a clear and organized manner, but it also provides suggestions for teacher follow-up. And remember this prompt is a simple one. If I wanted a different presentation of the data, or to focus on a particular area, it could do that. (Note: I also like the way it complimented my "dedicated guidance.")

Math Example

Let's consider another practical example. Imagine you're an algebra teacher, swamped with assignments. Instead of spending hours spotting common errors, what if you could let ChatGPT take a quick look? Think about the potential of AI in highlighting frequent mistakes. Let's see how ChatGPT can make feedback more efficient for both teachers and students.

Mr. Jim Prompt

Here are 2 Algebra problems I gave a student and the answers she provided. Did my student get the right answer on this? If not, what mistakes are they making and what can I suggest to help them?

Problem 1: Solve, (x-1)2 = [4√(x-4)]2

Solution: x2-2x+1 = 16(x-4)

x2-2x+1 = 16x-64

x2-18x+65 = 0

(x-13) (x-5) = 0

> Hence, x = -13 and x = -5.
>
> Second problem: "There are 47 boys in the class. This is three more than four times the number of girls. How many girls are there in the class? Solution: Let the number of girls be x
>
> As per the given statement,
>
> $4x + 3 = 47$ $4x = 47 - 3$ $x = 50/4$ $x = 12.5$

ChatGPT

The algebraic solutions provided by your student contain errors in both problems. Let's take a look at each one.

Problem 1:

Your student correctly set up the equation $(x-1)^2 = [4\sqrt{(x-4)}]^2$, and correctly simplified it to $x^2 - 2x + 1 = 16(x - 4)$. This simplifies to $x^2 - 18x + 65 = 0$. However, when finding the roots of the equation, they made a sign error.

From the equation $(x - 13)(x - 5) = 0$, the roots should be $x = 13$ and $x = 5$, not $x = -13$ and $x = -5$.

Recommendation: To help the student avoid such errors, emphasize the importance of double-checking the work and remind them that when an equation is set to 0, the solutions will be the positive value of x, not negative.

Problem 2:

The student's set-up of the equation from the word problem is correct, but they made an error in calculation. The correct steps are:

$4x + 3 = 47$

$4x = 47 - 3$

$4x = 44$

$x = 44/4$

$x = 11$

So, there are 11 girls in the class, not 12.5.

Recommendation: Encourage students to take their time with calculations, as small mistakes can drastically change the outcome. Reinforce the point that the number of students (girls, in this case) should be a whole number, not a fraction or decimal.

This type of analysis can be remarkably useful, especially if AI can pinpoint common mistakes a student is making across several problems. Moreover, it is feasible for students to self-correct their work in the classroom (if your teaching approach and district allows it). Students can directly input their work into ChatGPT to review their work and the process they used.

However, we also must acknowledge that AI, while advanced, isn't flawless. As we'll discuss later in more detail, it does make math mistakes. I was particularly surprised to see reports of mistakes that most non-AI programs get right. But at its core, this is a large language model that was optimized for generative conversation, not mathematics.

To add an interesting twist to using AI, you could consider offering a class reward for a student who determines that their solution is actually correct and that ChatGPT made an error. This tactic may motivate certain students to challenge AI and exhibit their own intellectual prowess.

Sharing Insights with Parents

Thus far, we have painted a picture of how ChatGPT can help educators unlock deeper insights from student data. But as every teacher knows, the classroom is not an island. The home plays a pivotal role in a child's education, and communication between teachers and parents is key to fostering this collaborative environment.

With ChatGPT, you can craft well-written, informative letters for parents, translating the insights gained from the data into understandable, actionable language.

This is not about conveying test scores. It is about bridging the gap between school and home, sharing a narrative of the child's academic journey in a language parents can understand. ChatGPT can help you write a letter summarizing the student's progress, highlighting their achievements, pointing out areas they need to work on, and suggesting ways parents can help at home.

> **Mr. Jim Prompt**
>
> Now craft a parent letter that shares in simple language, how Student 07 is doing and what her parents can do to support her at home. Put the specific results in a chart of what she got correct and what she got wrong.

ChatGPT

Dear Parents,

I hope this message finds you well. As [Student07]'s teacher, I am excited to share some updates on her progress in our ELA classes over the last two weeks. I've been thrilled to witness her enthusiasm for learning and the strides she's making in her education. In this letter, I will highlight some of her achievements and identify areas where some extra support could enhance her learning journey.

[Student07] has been doing remarkably well in many areas. She has shown a strong understanding of lowercase sounds and letters, an impressive grasp of sight words, and a commendable knowledge of uppercase letters. However, there are a few areas where she could use a bit more practice to achieve mastery.

Please find below a summary of her test results:

Test	Correct	Needs Practice
Lowercase Sounds	m, u (short), u (long), e (short), e (long), s,f,r,h,w, z,c,d,t, j, k, y,x, i Long, o short, o long	a short, a long, E, N, V, b,g,q,l (short)
Lowercase Letters	E, T, S, H, a (book), r, o, B, D, Q, J, P,F,K, G,L,I	y, v,w, z, x, n
Sight Words (Test #1, #2, #3)	Improved significantly from test to test. Most words correct by Test #3	'there' remained challenging across tests
Uppercase Letters	Most letters	Q, H

Here's how you can support [Student07]'s learning journey at home:

1. **Letter Practice:** Spend some time together playing with flashcards or letter magnets focusing on the sounds and recognition of the letters she finds challenging.
2. **Sight Words Fun:** Keep practicing sight words, especially the word "there." Make it a fun game to spot sight words in her favorite books or everyday items around the house.
3. **Writing Letters:** Encourage [Student07] to write uppercase "Q" and "H" during drawing or note-writing activities. This can help familiarize her with these letters.
4. **Reading Together:** Enjoy a good book that's appropriate for her reading level. This not only enhances her familiarity with letters and words but also promotes a love for reading.

[Student07] is making fantastic progress, and I am confident that with your support at home coupled with our efforts at school, she'll continue to thrive in her learning journey. Please do not hesitate to reach out if you have any questions.

Thank you for your ongoing support.

Warm Regards,
[Your Name]

The moment I showcased this capability to teachers during a webinar I was conducting, excitement rippled through the crowd. Teachers can genuinely see the transformative potential in this technology. The task of crafting individualized, meaningful emails for each student can often be a lengthy process, but with AI, this task becomes more manageable and efficient.

Would I send this letter home to parents? No. Not without my personal editing. But it's an excellent foundation to begin crafting my message. This efficiency, in turn, frees up more of your time for direct student interaction and instruction.

Furthermore, with precise prompts, you can shape the email to fit any format you prefer. You have the control to set the reading level, suggest phrases, and dictate the length of the email. This tool even translates these messages into other languages. And of course, if you prefer a more traditional approach, you can still edit any email in Word or Docs.

Other Data Analysis Possibilities

While the use of ChatGPT for student data analysis and generating reports is an exciting development, there are numerous other ways this tool could help teachers in testing, assessing, evaluating, and analyzing student achievement. Here are a few more possibilities:

1. **Generating Assessment Questions:** AI could be utilized to automatically generate quiz or test questions based on the curriculum and learning objectives. This could save you significant time in preparing assessments.

2. **Simulating Peer Review:** Students could use AI to receive instant "peer review" feedback on their essays or assignments. While not a substitute for human feedback, it could provide immediate and objective input for your students, highlighting areas for improvement and reinforcing successful approaches.

3. **Facilitating Self-Assessment:** By interacting with AI, students can gauge their understanding of a topic. It could provide them with questions and problems to solve, helping them realize areas they may need to focus on.

4. **Creating Personalized Learning Journeys:** Based on student performance and the challenges they face, AI could suggest personalized learning paths. This could include additional resources to focus on weaker areas or more advanced materials to challenge high achievers.

5. **Understanding Misconceptions:** You could use AI to explore potential misconceptions or areas of confusion within a topic. This could provide insight into common mistakes students make and help teachers prepare interventions or supplemental lessons.

6. **Benchmarking Student Progress:** By comparing student progress over time, AI can help identify patterns or trends in a student's learning journey. This could offer valuable information to guide teaching strategies and interventions.

7. **Analyzing Group Dynamics:** For projects that involve group work, data on individual contributions and group

interactions could be analyzed to assess both individual and collective performance.

The Power of ChatGPT in Crafting Tables

Analyzing data is merely the beginning in turning information into valuable insights for teachers and students. However, as all educators recognize, understanding is just half the challenge; effective communication completes the picture. In the world of education, how we present data is equally crucial as how we interpret it.

Using structured and clear tables is one undeniably effective method. Tables have an inherent power to transform abstract numbers into comprehensible patterns, making the unseen seen. And the good news is that ChatGPT can assist you in one very specific way: creating tables effortlessly.

But crafting the perfect table, especially one that resonates with students, is an art and science unto itself. To provide a sense of how ChatGPT can assist, let's just ask.

Let's take a look at how to employ ChatGPT for creating tables and what the generated tables might look like, using our five classroom examples:

> **Mr. Jim Prompt**
>
> Please provide 5 five classroom examples on the types of list where ChatGPT can be employed for creating tables.

1. Vocabulary Lists:

Creating tables to structure vocabulary lists is a fantastic idea, especially for language classes. You could craft a table with columns for the "word," "definition," "synonym," and "use in a sentence." This will help students better understand and remember new vocabulary.

To make one, simply provide the information to ChatGPT. Or you could just provide the titles and let ChatGPT to create the measurements:

> **Mr. Jim Prompt**
>
> Construct a table with the following column headers: 'Word', 'Definition', 'Synonym', and 'Use in a Sentence'. Fill the table with the details provided below: For the second row, the 'Word' is 'apathy', its 'Definition' is 'lack of interest', its 'Synonym' is 'indifference', and its 'Use in a Sentence' is 'His apathy towards the subjects led to his poor grades.'
>
> For the next row, the 'Word' is 'zealous', its 'Definition' is 'having great energy or enthusiasm', its 'Synonym' is 'passionate', and its 'Use in a Sentence' is 'Her zealous nature often inspired others.'

ChatGPT

Sure, here's a simple table following your format:

Word	Definition	Synonym	Use in a Sentence
Apathy	Lack of interest	Indifference	His apathy towards the subjects led to his poor grades.
Zealous	Having great energy or enthusiasm	Passionate	Her zealous nature often inspired others.

2. Historical Timelines:

For social studies or history classes, tables that outline key events, dates, involved parties, and outcomes can serve as a valuable resource. To create a timeline for historical events in a table format, you might input:

> **Mr. Jim Prompt**
>
> Create a table detailing major World War II events. The table should include columns for the event name, date, involved parties, and outcome. Include entries for the Battle of Midway, which took place in June 1942 between the USA and Japan, resulting in a decisive US victory, and the Invasion of Normandy in June 1944, where allied forces faced Germany, successfully establishing a Western front.

ChatGPT

Here's a table detailing the requested major events in World War II:

Event	Date	Involved Parties	Outcome
Battle of Midway	June 1942	USA vs. Japan	Decisive US victory
Invasion of Normandy	June 1944	Allied forces vs. Germany	Successful opening of a Western front

3. Scientific Elements:

In science class, particularly chemistry, you can use tables to list various elements, their atomic numbers, symbols, and atomic weights. For a chemistry class, you might command:

> **Mr. Jim Prompt**
>
> Generate a table listing the elements along with their atomic number, symbols, and atomic elements along with their atomic number, symbols, and atomic weight. Include the elements Hydrogen and Oxygen in the table.

ChatGPT
Here's the table with the element names included, for Hydrogen and Oxygen:

Element Name	Atomic Number	Symbol	Atomic Weight
Hydrogen	1	H	1.008
Oxygen	8	O	15.999

4. Math Problems:

Tables can be an excellent tool to illustrate and solve math problems. For instance, a table depicting multiplication facts can be a handy reference for younger students.

To create a table with multiplication facts, you could use:

> **Mr. Jim Prompt**
> Create a table that illustrates the basic multiplication facts for the numbers 1 and 2.

ChatGPT
Sure, here's the table with just the header and the first two rows filled in:

Factor	1	2
1	1	2
2	2	4

5. Literature Overview:

In literature or language arts classes, a table highlighting different authors, their works, genres, and publication dates can provide an organized overview of various literary pieces. For an organized overview of literary pieces, instruct ChatGPT like so:

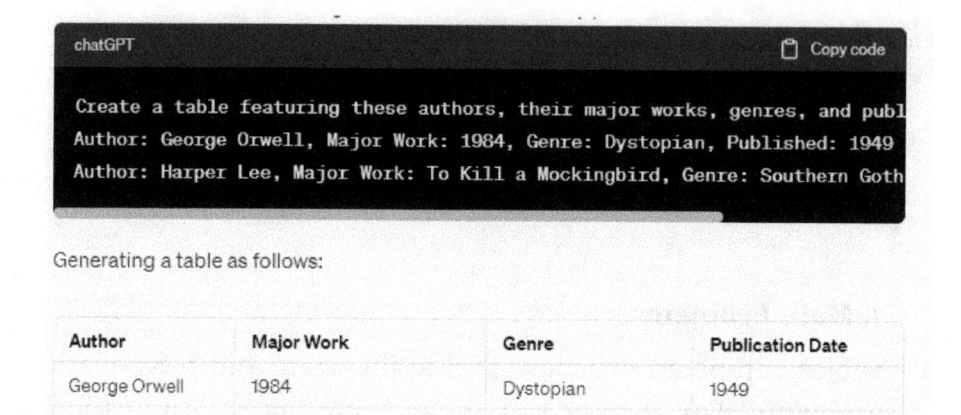

> **chatGPT** 📋 Copy code
>
> Create a table featuring these authors, their major works, genres, and publ
> Author: George Orwell, Major Work: 1984, Genre: Dystopian, Published: 1949
> Author: Harper Lee, Major Work: To Kill a Mockingbird, Genre: Southern Goth

Generating a table as follows:

Author	Major Work	Genre	Publication Date
George Orwell	1984	Dystopian	1949
Harper Lee	To Kill a Mockingbird	Southern Gothic	1960

Excel and ChatGPT

The versatility of AI doesn't end there. In addition to producing tables from shared data, ChatGPT can also format these tables for input into spreadsheet software such as Excel, further expanding its utility and adaptability.

To create a table that can be used in Excel, you would want to use the CSV (Comma Separated Values) format. This is a simple and universally accepted format that can be easily imported into Excel. Here's how to command ChatGPT to generate a CSV format table:

Mr. Jim Prompt

Create a CSV table for these fruits with their colors and prices:

Fruit: Apple, Color: Red, Price: $1

Fruit: Banana, Color: Yellow, Price: $0.50

ChatGPT

Fruit,Color,Price

Apple,Red,$1

Banana,Yellow,$0.50

Each row in the output represents a row in the table, and the values are separated by commas. The first row usually contains the column headers.

ChatGPT now creates Excel workbooks, too. You can request any table, chart or csv file to be converted to Excel for download.

Remember, you should always review and potentially clean up the data as necessary before using it for analysis, as AI outputs may not always be perfect or match your expectations perfectly.

Other Formats

As a dynamic language model, the beauty of ChatGPT lies in its flexibility – the ability to craft responses in various formats, tailoring the output to best match the user's needs and the nature of the inquiry. As we've seen, whether you're looking for a structured table of data, a dialogue simulation, or a poem, AI can meet your need. Here are a few of the formats we have already discussed and a few others that you might experiment with.

1. Bullet Points: An effective way to display concise information or list items.

Prompt 1: "List the top five most populated countries in the world."

Prompt 2: "What are the steps to bake chocolate chip cookies?"

Prompt 3: "Summarize the benefits of regular exercise."

2. Dialogues: Great for simulating conversations or script writing.

Prompt 1: "Create a dialogue between a detective and a suspect."

Prompt 2: "Simulate a conversation between two friends discussing their favorite books."

Prompt 3: "Write a dialogue between a customer and a restaurant waiter."

3. Poems and Songs: Perfect for when creativity calls.

Prompt 1: "Write a sonnet about the changing seasons."

Prompt 2: "Create a cheerful song about friendship."

Prompt 3: "Craft a haiku capturing a sunset scene."

4. CSV: Ideal for data organization and import/export tasks.

Prompt 1: "Generate a CSV file with 5 columns labeled: Name, Age, Occupation, City, Country."

Prompt 2: "Create a CSV formatted table with data for 10 different fruits, including their name, color, and average weight."

Prompt 3: "Produce a CSV output for a list of books, their authors, and publication year."

5. Programming Code: Helpful for beginners or anyone in need of basic code snippets.

Prompt 1: "Write a simple 'Hello, World!' program in Python."

Prompt 2: "Show me how to declare a variable in JavaScript."

Prompt 3: "Create a basic HTML structure for a webpage."

The Promise of What Is to Come

You might be thinking, "All of this sounds fantastic, but pulling data, feeding it into ChatGPT, tweaking the outputs... That's quite a bit of work." Yes, it may be. While I would argue that using AI to do regular analysis will save you time and provide great insights, as it stands, employing ChatGPT does require time to save time.

However, we're living in a dynamic world where the pace of technological advancements can leave us breathless. So, what does the future hold for ChatGPT and the broader field of AI in education?

As we speak, developers across the globe are working on application programming interfaces (APIs) for tools like ChatGPT. These APIs will allow for direct interaction between ChatGPT and various educational platforms and data sources. Imagine a very near future where instead of manually feeding student data into ChatGPT, an API automatically pulls this information from your school's student management system or your classroom's learning management system. This data can then be analyzed by AI, which will produce detailed student performance analyses and tailor-made educational strategies.

But why stop there? Once a comprehensive analysis is complete, these APIs could then allow you to press a button and receive individualized, well-crafted parent letters for each student. Just like that, you'll have an informative, respectful, and easy-to-understand communication for parents that outlines their child's academic progress, all thanks to the intricate dance between ChatGPT and these new APIs.

While I can't share company secrets, companies like Riverside Insights are working on tools that do just that. With these advancements, the role of AI in education is set to be transformative.

Rubrics

Another task that teachers might not initially consider for AI is rubric creation. Rubrics are a set of guidelines or criteria used to assess student performance. They provide a clear, concise framework for both teachers and students, outlining expectations and standards for assignments and projects.

ChatGPT-Enhanced Rubrics

Imagine a classroom where rubrics are not just static documents but dynamic, adaptive tools, co-created by teachers and an AI assistant. ChatGPT, with its advanced language understanding and generation capabilities, can assist educators in crafting rubrics that are both comprehensive and tailored to individual learning objectives.

To create a basic rubric, it's simple. You can approach it the same way you would create any rubric from scratch.

1. Identify the Learning Objectives and Scoring Range

Start by defining the assignment for which the rubric is needed. For instance, a 5th-grade writing assignment might focus on narrative skills, grammar, and creativity. A typical scoring range could be 1-4, where 1 is "Needs Improvement" and 4 is "Exemplary."

2. Consult ChatGPT: Input these objectives into ChatGPT. For example, you might ask, "ChatGPT, help me create a rubric for a 5th-grade writing assignment focusing on narrative skills, grammar, and creativity with this scoring range."

3. Use ChatGPT to Complete Details

Ask ChatGPT to suggest descriptors for each level of performance for the different components. For example, "What are descriptors for a score of 1 to 4 in 'Story Structure' for a 5th-grade writing assignment?"

4. Compile and Review

Review and adjust as needed to ensure it aligns with your educational goals and the needs of your students.

Mr. Jim Prompt

I need to create a rubric for a 5th-grade writing assignment. The assignment is a short story. The rubric should assess the following components: 'Story Structure', 'Grammar and Spelling', 'Creativity and Originality', and 'Use of Language'. Please suggest detailed descriptors for each scoring level from 1 to 4 for each component."

Example of a Simple Rubric for 5th Grade Writing

Criteria/Scoring	1 - Needs Improvement	2 - Developing	3 - Proficient	4 - Exemplary
Story Structure	Limited organization, lacks clear beginning, middle, and end.	Some organization, but missing elements in the structure.	Well-organized with clear beginning, middle, and end.	Exceptionally well-organized, engaging structure, and flow.
Grammar and Spelling	Numerous grammatical and spelling errors.	Some grammatical and spelling errors.	Few grammatical and spelling errors.	No grammatical and spelling errors.
Creativity and Originality	Limited creativity, uses clichés, lacks original ideas.	Some creative elements, but lacks originality.	Creative and original ideas are evident.	Highly creative and original, captivating ideas.
Use of Language	Limited vocabulary, simple sentences, lacks variety.	Adequate vocabulary, some sentence variety.	Good use of vocabulary, varied sentence structure.	Rich and varied vocabulary, sophisticated sentence structure.

This rubric serves as a foundation. Teachers can further customize it based on their specific classroom dynamics and the individual needs of their students. The beauty of using AI like ChatGPT in this process is its adaptability and the potential for continuous improvement.

A Guide to AI-Enhanced Rubrics

By leveraging ChatGPT, teachers can develop rubrics that are not only tailored to specific educational objectives but also responsive to the diverse learning styles and needs of students. Here are examples.

1. Grade School Example: Storytelling Project
- **Traditional Rubric Components:** Creativity, coherence, grammar, and use of language.

- **ChatGPT's Role:** The teacher inputs the basic objectives of the storytelling project into ChatGPT. The AI then suggests additional criteria such as narrative structure, character development, and cultural sensitivity, which might not have been initially considered.

2. **High School Example: Science Fair Project**
   - **Traditional Rubric Components:** Scientific method adherence, data analysis, presentation skills.
   - **ChatGPT's Role:** For a more advanced project, ChatGPT can assist in developing a rubric that includes criteria for innovative problem-solving, ethical implications of the scientific work, and interdisciplinary connections, fostering a more holistic assessment approach.

ChatGPT's can also create a rubric from scratch with just the topic and grade level provided. This feature is particularly valuable for teachers facing complex or specialized topics where they might lack specific expertise.

For instance, a teacher might be unsure about what criteria to use for pre-screening students for dyslexia. In such cases, ChatGPT can suggest components and measurements appropriate for the grade level and subject matter. By inputting the need for a dyslexia pre-screening rubric, the teacher has a reliable and educational tool to support their students' diverse needs.

> **Mr. Jim Prompt**
> Create a dyslexia pre-screening rubric for my 2nd-grade class. Provide the criteria measurements and scoring criteria that I can use with observational assessment.

Sample Rubric for Pre-Screening Dyslexia in 2nd Grade

Criteria/Scoring	1 - No Concern	2 - Slight Concern	3 - Moderate Concern	4 - High Concern
Letter Recognition	Correctly identifies almost all letters.	Occasionally confuses similar letters.	Frequently confuses letters, especially similar ones.	Struggles to recognize many letters.
Phonemic Awareness	Accurately associates sounds with corresponding letters.	Some difficulty in associating sounds with letters.	Often unable to associate sounds with corresponding letters.	Regularly struggles with phonemic awareness.
Reading Fluency	Reads age-appropriate texts smoothly with few errors.	Reads slowly with some hesitations and errors.	Often reads haltingly, mispronounces words, and loses place.	Struggles significantly with fluency, frequent mispronunciations.
Writing and Spelling	Writes and spells age-appropriate words correctly.	Makes occasional spelling errors, simple words correct.	Often makes spelling errors, including simple words.	Regular and significant spelling errors, even with simple words.
Sequencing Abilities	Can easily sequence events and concepts.	Sometimes struggles with sequencing events in stories.	Frequently mixes up sequences in stories or tasks.	Consistently unable to sequence events or tasks correctly.

The use of AI tools like ChatGPT in developing rubrics simplifies the process for teachers, enhancing their ability to employ rubrics more effectively with students. This advancement also enables teachers to craft rubrics for a variety of activities needing observational assessment, such as collaborative projects, classroom activities, or social-emotional behavior. Specialists and interventionists can leverage these tools for observing students in individual sessions. Moreover, coaches and administrators have the opportunity to design rubrics for evaluating professional development and teaching strategies.

While I recommend consulting with a specialist to refine and validate the rubric before implementation, these tools offer a robust starting point. Such AI-enhanced rubrics pave the way for more personalized, adaptive, and all-encompassing assessment methods, empowering educators to cater to the varied needs of their students more effectively. You have the ability to customize the flashcards for your whole class, groups or even specific students.

Flashcards

Teachers recognize the timeless value of flashcards as a learning aid. We can now leverage AI to create more targeted and interactive flashcard resources. These aren't just traditional flashcards; they are smarter, more adaptable, and tailored to the specific learning needs of our students. For example, here are ten flashcard ideas, crafted with the help of AI, designed to support, and enrich areas that students have yet to master.

1. **Sight Words Flashcards**: For emerging readers, flashcards featuring common sight words to enhance reading fluency.
2. **Math Facts Flashcards**: Basic addition, subtraction, multiplication, and division facts for practice and mastery.
3. **Phonics Flashcards**: Cards focusing on phonetic sounds, blends, and digraphs to support reading skills.
4. **States and Capitals Flashcards**: For learning U.S. states and their capitals, or similar geography-based content.
5. **Historical Figures Flashcards**: Important figures in history with key facts and contributions.

6. **Science Concepts Flashcards**: Basic science terms and concepts, like parts of a plant, animal classifications, or the water cycle.
7. **Vocabulary Builder Flashcards**: New words with definitions and example sentences to enhance language skills.
8. **Fraction Flashcards**: Visual representations of fractions to teach basic fraction concepts and equivalencies.
9. **Language Translation Flashcards**: For bilingual education, featuring words in two languages to enhance language skills.
10. **Emotion and Social Skills Flashcards:** Cards showing different emotions or social scenarios, helping students to identify feelings and appropriate responses.

Prompts for the Everyday Teacher

Here are some suggestions you might consider for targeted rubrics or observational evaluations.

Elementary School Rubric Creation Prompts
1. **Storytelling Skills:** "Create a rubric to assess 3rd-grade students' storytelling skills, focusing on creativity, coherence, and use of language."
2. **Science Project:** "Develop a rubric for a 4th-grade science fair project, evaluating research quality, experiment design, and presentation skills."
3. **Math Problem-Solving:** "Formulate a rubric to assess 2nd graders on their problem-solving abilities in math, including understanding the problem, the process used, and the accuracy of the solution."

4. **Reading Comprehension:** "Construct a rubric for assessing 1st-grade reading comprehension, including fluency, ability to recall facts, and understanding of the main idea."
5. **Art Project:** "Create a rubric for evaluating a kindergarten art project, considering creativity, effort, and use of materials."
6. **Emotional Recognition and Response:** "Design a rubric to assess elementary students' abilities in recognizing and appropriately responding to their own emotions and the emotions of others."
7. **Language Acquisition Progress:** "Create a rubric for assessing the progress of ELL students in elementary school, focusing on vocabulary development, sentence construction, and basic communication skills."
8. **Individualized Learning Goals:** "Establish a rubric for elementary special education students, tailored to individual IEP (Individualized Education Program) goals, assessing progress in areas like cognitive skills, motor skills, and communication abilities."

High School Rubric Creation Prompts

1. **Literature Analysis Essay:** "Develop a rubric for assessing a high school literature analysis essay, focusing on thesis clarity, evidence support, and writing style."
2. **Chemistry Lab Report:** "Create a rubric to evaluate a chemistry lab report, considering accuracy, analysis, and presentation of data."
3. **Mathematical Modeling:** "Formulate a rubric for a high school math modeling project, assessing understanding

of concepts, application of methods, and clarity of explanation."

4. **Foreign Language Oral Exam:** "Construct a rubric for a foreign language oral exam, focusing on fluency, pronunciation, and conversation skills."
5. **Computer Science Project:** "Establish a rubric for assessing a computer science project, considering code efficiency, innovation, and problem-solving skills."
6. **Physical Education Fitness Assessment:** "Create a rubric for a high school physical education fitness assessment, including endurance, strength, and flexibility."
7. **Advanced Language Proficiency:** "Formulate a rubric to evaluate high school ELL students' proficiency in advanced language skills, such as nuanced understanding, idiomatic expressions, and complex sentence structures."
8. **Social Interaction and Inclusivity:** "Develop a rubric for high school special education students, focusing on assessing and encouraging social interaction, inclusivity in group settings, and self-advocacy skills.

ThinkFives Top 5 Most Admired Teachers in Film & TV

The world of film and television has given us many memorable teachers. They inspired audiences and showcased various facets of the teaching profession. ThinkFives asked ChatGPT who it would include on the list, and from that list we asked teachers to pick their favorites. Here are their Top 5.

5. Ms. Frizzle - *The Magic School Bus*

Voiced by the iconic Lily Tomlin, Ms. Frizzle isn't your average science teacher. With the help of her enchanted school bus, she took her students on whimsical adventures, from the depths of the ocean to the vastness of outer space, making science both accessible and exhilarating.

4. Mr. Feeny - *Boy Meets World*

As portrayed by William Daniels, Mr. Feeny is more than just a teacher; he's a mentor and guide. Positioned both as a classroom educator and wise next-door neighbor, he dispenses lessons that extend beyond academics, touching on life's greater truths and challenges.

3. Jaime Escalante - *Stand and Deliver*

In a role that resonated with educators everywhere, Edward James Olmos brought to life the true story of Jaime Escalante. This determined teacher introduced calculus to an underfunded high school, defying societal expectations and showcasing the boundless potential within every student.

2. Erin Gruwell - *Freedom Writers*

Hilary Swank's portrayal of Erin Gruwell serves as a testament to the transformative power of writing and personal reflection. Based on a true story, Gruwell's unyielding dedication helps a group of at-risk students find their voices, fostering not just academic growth but profound personal change.

1. John Keating - *Dead Poets Society*

Robin Williams's role as John Keating remains etched in cinematic history. With an infectious passion for poetry and literature, Keating encourages his students to challenge the status quo, seize the day, and embrace the boundless realms of thought and emotion within themselves.

#7 COLLABORATE

"Fight for the things that you care about, but do it in a way that will lead others to join you."
- Ruth Bader Ginsburg

Homework has always been a bridge between the classroom and the home, a space for students to reinforce what they've learned and explore new concepts. For those fortunate enough, homework help has always existed as well – whether that be with the assistance of a parent, sibling, or neighbor.

I can remember the good old days of seeking help from my well-intentioned dad. It was an adventure, as innocent questions about the Civil War would inevitably lead us down a winding path through the history of the entire world. The poor Civil War never stood a chance against my dad's unwavering commitment to providing comprehensive historical context. Starting with the Big Bang and the formation of the universe, weaving through ancient civilizations like a master storyteller, he'd eventually circle back to the American Civil War. My dad would provide context. While I did appreciate his genuine enthusiasm and passion, my attention waned with each new era explained, and his frustration grew with my lack of attention.

For good or bad, the role of a dad's homework help may soon be facing the fate of dinosaurs. With ChatGPT by our sides now, homework can be targeted, immediate, and thorough. A student can have their very own tutor. But is that good or bad?

The Conflicted Views of AI Homework Help

With AI's ability to provide instantaneous answers, we risk transforming the school-to-home learning bridge into a shortcut. The rollout of ChatGPT saw a divided reaction from educational institutions across the nation. On one hand, we had the largest school districts swiftly raising the alarm, banning this AI marvel, and echoing concerns of academic integrity. Los Angeles, Baltimore, Seattle, and New York City were just a few of the districts that feared the ease with which students might be tempted into the darker alleys of academic compromise. On the other hand, tech educators argued that shying away from such tools is not an answer but the lack of an answer. If AI is the future, then that future should start in today's classrooms, which should be focused on what is possible.

The promise of a personal homework helper is compelling. It can offer students round-the-clock assistance, personalized explanations, and instantaneous feedback. Yet, like any powerful tool, it holds the potential for misuse. As teachers, we may find ourselves questioning: "Will AI merely spoon-feed answers to students, undermining the very essence of learning?"

Let's consider Lori, a tenth-grade student. Struggling with a complex math problem late in the evening, she turns to her AI-powered homework assistant. In seconds, the solution appears on the screen. Lori copies it down, feeling relieved but with little knowledge of what she writes. The solution has been provided, yes, but the journey to it has been circumvented. Is Lori learning or merely transcribing?

On the other hand, there's Max, a sixth grader. Faced with a history assignment, he interacts with his AI tool, asking it to explain the contribution of the Aztecs on developing the calendar. The AI responds, providing a detailed narrative and links to further resources. Max reads, takes notes, asks more questions. He's engaged, curious, and his understanding deepens. In Max's case, AI has facilitated learning, not undermined it.

Elementary Example

The challenge, therefore, lies not in the technology itself but in how it is used. Can we teach students to use AI as a tool for understanding, not just for obtaining answers? Can we shift the focus from the end result to the learning journey? In this quest, we, as fearless educators, have a critical role to play.

Instead of just asking for direct answers, we can guide them to craft questions that lead to more thoughtful discussions and deeper exploration of the topic.

If we teach students to ask probing questions, a resultant dialogue between a 3rd-grade student and ChatGPT might look like this.

Student: Hi there, ChatGPT! I need to ask you something. Can you tell me what makes a noun different from a verb?

ChatGPT: That's a wonderful question, my friend! Nouns and verbs are like puzzle pieces that help us make sentences. They each have their own job. Let's start with nouns. Nouns are special words that name people, places, or things. So, if you think about your favorite toy or your best friend, their names are nouns. Words like "dog" or "cat" are nouns because they name kinds of animals. Can you give me more examples of nouns?

Student: Oh, I see! So, words like "car" and "book" are also nouns because they name things, right?

ChatGPT: Exactly! You're really catching on. "Car" and "book" are perfect examples of nouns because they name objects that we can touch. Now, let's look at verbs. Verbs are action words. They show us what someone or something is doing. If you think about actions like running or jumping, those are verbs. Can you think of some verbs?

Student: Yes, I can! Words like "sing" and "dance" are verbs because they show actions.

ChatGPT: Fantastic! You've got it. You've named actions that people can do, which are verbs. So, when we think about it, nouns are like the names of actors on a stage, and verbs tell us what these actors are doing. Remembering this can help you make great sentences when you write. Do you have any more questions about this or something else?

Student: Thank you, ChatGPT! You've made it very clear. I understand the difference between nouns and verbs now.

Social Studies Example.

Student: Hi, ChatGPT! I'm working on a social studies assignment about George Washington, specifically about how he set a good example for future presidents. Can you help me brainstorm some ideas?

ChatGPT: Of course! I'd be happy to help you brainstorm some ideas about how George Washington set a good example for future presidents. Let's work together on this. What are your initial thoughts on how he demonstrated exemplary leadership?

Student: Well, I know that George Washington voluntarily stepped down after serving two terms as president, which established the precedent of a peaceful transfer of power. I think that's an important example he set.

ChatGPT: Absolutely! That's an excellent point. Washington's decision to voluntarily step down after two terms established the principle of term limits and a peaceful transition of presidential authority, which subsequent presidents followed. This commitment to democratic ideals is certainly worth highlighting in your assignment. Can you think of any other ways for him to set a good example?

Student: Hmm, I also remember learning about Washington's leadership during the American Revolutionary War. He showed courage and determination as the commander of the Continental Army. Maybe that's another example?

ChatGPT: Absolutely! George Washington's leadership during the Revolutionary War is a fantastic example. He demonstrated courage, strategic thinking, and the ability to inspire and rally troops in the face of challenging circumstances. His actions helped foster a sense of unity and patriotism among Americans. This leadership example during times of crisis is certainly noteworthy. Can you think of any other ways he set a good example for future presidents?

Student: I think Washington emphasized integrity and ethical conduct. He prioritized the interests of the nation over personal gain, and his commitment to honesty and transparency was commendable.

ChatGPT: That's an excellent point! Washington's emphasis on integrity and ethical conduct is crucial. By upholding high moral standards, he established a precedent for future presidents to prioritize the nation's well-being and maintain public trust. His ethical leadership serves as an important example for future leaders. Are there any other aspects you would like to explore, or do you feel we have covered the main points?

Student: I think those are the main points I wanted to discuss. Thank you so much for helping me brainstorm these ideas. It's much clearer to me now how George Washington set a good example for future presidents.

ChatGPT: You're very welcome! I'm glad I could assist you in brainstorming ideas. Remember to organize your thoughts and expand upon these examples in your assignment. If you have any more questions or need further assistance, feel free to ask. Good luck with your assignment!

Student: Thank you! I'll do my best.

With guidance and the right set of instructions, students can have engaging conversations with AI, extending their learning experience beyond traditional teaching methods. It's all about asking the right questions and encouraging our students to do the same.

High School Example

In this example, a fearless teacher asks a high school student to write an essay on the effects of climate change on ocean levels and weather. Students have the choice to affirm or contest the prevailing views on this issue, yet their standpoint must be underpinned by supporting data and scientific evidence.

For the first phase of the assignment (and to be turned in), the teacher instructs the student to engage in a dialogue with ChatGPT to create an outline and develop a point of view for this paper. This approach enables the teacher to observe the critical thinking skills the student employed in conjunction with ChatGPT to construct the outline.

Student: Hi, ChatGPT. I have been given an assignment on the effects of climate change on ocean levels. I need to agree or challenge the prevailing views and back up my stance with statistics and science. Can you help me write an outline?

ChatGPT: Absolutely, happy to assist! Let's start with the basics: Do you have a stance on this issue yet? Do you think climate change significantly impacts ocean levels?

Student: Yes, I believe it does. Climate change is causing glaciers to melt, leading to rising ocean levels.

ChatGPT: That's an excellent starting point. Now, if you were to divide your paper into three main sections to guide your reader through your argument, what could they be?

Student: I suppose the first part should give background information on climate change and ocean levels. The second part could present evidence supporting my viewpoint, and the third could address opposing viewpoints and refute them.

ChatGPT: Great! You've got a clear structure. Now, when it comes to providing evidence to support your argument, what kind of data and scientific reasoning do you think could be useful?

Student: I think citing studies about rising temperatures leading to glacier melts and statistical data about rising sea levels over the years could help. I could also mention the impact on marine life and coastal communities.

ChatGPT: Fantastic ideas! That will provide compelling evidence to support your stance. Now, when you address opposing viewpoints, remember it's not just about proving them wrong. Can you think of why this is important?

Student: I guess it's important because it shows I understand the other side of the argument. It also gives me an opportunity to strengthen my own argument by addressing and rebutting these opposing points.

ChatGPT: Exactly. By acknowledging counterarguments, you can present a balanced view and then use scientific evidence to support your thesis. Speaking of which, what would you say your thesis or main argument is based on what we've discussed?

Student: My thesis would be: Climate change, due to its effect on glaciers, is a significant factor in rising ocean levels, impacting marine life and posing a threat to coastal communities.

ChatGPT: That's a robust and well-articulated thesis! Remember to keep reinforcing it with your evidence and counterarguments. Ready to get started on your research?

Student: Yes, definitely! Thanks for your help, ChatGPT!

In this interaction, ChatGPT acts as a sounding board for the student's ideas, methodically guiding them and asking questions that help them structure their thoughts and develop their thesis. This way, the student plays an active role in their learning process, engaging more deeply with the topic and taking ownership of their work.

A Math Example

In this scenario, the student is seeking assistance from ChatGPT to function as a math tutor in solving the equation. A fearless teacher could assign several equations for homework and also require that the students engage with ChatGPT during the problem-solving process and submit that work.

Student: Hi, I need some help with this problem: $7X + 3XY = 42$.

ChatGPT: Sure, I'd be happy to help! Are you familiar with the Distributive Property?

Student: Kind of. Isn't that when you multiply a number outside of parentheses by everything inside the parentheses?

ChatGPT: That's correct! We can apply that concept here by factoring out the X. Try that and tell me what you get.

Student: Okay, let me see. So, I'll take out the X and I get $X(7 + 3Y) = 42$.

ChatGPT: Perfect! Now, to isolate X, you can divide both sides of the equation by the expression in parentheses. Go ahead and do that.

Student: Alright, so that means $X = 42 / (7 + 3Y)$.

ChatGPT: You've got it! Do you have a value for Y that you can substitute into the equation?

Student: Yes, I have that $Y = 9$.

ChatGPT: Great, now you can substitute $Y = 9$ into your equation to solve for X. Can you try that?

Student: Sure. So, I get $X = 42 / (7 + 3*9)$, so $X = 42 / (7 + 27)$, which means $X = 42 / 34$.

ChatGPT: That's correct! And if you simplify that, you'll find that $X = 42 / 34$, which approximates to $X = 1.235$. Well done! You've now solved for X given the value of Y.

This way, the student is guided through the process, allowing them to learn the steps and develop their problem-solving skills.

In these examples, it becomes clear that thoughtfully crafted questions can invite students to engage in deeper thinking and understanding, even while they leverage AI tools for support.

Teachers can create assignments that require critical thinking, creativity, and complex problem-solving – tasks that cannot be simply solved by AI. This pushes students to engage with the material at a deeper level, rather than just scratch the surface in search of a quick answer.

Homework Questions That Do Not Encourage Critical Thinking

1. (For younger students) "What is the capital of Australia and its most famous cities and animals?" – This is a simple factual question that doesn't encourage deeper engagement or understanding.

2. "Who wrote *To Kill a Mockingbird* and what was her background?" – Again, this fact-based question has a straightforward answer that an AI could quickly provide.

3. "When was the Magna Carta signed and who signed it?" – A straightforward historical fact that an AI could provide instantly.

4. "Solve the equation $2x + 3 = 7$." – This simple algebra problem has a direct solution which an AI could solve without any need for conceptual understanding from the student.

5. "Translate 'Hello, how are you?' to French." – A simple translation request that doesn't prompt any deeper learning.

Homework Questions That Encourage Critical Thinking

1. "Imagine you are planning a trip to Australia. What things would you think about when choosing your places to go and what you want to do? How might the land, the weather and the animals help your decisions?" – While an AI might provide some basic facts, the student would need to synthesize this information to form a cohesive argument.

2. "Harper Lee's *To Kill a Mockingbird* explores the theme of racial injustice. Provide examples from the book that illustrate this theme and discuss their significance." – While an AI could provide some examples, the student would need to engage with the text and interpret the significance of these examples themselves.

3. "Explain the historical context and the implications of the signing of the Magna Carta. How did it influence feudalism?" – An AI could provide some context, but the student would need to analyze and articulate the implications themselves.

4. "Consider the equation $2x + 3 = 7$. Solve it and then explain how changing the values of the constants could influence the solution. Provide three examples with different constants." – An AI could help solve the equation, but the student would have to understand and articulate the impact of changing constants.

5. "Translate 'Hello, how are you?' to French. Then, discuss how greeting customs in French culture might differ from those in your own culture." – After getting the translation

from the AI, the student would need to engage in cultural exploration and reflection.

As teachers, we must redefine our approach to homework. Our mission is not to ask questions that simply test students' ability to recall facts or perform straightforward calculations, tasks an AI can easily accomplish. Instead, our questions should provoke thought, stimulate curiosity, and inspire deeper understanding. They should leverage the power of AI as a tool for exploration, not as a shortcut to answers.

The Flipped Classroom

There is no argument that AI has complicated the lives of teachers in terms of plagiarism. Even the best of assignments now become a test of ethical boundaries. Worse yet, homework assignments that were not very good (i.e., who was Madame Curie and what did she do?) are still prevalent. The advent of AI in schools should only hasten the debate on the role of homework in education. The flipped classroom may be the answer, particularly for high schools.

A flipped classroom is an instructional strategy that reverses traditional teaching methods. Instead of whole class instruction occurring in the classroom and assignments being done at home, the flipped classroom model moves instructional content outside of the classroom. This enables students to review core content at their own pace. Struggling students are not embarrassed to interrupt teachers, and bored students can move right to chapter extensions.

In this model, classroom time is used for interactive exercises, projects, and discussions that enhance comprehension and application of the material. The teacher's role in a flipped classroom shifts from a dispenser of information to a facilitator or guide, helping students apply what they've learned online to real-world situations.

When students engage with new material at home via AI, they come to class armed with specific questions, confusions, and insights. The teacher facilitates discussions that make the collective wisdom in the room greater than the sum of its parts. They walk around, listen to group discussions, pose counterarguments, and challenge students to think differently. The classroom becomes a forum of ideas, where students not just digest information but gain perspectives.

This model places a premium on creative and critical thought. Freed from the shackles of rote note taking and passive absorption, students get the chance to apply, analyze, and synthesize what they've learned. They engage in hands-on projects, peer-to-peer teaching, and real-world problem-solving—activities that demand a level of creativity and critical reasoning that AI, at least for now, cannot replicate. With the teacher steering these activities, the classroom turns into a laboratory for life skills: how to negotiate, how to think critically, how to solve problems, and even how to fail and try again.

Let's not forget emotional intelligence, an arena where teachers hold an undisputed edge over machines. Teachers in a flipped classroom can focus more on the "soft skills" that are crucial for a well-rounded education. Reading the room, sensing conflicts, instilling teamwork—these human elements are nurtured in the fertile ground of a flipped classroom. Struggling with a math problem? A teacher will detect your frustration and offer encouraging words or even suggest a break. Feeling disengaged? A good teacher can nudge you back into focus. The teacher becomes a coach, helping each student understand not just the subject matter but also themselves.

Examples – Flipping the Classroom

How do fearless teachers reimagine learning in the age of bots? Here are a few examples in various disciplines that may spark your imagination. Each lesson encourages students to use AI with their homework assignments.

Social Studies Topic: The Renaissance

Pre-Class: Home Study

- **Video Lecture**: Introduction to the Renaissance, highlighting its significance and major figures like Leonardo da Vinci, Michelangelo, and Copernicus.
- **Reading Assignment**: A short e-book or online article detailing the societal and cultural changes during the Renaissance.

- **AI Tool**: Use ChatGPT or similar AI platforms to answer any queries, clarify doubts, or to delve deeper into certain topics or figures.

In-Class Activities

- **Artistic Expression**: Students recreate or interpret famous art pieces or inventions from the Renaissance.
- **Discussion & Debate**: Engage in a dialogue about the impact of the Renaissance on modern society, art, and science.
- **Role-Play**: Students take on the personas of famous Renaissance figures and stage a "meet and greet" to introduce their contributions and ideologies.

Science Topic: Plant Photosynthesis

Pre-Class: Home Study

- **Diagrammatic Explanation**: Visual content detailing the process of photosynthesis, including the light and dark reactions.
- **Interactive Game**: An online game where students guide a plant through the photosynthesis process.
- **AI Tool**: AI chatbot for clarification on complex processes and terms.

In-Class Activities

- **Leaf Chromatography**: Students extract pigments from leaves to see the different colors involved in capturing sunlight.

- **Discussion**: Dive deep into the importance of photosynthesis in the food chain and global oxygen supply.

Civics Topic: The Importance of Voting and Civic Participation

Pre-Class: Home Study

- **Video Lecture**: A historical overview of the evolution of voting rights, highlighting major milestones such as the suffrage movement, the civil rights movement, and recent voting rights discussions.
- **Reading Assignment**: Articles or short readings that present both national and international perspectives on voting, detailing its significance and the consequences of civic apathy.
- **AI Tool**: Use ChatGPT or another AI platform to clarify doubts, provide deeper context on certain events, or answer questions about voting systems around the world.

In-Class Activities

- **Role-Playing Simulation**: Students participate in a mock election, taking on roles such as campaign managers, candidates, voters, and election commission members. This can be based on real-life issues or fictional ones created for the classroom.
- **Discussion**: Facilitate a dialogue on the barriers to voting in modern times, the influence of social media on elections, and the importance of staying informed.
- **Civic Action Plan**: Working in groups, students devise a plan or campaign to increase voter turnout in their community or advocate for an issue they find pressing.

This could involve social media strategies, community outreach, or educational events.

World Literature Topic: Gabriel García Márquez's *One Hundred Years of Solitude*

Pre-Class: Home Study

- **Reading Assignment**: Extracts or specific chapters from *One Hundred Years of Solitude* that introduce the Buendía family and the town of Macondo.
- **Video Lecture**: Overview of Magical Realism, its origins, and its significance in Latin American literature. Emphasis on how Márquez exemplifies this genre.
- **AI Tool**: Utilize ChatGPT or a similar AI system to provide clarity on the complex family relations, historical references, or to decode some of the symbolic elements present in the narrative. Ask ChatGPT to assist in displaying the key family figures.

For the latter assignment, I can share how a student might interact with ChatGPT. Personally, when I read the book, I found it profound but also particularly challenging to keep track of the characters and discern which generation each belonged to."

> **Mr. Jim Prompt**
>
> We are reading "One Hundred Years of Solitude" in class and there are so many characters, many of whom share similar or even the same names across multiple generations. Can you create simplified table to help me understand the main characters in the Buendía family?

ChatGPT

Name	Relationship & Description
José Arcadio Buendía	Patriarch and founder of Macondo. Married to Úrsula.
Úrsula Iguarán	Matriarch, married to José Arcadio Buendía.
José Arcadio	Their firstborn son. Inherits his father's impulsive tendencies.
Colonel Aureliano Buendía	Their second son. Becomes a revolutionary leader.
Amaranta	Their daughter. Never marries and maintains a rivalry with Rebeca.

Rebeca	Adopted daughter of José Arcadio Buendía and Úrsula.
Remedios the Beauty	Daughter of Santa Sofía de la Piedad and Arcadio. Renowned for her beauty.
Renata Remedios (a.k.a. Meme)	Daughter of Fernanda and Aureliano II. Sent to a convent after a scandal.
José Arcadio (II)	Son of Santa Sofía de la Piedad and Arcadio. Inherits his uncle's name and his grandfather's impulsive tendencies.
Aureliano II	Son of Meme and Mauricio Babilonia. Marries Renata Remedios.
Aureliano (III)	Son of Meme and Mauricio Babilonia. Last of the Buendía lineage.
Amaranta Úrsula	Daughter of Fernanda and Aureliano II.

There are, of course, many other characters in the novel, both within the Buendía family and outside of it. I can provide more if you would like. This table, however, covers the most prominent members and should help in understanding the family's complex relationships.

In-Class Activities

- **Character Web**: Given the intricate web of characters in the novel, students work in groups to create visual

representations (charts, mind maps) of relationships and key events associated with each character.
- **Discussion**: Dive deep into the themes of the novel, such as solitude, love, passion, power, and the cyclical nature of history.
- **Magical Realism in Modern Context**: Students are encouraged to write or narrate short stories in the style of magical realism, based on their own experiences or current global events, showing the blending of the magical and the ordinary.

Prompts for the Everyday Teacher

Here are more prompts that students can use for assignments. For each of these questions, students must show how they dialogue with AI to guide in creating their outline and share the prompts they used to get the data to support their position.

1. Investigate the role of bees in global ecosystems. How do they impact our world, and what are the consequences of declining bee populations? Show how you use AI to create an outline and what prompts you used to get your data.

2. Explore the socio-economic implications of automation and AI on the job market. Is the rise of AI beneficial or detrimental for future employment opportunities?

3. Assess the impact of fast fashion on the environment. What is the environmental footprint of the fast-fashion industry?

4. Analyze the cultural significance of the Silk Road in ancient civilizations. How did it influence the exchange of goods, ideas, and the growth of empires?

5. Evaluate the health impacts of processed foods. What are the nutritional components and their long-term effects on human health?

6. Dive into the artistic movements of the 20th century. How did art evolve during this period, and what were the societal influences on major movements?

7. Examine the influence of classical music on modern genres. How have contemporary music genres borrowed elements from classical compositions?

8. Delve into the mechanisms of genetic inheritance. How do dominant and recessive genes determine the traits we inherit?

9. Probe into the world of quantum mechanics. Can you demystify key principles like superposition and entanglement?

10. Investigate the dynamics of ecosystems and biodiversity. Why is biodiversity essential, and what are the consequences of reduced species diversity?

ThinkFives Top 5 Elementary Homework Projects

Nostalgic school projects can evoke heartwarming memories from simpler times. ThinkFives asked hundreds of teachers which elementary school projects they remembered fondly. Here are their Top 5. Do you remember these?

5. Popsicle Stick Crafts

These crafts harnessed the structural versatility of popsicle sticks. Whether it was a picture frame adorned with colorful patterns, intricately woven coasters that provided a functional household item, or small trinket boxes built by stacking and gluing the sticks in creative arrays, these projects allowed students to build simple and fun structures.

4. Macaroni Jewelry

Transforming simple pasta into elegant jewelry, students would string together macaroni that had been either painted or dyed in vibrant colors. The result? Unique necklaces and bracelets that served as a testament to their artistic abilities – and great gifts.

3. Paper Mâché Globes

Using balloons as a base, students would layer them with strips of newspaper dipped in a glue mixture, creating a hard shell once dried. These spheres were then painted blue and adorned with the green of continents, with some students labeling countries, oceans, and cities.

2. Handprint Turkeys

A festive craft, especially around Thanksgiving. Students would lay a hand flat on a sheet of paper, fingers spread out, and trace its outline. The result bore a striking resemblance to a turkey. Crayons, markers, or paint, students would bring their turkeys to life,

1. Shoebox Dioramas

Taking a simple shoebox, students would transform its interior into a three-dimensional scene. Using a mix of handcrafted items, drawings, and sometimes even miniature figures, they'd recreate scenes from their favorite books, depict significant historical events, or showcase natural habitats. Probably every teacher remembers these from their childhood.

#8 PIONEER

> "Never doubt that a small group of thoughtful, committed citizens can change the world; indeed, it's the only thing that ever has."
> – Margaret Mead

While OpenAI's ChatGPT has garnered the most attention since its launch (and became one of the most downloaded apps in history), it comes as no surprise that other technology giants are venturing into the rapidly evolving landscape of AI chatbots. Microsoft, with its integration of ChatGPT with Bing and Google's development of Google Gemini, demonstrate how industry leaders are actively contributing to the field of conversational AI.

While most of this book uses ChatGPT for my examples, the principles of using AI apply to Bing and Gemini as well.

As they evolve, each will develop its strengths and focus, and certain teachers may prefer one over another. As the demand for sophisticated chatbots continues to grow, we expect others known for their technological prowess to also bring their specific expertise and resources to create innovative AI-driven solutions. Certainly, educational technology companies will introduce solutions built on these platforms and focus more on meeting K-12 challenges.

Microsoft's ventures into AI are transforming the landscape of digital tools available for educators. Since the launch of OpenAI's ChatGPT last fall, Microsoft has significantly invested in the company. Rather than focusing solely on the AI chatbot, Microsoft has channeled these investments into enhancing its own search engine, Bing, with generative AI capabilities. This strategic move has led to the birth of a new and improved platform, now called Copilot.

Meanwhile, Google has developed its own AI chatbot, Google Gemini, which presents a unique approach to conversational AI by leveraging new advanced technologies.

With these developments, the stage is set for an exciting competition between ChatGPT, Microsoft Copilot, and Google Gemini. As users explore the capabilities of these AI chatbots, it becomes crucial to understand their distinct features, strengths, and limitations. Teachers should examine the challenges and opportunities presented by these advancements, considering factors such as accuracy, availability, and integration into existing platforms.

One final caveat. This book that you read is created using a technology invented by Gutenberg in 1436. A manuscript is created, then proofed, then printed long before reaching your hands or Kindle. That's a long way of saying that in the ever-changing world of AI, the features offered by OpenAI, Microsoft, and Google are evolving daily. The passages that follow are our best effort to show the power and differences of each. However, best to check online information (or our website at engaiged.ai) for the latest. Who knows, maybe Elon Musk has bought OpenAI by now.

The Collaboration of Bing and OpenAI

In January 2023, Microsoft announced a multiyear, multibillion-dollar investment in OpenAI, expanding their existing partnership to incorporate more artificial intelligence into Microsoft's product suite. The partnership began in 2019 when Microsoft initially invested $1 billion in OpenAI, followed by an additional $10 billion in January.

Partnerships with large search engines can further break down the walls of the classroom, providing access to real-time information from around the world. By combining the power of ChatGPT's large language models with Bing's comprehensive database, teachers no longer rely solely on static textbooks and outdated resources. Bing and Copilot can access information that is current, unlike the April 2023 limitation that ChatGPT currently has (although the latest paid version of ChatGPT can access Bing).

With this access to current data, teachers can supplement their lessons with the latest research, current events, and diverse perspectives. Imagine a geography lesson where students explore the Amazon rainforest not just through textbooks but with access to the latest information. With ChatGPT and Copilot, teachers can share updates on conservation efforts, scientific discoveries, and Indigenous cultures, providing a dynamic understanding of the subject.

The implications of this collaboration extend far beyond education alone. With Copilot's search engine capabilities seamlessly integrated with OpenAI's advanced technology, users can blend current events and business performances with artificial intelligence, unlocking new possibilities.

Here are examples of what users can do with Bing's OpenAI implementation:

Access Real-Time Information: Users can ask for the latest information on movies, events, personalities, controversies, book releases, and more. This expands teaching materials beyond ChatGPT's static training data, ensuring up-to-date and relevant content.

Choose the Conversation Style: Users can ask questions of Bing and receive contextual answers without having to read an entire webpage. Bing AI comes in three flavors: Creative, Balanced, and Precise. Balanced is the default style suitable for all kinds of search queries. Creative is ideal for generating ideas and writing assignments, while Precise provides shorter answers focusing on facts.

Create Charts: Copilot's data analytics capabilities allow users to find products, generate charts with reviews, weigh pros/cons, and make informed decisions. It aids in evaluating choices and sharing findings with others.

Provide Inspiration: Users can ask Copilot for suggestions and new ideas, overcoming writer's block and exploring fresh perspectives for storytelling. Copilot's ability to generate new ideas using current events challenges users to think creatively.

Create Itineraries: Users can plan personalized itineraries for educational trips and adventures using Bing AI's travel companion features. By entering interests, food preferences, and timeline, Copilot generates customized plans with sightseeing recommendations and suggested restaurants.

Access to real-time data is a huge benefit to users. However, it is essential to note that, like the warnings regarding ChatGPT, Copilot also has challenges with inaccuracies and inappropriate responses. Due to access to a vast array of data (including all search results and more recent data), Microsoft faced initial growing pains in implementing its AI. It is crucial to review all results before sharing them with students.

ChatGPT vs Bing

One might be asking, if Copilot now accesses ChatGPT what is the difference? There are significant distinctions between the two prominent players. When deciding between ChatGPT and Copilot, consider your specific requirements and objectives.

ChatGPT

If you desire a chatbot with established name recognition, widespread usage, and the ability to provide detailed responses on a diverse array of topics, ChatGPT is an excellent choice. Its benefits include:

- Ability to deliver detailed, conversational responses to inquiries related to events and topics predating 2023.
- Explanations akin to a tutor make it a valuable resource for learning and research purposes.

- Expansive informational data makes it particularly valuable for historical inquiries and comprehensive explanations.
- Free to use, but there are limitations. It allows users on its free tier to access the GPT-3.5-based version. It can be accessed via the website on a desktop or mobile browser. OpenAI's ChatGPT Plus subscription plan costs $20 per month. It comes with exclusive new features and priority access in peak traffic, and access to GPT- 4.

Additionally, ChatGPT has released several new features in the last six months. This includes:

- **New Knowledge Cutoff:** The knowledge cutoff for ChatGPT has been extended to April 2023. This update will allow ChatGPT to provide more current and relevant responses to your prompts, making it a more effective tool for both teaching and learning.
- **Input Longer Prompts:** GPT-4 Turbo supports up to 128,000 tokens of context. This allows for much longer and detailed prompts, akin to the content of around 300 book pages. This feature is particularly useful for analyzing extensive documents or detailed educational material.
- **Voice Capabilities:** ChatGPT now features voice interaction, allowing for real-time verbal communication with the AI, ideal for clarifying lesson plans, conducting interactive storytelling, or facilitating classroom debates. It can be a great tool for engaging students in auditory learning experiences.
- **Image Capabilities:** The newer integration of image capabilities into ChatGPT opens venues for visual

learning in the classroom. Educators can upload images directly to ChatGPT for a more engaging and interactive discussion. This feature is perfect for exploring visual materials, from historical photographs to science diagrams, and is available on all platforms.

- **Enhanced Focus with Image-Based Interactions:** Beyond basic image uploads, ChatGPT now allows educators to focus on specific parts of an image using the drawing tool in the mobile app. This is particularly useful for detailed discussions or analyses, such as highlighting specific areas in a complex diagram, focusing on parts of a map, or examining certain elements in a science experiment photo.

These new functionalities in ChatGPT, all announced in the latter part of 2023, provide educators with more dynamic and interactive ways to incorporate AI into their teaching methods. It will be exciting to explore these tools and imagine the lessons that you can create once you have mastered basic prompting.

Copilot

On the other hand, if you prioritize real-time information, access to current events, and the ability to verify sources, Copilot proves to be a valuable companion. Its key benefits include:

- Free integration with the Bing search engine, granting users the ability to browse the web to help answer questions.
- Ability to analyze websites or local documents if used in the side bar.
- Incorporation of footnotes makes it great for users interested in confirming the accuracy of responses.
- Provision of sources that lead directly to the web articles from which responses are derived, enables users to verify and validate information.

Additionally, Copilot has announced many new features:
- **Image Upload Capability**: Similar to Google Lens and GPT-4, Copilot allows the uploading of images

for AI processing, adding a visual dimension to your interactions with the tool.

- **Voice Command Feature**: For hands-free operation, Copilot includes a microphone option. Simply speak your prompts to the AI chatbot for an even more interactive experience.
- **New Topic Functionality**: This feature clears previous conversations, allowing you to start fresh with a new topic, keeping your workflow organized and focused.
- **AI-Powered Search with Sources**: While Copilot operates more like a conversational AI than a traditional search engine, it still sources most of its information from the web, citing sources and links for comprehensive understanding.
- **Suggested Follow-Up Questions**: After receiving a response, Copilot offers suggestions for additional questions, fostering a deeper exploration of topics relevant to your teaching needs.
- **Versatile Conversation Styles**: Choose from three response formats - more creative, more balanced, and more precise - to tailor Copilot's replies to your specific educational context, whether you're seeking imaginative ideas or straightforward information.
- **Integration with Outlook**: Reduce time spent managing emails with Copilot in Outlook. It can summarize email threads and draft responses, with options to adjust the tone and length to suit your communication style.

Introducing Google Gemini: Another Option

Not wanting to be overshadowed by the emergence of ChatGPT and Microsoft's partnership, Google developed its own AI engine called Gemini, aiming to become a formidable competitor to both. While Gemini shares similarities with ChatGPT, it boasts distinct features that set it apart. Gemini offers a wide range of functionalities, including event planning, email drafting, answering complex questions, coding assistance, and an AI image generator powered by Adobe.

Google Gemini is an AI chatbot like ChatGPT, albeit employing a different language model (PaLM 2) for advanced capabilities such as coding and upcoming search features. Like other chatbots, Gemini is designed for conversational engagement. Users interact with Gemini by typing queries or requests into a text box, and the AI responds in a conversational tone.

For instance, if you ask Gemini to share discoveries from the James Webb Space Telescope with a nine-year-old student, Gemini will search its trained information and provide a response containing relevant information and recent discoveries.

Gemini expands the horizons of AI interaction, encompassing a wide array of functionalities from event planning to coding. Here's a closer look at the key features of Google Gemini.

- **Accuracy and Google Search Integration**: Google provides information from its vast array of Google-indexed sites. It is heavily trained on multilingual text, spanning more than 100 languages. This has significantly improved its ability to understand, generate and translate nuanced text.
- **Versatile Chatbot Capabilities**: Gemini allows users to perform a variety of tasks, including planning events like

birthday parties, drafting emails, and tackling questions on complex subjects. Its versatility makes it a useful tool for both classroom activities and administrative tasks.

- **Google It**: Google does acknowledge that some of Gemini's responses may be inaccurate. To counter this, a "Google It" button is provided alongside responses, directing users to Google Search for additional information and verification.

- **Multimodal Functionality**: Thanks to its integration with its next generation language mode, PaLM 2, Gemini can process image-based prompts, enhancing its multimedia capabilities. This feature will soon allow Gemini to respond with images and videos, further enriching the interactive experience.

- **YouTube Video Understanding**: Gemini is taking steps to comprehend YouTube videos. This feature can be a significant benefit for educators looking to integrate multimedia content into their lessons, such as querying specific details from instructional videos.

- **Collaboration Across Google Workspace**: Gemini can interact with information from your Gmail, Docs, and Drive, enabling you to find, summarize, and answer questions across your personal content. This integration allows for seamless collaboration and content management within the Google ecosystem.

- **AI Image Generation**: The chatbot is also gearing up to include an AI image generator, thanks to a collaboration with Adobe. This feature will be especially beneficial for creative and technology-based education.

While slower to enter the market than OpenAI and Microsoft, Google's Gemini is emerging as a formidable tool in the realm of

AI chatbots. It offers educators and students a versatile platform for learning, creativity, and productivity. Many school districts already utilize a range of Google products, and integration with these could provide numerous advantages for using Gemini. For more updates tailored to teachers on these features, check out our website at engAiged.ai. These features are expected to roll out in the coming months

Jim Bowler

Khan Academy Enters the World of AI

A Free Virtual Classroom: The Genesis of Khan Academy

For teachers not yet ready to fully introduce AI solutions in the classroom, there are other alternatives like Khanmigo from Khan Academy. Anyone familiar with K-12 education knows that Khan Academy stands as a testament to free, world-class education for anyone, anywhere. Founded in 2008 by Sal Khan, the not-for-profit organization has revolutionized the tutoring landscape. Using a vast digital library of instructional videos, interactive exercises, and a personalized learning dashboard, Khan Academy has empowered millions of learners—from kindergarten to college and beyond—to master subjects at their own pace.

The platform covers a multitude of subjects, including math, science, computing, history, and art. All resources are offered free of charge, ensuring that socio-economic factors don't inhibit a student's access to quality education.

Meet Sal Khan

The man behind this commitment of democratizing education is Sal Khan. With three degrees from MIT and an MBA from Harvard Business School, Khan began by tutoring his cousin in mathematics over the Internet. Realizing the immense potential to scale this kind of learning, he launched Khan Academy to bring education to the fingertips of eager learners globally. But what truly sets him apart is his commitment to education for all and his uncanny ability to simplify complex topics into easily digestible lessons. Soft-spoken yet compelling, Khan has become a household name in the realm of online education.

Khan Academy Meets OpenAI: The Birth of Khanmigo

It shouldn't be surprising then that Khan Academy is also a pioneer in providing students with access to AI tutors. Khanmigo, a collaboration with OpenAI, is designed to make online learning more interactive and personalized. Powered by the GPT-4 technology, Khanmigo serves as a sophisticated virtual tutor and guide to assist students in their learning journey. It is currently a paid service.

Unlike ChatGPT, Khanmigo is explicitly tailored for educational contexts. It doesn't merely provide answers but engages students in dialogue, asking them to explain their reasoning and offering nuanced feedback. By doing so, Khanmigo helps students understand where they might have gone wrong and encourages them to correct their mistakes independently. It can even co-write lesson plans with teachers, assist in administrative tasks, and act as a virtual debate partner.

Sal Khan's initial skepticism toward AI faded upon witnessing the capabilities of GPT-4. Its sophisticated conversational abilities and reduced error rate convinced him of its utility in educational settings. Now, Khan Academy is collaborating with school districts for broader implementation of Khanmigo, taking careful steps to ensure this new venture retains the mission of providing a free, world-class education to all.

For teachers or schools hesitant about allowing students to use AI for homework help, Khanmigo might provide a safe and secure environment to introduce the possibilities.

The Power of Plugins: Customizing Your Classroom

Even with these sophisticated large language models, it is not surprising that no single platform solution can ever meet the needs of all market segments. Users expect targeted functions that meet their specific needs. In the realm of technology, "plugins" fill that requirement. ChatGPT and other AI solutions offer numerous helpful plugins. But what exactly are plugins, and why should a teacher care?

The creators of software like ChatGPT cannot possibly predict every need of every user. Nor do they have the time to build apps that may only be useful to a subset of their audience. Third party companies see this need and also a business opportunity, and create plugins that have narrow functionality. Have you ever added an extension to your web browser that helps you organize your bookmarks, block ads, or correct your grammar as you type? That's a plugin at work.

One might wonder, "If these plugins are so useful, why don't software creators just integrate all these features from the start?" The answer is both simple and complex. At the most basic level, it's about avoiding unnecessary bulk. Imagine a textbook that had every possible topic under the sun – not very efficient, right? Software can get heavy, slow, and cumbersome when loaded with too many features. Not every teacher will need every bell and whistle, much like not every student will need every tool.

More deeply, it's about innovation. By allowing third-party creators to develop plugins, software companies are encouraging a culture of collaborative progress. Different experts can create tools that cater to specific needs, allowing for a richer, broader, and more diversified set of functionalities.

Types of Plugins

For teachers, plugins empower us to access unique productivity tools. This might sound challenging, especially if you're not particularly tech-savvy, but most plugins are easy to install.

These plugins can solve specific problems for teachers and individual student needs, ensuring that education is more personalized, interactive, and accessible than ever before. Here are examples of the type of plugins that may be beneficial for teachers. Some are currently available, and others are in development.

To access these plugins, you go to the AI solutions (ChatGPT, Gemini, Bing), find the plugin button and then install the plugin. It will then work within your browser or app.

Here are examples of the types of plugins that could help teachers.

Personalized Feedback and Assessment

Assessment plugins are designed for grading and assessment, enabling educators to receive detailed, personalized feedback on student assignments, essays, and exams. These plugins analyze student responses and offer insightful evaluations, helping educators provide targeted guidance for improvement.

Content Generation and Lesson Planning

Plugins equipped for content generation assist educators in developing interactive and engaging lesson plans, assignments, and teaching materials. These tools offer valuable resources, from educational articles to problem-solving exercises, streamlining the curriculum development process.

Interactive Learning Experiences

Plugins that foster interactive learning experiences enable educators to create dynamic, gamified lessons that captivate students' attention and encourage active participation. These extensions promote collaborative learning and critical thinking through immersive activities.

Language Translation and Support

AI plugins designed for language translation and support bridge communication gaps in diverse classrooms, offering multilingual assistance to students and educators alike. These tools ensure inclusivity and accessibility in the learning environment.

Virtual Tutoring and Extra Help

With plugins for virtual tutoring, students can receive additional support outside traditional classroom hours. These extensions function as digital tutors, providing explanations, answering questions, and offering guidance whenever needed.

Creative Writing and Storytelling

Plugins designed for creative writing and storytelling inspire students' imagination and nurture their writing skills. These extensions generate prompts, plot ideas, and character development suggestions, fostering creativity in young minds.

These are just a few examples of the wide array of plugin types that extend AI. Many plugins have been added to Ai chatbots since their inception, and the list is growing. At the end of this chapter, ThinkFives shares a list of the more popular plugins that might appeal to teachers. The best way to find out about the newest plugins would be to search online.

Prompts for the Everyday Teacher

For Grade School Students

1. Explain what an AI plugin is and how it can make using technology more enjoyable or easier.
2. Describe an AI plugin that could help you with homework. What kind of assistance would it offer?
3. Discuss how AI plugins in educational apps can make learning more fun and interactive.
4. Think of creative projects or artworks you could create with the help of AI plugins.
5. Talk about the importance of safety and privacy when using AI plugins. What precautions should be taken?
6. If you could design an AI plugin, what would it do and how would it help kids your age?
7. Find examples of AI plugins that help people with disabilities. Discuss how technology can be more inclusive.

For High School Students

1. Delve into the concept of AI plugins and their role in enhancing software applications. How do they function?
2. Investigate various AI plugins, from those improving productivity tools to those aiding creative software.
3. Discuss the advantages of AI plugins in professional environments. How do they foster efficiency and innovation?
4. Analyze the influence of AI plugins on sectors like healthcare, finance, and e-commerce. What changes are they bringing?

5. Examine ethical issues related to AI plugins, including data privacy and security. How can these be managed?
6. Research AI plugins aiding in content creation, like writing, design, or music. How are they reshaping creativity?
7. Debate the need for regulations or standards for AI plugins to ensure their quality and safety. Present arguments for and against.

ThinkFives Top 5 Most Popular Plugins for Teachers

We asked ThinkFives to survey its experts and provide our readers with what they thought would be the most helpful or innovative ChatGPT plugins for teachers. Here are their top picks, grouped into two categories:

Category 1: Research and Learning Enhancement
1. **AskYourPDF**: Transform your PDF documents into interactive, conversational formats. Review and learn from PDFs in a more engaging way, asking questions directly from the document.
2. **Wolfram**: A lifesaver for math and science tasks, it enhances ChatGPT's computational capabilities, making complex algorithms and math problems easier to tackle.
3. **Minihabits: Nurturing Lifelong Learning:** Minihabits encourages the cultivation of productive learning habits and mental well-being. Set small, achievable daily goals, monitor your progress, and see your knowledge, teaching skills, and mental health improve with each passing day.
4. **Science: Fueling Curiosity:** With access to scientific articles and detailed explanations, this tool allows you to delve deeper into any topic with ease. It's an incredible resource for sparking curiosity and diving into the depths of scientific exploration.

5. **Zeno Assistant**: This tool aids in various writing tasks, including fixing spelling and grammar, simplifying language, creating essays, and summarizing content. It's integrated into over 4000 websites.

Category 2: Document and Presentation Creation

1. **Canva with ChatGPT Plugin:** Canva, a popular graphics program, has an integration that allows users to easily craft professional-quality designs by simply inputting prompts into ChatGPT, like "Create a classroom graphic on the solar system." You'll receive several design options from which to choose.

2. **Doc Maker:** Easily converts text inputs into various document formats like Docx, PDF, CSV, etc., perfect for teachers and students who need quick document conversions.

3. **Smart Slides:** Simplify the creation of presentations with this plugin. Generate engaging slides quickly by entering commands and prompts.

4. **Roshi:** Your Personal Lesson Resource Planner: Roshi seamlessly generates engaging lesson content from websites and videos, including YouTube. For teachers who invest hours in research and lesson planning, Roshi can be a significant time-saver, enriching your teaching resources with minimal effort.

5. **Prompt Perfect:** Ideal for generating writing or conversation prompts, helping teachers encourage creativity and engagement in writing exercises or discussions.

#9 VISUALIZE

"The one thing the world will never have enough of is the outrageous." — Salvador Dali

The bells of Kahlo High signaled the start of yet another period, and in Mrs. Tennant's 9th-grade English class, the wonder was just beginning. The students were delving into a chapter on magical realism, their minds swirling with tales where the ordinary met the extraordinary, a dance between the mundane and the fantastical.

"Imagine," Mrs. Tennant began, her voice tinged with excitement, "a flamingo with the head of a lion, dancing on a cloud made of cotton candy." The room filled with giggles and curious glances. "Now, think of the most unusual characters, the wildest combinations of creatures, objects, and places you can envision."

EngAIged

Pencils began to scribble, ideas flowed, and the room buzzed with energy. "A kangaroo playing a violin on the moon while a parade of starry jellyfish floats by," said one student. "A chocolate waterfall cascading from a floating island made of waffles, with penguins riding down on candy cane surfboards," shared another. "An octopus librarian reading a bedtime story to a circle of enchanted books that flutter their pages in glee, all of this taking place on a sandy beach inside a giant seashell," offered yet another.

Mrs. Tennant's journey of imagination wasn't done yet. "Now," she said, turning to the projector, "let's bring your imaginations to life." She projected on the screen and logged in to Midjourney, an AI graphic generator capable of translating their words into vivid visuals. She promptly typed in the first suggestion from her students, and they watched in awe as their whimsical ideas materialized on screen.

The room was electric with amazement and joy. With each generated image, a collective laugh or cheer erupted. The AI-driven graphics weren't just pictures; they were visualizations of her students' creativity, giving form to their wildest dreams.

The combination of magical realism literature and AI-powered imagination turned an ordinary English class into an extraordinary adventure. The students couldn't stop talking about the experience even after the bell rang. They had felt, seen, and heard in a way they never had before. Mrs. Tennant had not only provided them with a platform to let their creative juices flow but also showcased a fusion of technology and creativity that resonated with their digital-native sensibilities. Many left the classroom already brainstorming their next imaginative descriptions, eager for another chance to meld words and art in the next session. And of course, this being an English class, they would be crafting an original story sparked by their image. For once, homework felt like a gift, not a chore, and they couldn't wait to dive deep into their next literary voyage with Mrs. Tennant.

As the year unfolded, this lesson remained etched in the students' memories, a testament to the wonders that emerge when classic education meets modern innovation.

AI Image Generators

You also may have already noticed the wonderful artwork brightening these chapters. All this original art was created by me, your author. I can design in many styles, in many mediums, in color or black and white, and do so with great efficiency. It may have taken Leonardo da Vinci twelve years to paint the Mona Lisa, but I created over twenty distinct pieces of art for this chapter in one evening on my iPad while watching *Stranger Things*.

However, I must confess, I possess no innate artistic talent – nor acquired for that matter. But with the aid of creative prompts and a few iterations, I now boast a portfolio worthy of an art graduate. How did I achieve this? Through AI image generators.

While our fearless journey in this book has focused on large language models, there are also remarkable graphic programs that captivate us with their artistic prowess. Two of the most popular are Midjourney and DALL·E. These innovative programs fall under the category of Generative Adversarial Networks (GANs), an exciting form of AI that has elevated the world of art and creativity to unprecedented levels.

Midjourney is an emerging player in the world of AI image generation, occupying a unique niche with its more dream-like, artful outputs as compared to some of its competitors. This tool brings about a more whimsical, surreal quality to its creations, opening a myriad of possibilities for classroom applications.

DALL·E, created by OpenAI, is a trailblazer in the realm of text-to-image generation. Unlike tools that bank on existing visuals, DALL·E gives birth to images. It creates, rather than curates, turning the nebulous thoughts of its user into tangible art.

Two additional players in this arena are Adobe and Stable Diffusion. Adobe, a household name in the design world, has expanded its solutions by introducing an AI tool called Firefly. With a legacy of embedding AI into its applications for years, Adobe's Firefly is a standout in their recent line-up. It's adept at crafting images from text descriptions, creating dynamic text effects, and enhancing photos with AI-driven elements.

While most of these require a subscription to cover the high server costs to create and store images, you can also search online as trial versions of Bing and Gemini implementations are now providing similar access.

For those seeking a more hands-on approach, there's an open-source solution called Stable Diffusion. As open source, this means anyone with the requisite technical skills can download it and run it locally on their own computer. It also means that you can train and fine-tune the model for specific purposes. It's the backbone of many services crafting portraits, architectural visuals, and more. While not for most educators, if you have the technical prowess to harness it, you can create awesome graphics.

How do AI Image Generators Work

All these generators are digital neural networks, similar to our brain but on a digital scale. Like Large Language Models, they're trained with billions of image-text pairs, teaching them about sunsets, daffodils, pop art, and so much more. After this extensive learning phase, the AI becomes adept at interpreting a myriad of prompts. The models then craft the image using a technique called diffusion, starting with a blank canvas and iterating to match the envisioned prompt. It's like molding clouds to fit the patterns of your imagination.

Creating an AI Image Generator typically entails the following phases:

1. **Digesting Art:** Initially, a rich collection of diverse artworks is chosen. This acts as the foundational lesson for our AI, helping it understand the essence and nuances of art styles and patterns.

2. **Teaching AI:** With the art collection in place, the next phase is akin to an intensive art history class. Here, the chosen artworks are introduced to the AI, allowing it to understand, recognize, and remember various art patterns.

3. **Crafting New Pieces:** Once equipped with this knowledge, the AI is all set to create its own canvas. Depending on the input or a creator's nudge, it stitches together elements it has learned to produce a unique artwork.

4. **Perfecting the Masterpiece:** Like a seasoned artist adding finishing touches, algorithms polish the generated piece, using techniques like style adaptations or image enhancements, ensuring it's not just art but customized art.

While these tools are groundbreaking, they aren't the answer to every visual need. For instance, a blogger might find it quicker to customize a stock photo than to generate an original work. And while creative, the graphic programs have minds of their own and sometimes generate graphics seemingly unrelated to your prompt.

Let's look a little deeper at the two most popular programs, Midjourney and Dall-E.

What is Midjourney?

Midjourney sets itself apart by focusing on a more abstract and artistic style. Instead of generating photo-realistic images like Dall-E, Midjourney aims to produce images that resemble more of a painting. Its objective is to provide a platform to "explore new mediums of thought and expand the imaginative powers of the human species," making it potentially interesting for art, literature, and creative writing classes.

Midjourney is a breakthrough in AI-generated imagery, particularly in realistic face synthesis. The program has redefined how we perceive computer-generated visuals, bringing virtual faces to life with stunning realism. Technically, it relies on a dual neural network system: the generator and the discriminator.

The generator is responsible for producing synthetic faces, while the discriminator acts as a critique, assessing the authenticity of these generated images against real photographs.

Through a constant feedback loop, Midjourney learns from this process, honing its skills until it can generate faces that are nearly indistinguishable from real ones.

Accessing Midjourney

Midjourney is different from the other AI apps when it comes to access. You'll have to start by visiting their website and signing up for the Beta version. You'll then need to access another program called Discord, a popular communication platform. Once you sign up there, you'll receive an invite to Midjourney Discord, where you can start using the image generator. Midjourney is no longer free, but you can get significant value from low-cost subscriptions. Midjourney has four subscription tiers with the basic plan $10 a month and the standard plan at $30. Full-year subscriptions receive a 20% discount.

When you're ready to dive into the world of Midjourney, simply type "/imagine" into the prompt box. From there, you are only limited by your imagination! Need a spark to ignite that creative flame? Borrow some prompts from Mrs. Tennant's class or peek at the end of this chapter for ideas.

For most of the art displayed in this book, I utilized Midjourney. I found it struck a good balance between the literal and creative aspects, offering me four options for each prompt and enabling me to explore additional variations of each. I could then upscale my final choice to a high-quality graphic.

Getting to Know DALL·E

DALL·E, crafted by OpenAI, is like a digital illustrator with an AI twist. In essence, DALL·E is a computer program that has the unique ability to turn textual descriptions into visual images. Think of it as having a student who, when you describe something verbally, promptly sketches it out for you.

While platforms like Midjourney excel in providing curated visual experiences, DALL·E sets itself apart by generating images and not accessing a bank of existing visuals. DALL·E creates, rather than curates, turning the nebulous thoughts of its user into tangible art. Powered by GANs and vast datasets, DALL·E transforms textual descriptions into vivid, high-quality images, demonstrating an unprecedented level of artistic imagination and creativity.

The beauty of DALL·E lies in its adaptability. It listens, interprets, and renders, offering visuals that range from the profoundly realistic to the gorgeously abstract. This spectrum of creativity offers educators and students alike a vast playground of visual expression.

Accessing Dall-E

DALL-E is easier to access than Midjourney. Teachers access Dall-E by using the same URL as ChatGPT (Openai.com). There you can choose DALL·E's web application and sign up. During your sign-up, you'll undergo a simple phone number verification to ensure the platform's integrity.

Upon entering, you'll see an option to "Buy Credits." DALL·E 2 functions on a credit-based system. Each credit lets you explore a new idea, which in turn provides you with four distinct images. These credits serve as your ticket to generating unique AI-artwork.

DALL·E 2's user interface is elegantly simple, showcasing a gallery of previous works and a space for you to introduce your prompts. On the home screen, you can type in a creative prompt and select "Generate." In moments, you'll be presented with four AI-derived images, each catering to your initial idea. Once your images are displayed, you have a world of options. Download, save for later, share, or even play around to create more variations. More recently, DALL·E 2 has been integrated directly into ChatGPT, providing a single interface for text or images.

AI Graphics and Education

For teachers, these programs provide yet another wave of innovation for learning, and it's set to revolutionize the way we think about art, creativity, and education. Our canvas of learning is expanding, allowing us to blend the traditional with the avant-garde. Here are a few examples:

Art & Design

With these programs, students can collaborate with AI, taking their artistic ventures to realms previously uncharted. Picture this: young minds crafting, iterating, and refining, with an AI partner suggesting innovative patterns and designs.

Literature and English

Dive into narratives like never before. With both Midjourney and DALL·E at their fingertips, students can visualize the haunting moors of Wuthering Heights or the bustling streets of Dickensian London. Literature becomes a multi-sensory experience.

Social Studies & History

Instead of solely relying on words, let Midjourney and DALL·E bring epochs to life. Whether it's a recreation of the Roaring Twenties or the elegance of ancient Chinese dynasties, AI can render the past in vibrant detail.

Science & Biology

Illustrating complex biological systems is now simplified. Using DALL·E, transform textbook definitions into striking visuals, making the wonders of biology accessible and engaging.

History & Geography

Use AI to breathe life into past events, figures, or even geographical wonders. Allow students to see, rather than just read about, the mysteries of ancient civilizations.

Creative Writing

When student authors describe their imaginative worlds, AI stands ready to illustrate, bridging the gap between abstract thought and tangible visualization.

Problem Solving & Critical Thinking

Challenge your students to express abstract concepts through visuals with Midjourney. Whether it's a mathematical conundrum or a philosophical idea, visual representation can foster deeper understanding.

Interdisciplinary Projects

Collaborate on projects where art meets science or literature melds with history. Midjourney can be the tool that ties varying subject matters together, fostering a holistic educational experience.

Let's Get Started

Wondering where to start as a teacher? Here are some sample prompts to ignite creativity and foster interactivity in the classroom, seamlessly blending academic concepts with cutting-edge AI visualization. Begin with something whimsical or magical, much like Mrs. Tennant did.

Think about playful takes on everyday scenes. How about envisioning a classroom filled with joyful students, perhaps depicted in cartoon form?

Now, let's have a little fun. We can take our playful classroom and visualize what it might have looked like if famous artists had created it. For example, how would this classroom appear if it were rendered by a Renaissance master?

In the Style of Rembrandt   In the Style of Michelangelo

Now that's impressive. We can see Rembrandt, characterized by deep contrasts between light and dark and his meticulous attention to human emotion and detail. We can also see the work of the renowned Michelangelo and his anatomically accurate sculptures and frescoes in the background. We almost hear the master emphasizing the beauty and strength of the human form with his students.

In the Style of Monet   In the Style of van Gogh

With these examples, you could introduce the school of impressionists. Monet, a pioneer of Impressionism, often depicts fleeting moments in nature, using loose brushstrokes and vibrant colors to capture the play of light and atmosphere. And we can see a quintessential Van Gogh, recognized by expressive and emotive use of color and bold, swirling brushstrokes. Even in this example, you can see how Van Gogh's works convey deep emotion and a unique perspective on the world around him.

In the Style of Mexican Modernism   In the Style of Cubism

Even more exciting for a class lesson might be exposing students to movements with which they may be less familiar. What would a classroom look like if it was painted in the style of Mexican modernism by someone like Frida Kahlo? This style combines traditional Mexican motifs with modernist aesthetics and might include a self-portrait of the artist herself. Or consider the wild imagining of a classroom from a cubist like Pablo Picasso, known for his fragmented and abstract forms. We can see how he innovatively deconstructs and reassembles objects in a single canvas.

In the style of Surrealism   In the style of Pop Art

From surrealism to pop art, students can explore the art of the 20th century. How might a Surrealist interpret the classroom? Perhaps Salvado Dali would characterize it by dreamlike landscapes, bizarre imagery, and mysterious detail. Or consider how Andy Warhol might interpret a classroom in a Pop Art style, marked by its celebration of consumer culture, using bright colors and recognizable imagery (and Marilyn Monroe as your teacher).

In the style of Pop Art   In the style of a street artist

And finally, you could consider artists who have painted in more recent times. Other pop artists like Roy Lichtenstein are known for their use of bold colors, thick lines, and Ben-Day dots similar to those found in comic strips. They are often infused with irony or commentary on modern culture. And imagine what the street art of the elusive Banksy's might look like. Characterized by its satirical and subversive nature, it often conveys political and social commentary through stenciled images and witty slogans.

The inclusion of AI graphic generators opens up a completely new avenue to draw student creativity into any lesson. Take a science class for example.

Title: Exploring Animal Adaptations through Digital Art

Objective:

By the end of this lesson, students will understand the concept of animal adaptations and how they help animals survive in their environments. They will demonstrate their understanding through digital art creation.

Materials:

- Computers or tablets with access to a graphic program like DALL-E or a simplified online drawing tool.
- Projector or interactive whiteboard for demonstrations.
- Reference materials on animal adaptations (books, websites, or videos).
- Art supplies (paper and colored pencils) for offline activity.
- Duration: Two 45-minute class periods

Lesson Plan:

Introduction (15 minutes):

1. Begin by discussing the concept of adaptations in animals. Ask students if they know what adaptations are and why they are important for animals.
2. Show some images of animals with unique adaptations (e.g., a chameleon's camouflage, a giraffe's long neck, a polar bear's fur) and discuss how these adaptations help the animals survive in their environments.

Digital Art Activity (25 minutes):

1. Explain to students that they will be using a graphic program (like DALL-E) to create their own imaginative animals with unique adaptations.
2. Demonstrate how to use the digital art tool for drawing and adding features to their animals. Encourage them to be creative and think outside the box.
3. Provide a list of environments or challenges (e.g., desert, deep ocean, cold tundra) and ask students to choose one. Their task is to create an animal that is well-adapted to survive in that environment.
4. Allow students time to work on their digital art creations, offering assistance as needed.

Discussion and Sharing (15 minutes):

1. Have students present their digital animal creations to the class. They should explain the adaptations they designed and how those adaptations help their animals thrive in their chosen environment.
2. Encourage discussion and questions from the class.

Offline Extension Activity (Homework) (Optional):

1. As homework, ask students to choose one real animal and research its adaptations.
2. They should create a traditional drawing (on paper) of the chosen animal and label its adaptations.

Conclusion (5 minutes):

1. Summarize the main points of the lesson: what adaptations are, why they are important, and how animals have unique features to survive in their environments.
2. Emphasize the creativity and critical thinking demonstrated by students during the digital art activity.

Fish Adapting to Environment   Tiger in Hiding

Having students choose animals and environments immerses them in learning, providing a richer experience than merely observing slides or pictures in a book. These examples illustrate how teachers can build lesson plans around the topics and standards they need to cover, integrating image generators to enhance critical thinking and engagement. How about exploring a few other lessons? Let's allow ChatGPT to provide us with ideas.

> **Mr. Jim Prompt**
>
> Provide great lessons for various grade levels that start by incorporating the student use of DALL-E or a similar graphic program in class. Start with tapping into student creativeness and use that to learn about the topic.

ChatGPT

Elementary ELA: AI-Generated Story Illustrations

Elementary students will improve their storytelling skills and create illustrated stories with AI-generated images.

AI Integration: Students will use AI graphic generators to generate images based on their story elements and incorporate these images into their narratives, enhancing their visual storytelling abilities.

Middle School Science: AI-Infused Ecosystem Models

Students gain understanding of the concept of ecosystems and create detailed ecosystem models with AI-generated flora and fauna.

AI Integration: Students will use AI graphic generators to populate their ecosystem models with AI-generated images of plants and animals, creating realistic and diverse representations of ecosystems.

Middle School Spanish: AI-Enhanced Cultural Posters

Students will learn about Spanish-speaking countries' cultures and create informative posters with AI-generated visuals.

AI Integration: Students will use AI graphic generators to generate images that represent cultural aspects (e.g., landmarks, traditional clothing) of Spanish-speaking countries. These images will be incorporated into their cultural posters, promoting a deeper understanding of the culture.

High School Computer Science: AI-Powered Game Design

Students learn the basics of game design and create a simple video game with AI-generated characters and elements.

AI Integration: Students will use AI graphic generators to design characters, objects, or backgrounds for their video games, introducing them to AI-assisted game development.

High School English Literature: AI-Enhanced Poetry

Students explore the world of poetry and enhance their creativity by incorporating AI-generated imagery into their poems.

AI Integration: Students will use AI graphic generators to generate images or visual metaphors that complement their poems, adding a visual dimension to their poetic expressions.

Cultural Poster: Traditional Spanish town square with flamenco dancers, classical Spanish guitarists, a historic fountain, and people enjoying tapas

Poetry interpretation: "Do not go gentle into that good night, Old age should burn and rave at close of day. Rage, rage against the dying of the light." (Dylan Thomas)

These examples from various grade levels should spark your own ideas. Do you need some more ideas for your classes? Consider these.

1. History class: students can create AI-generated depictions of historical events or figures, bringing the past to life through visual storytelling.
2. Geography lessons: students can design AI-enhanced maps that illustrate geographic features, climate zones, or population distribution.
3. Literature studies: students can craft AI-augmented book covers or character portraits that represent their interpretations of literary works.

4. Mathematics: students can use DALL-E to visualize complex geometric shapes or solve word problems with visual aids.
5. Foreign Language classes: students can generate AI-assisted flashcards with images to help reinforce vocabulary and language comprehension.
6. Art education: students can experiment with AI-generated elements to create unique, contemporary artworks or explore artistic styles.
7. Social Studies: students can design multimedia presentations with AI-generated infographics and visuals to explain historical or cultural concepts.
8. Music Classes: students can create album cover designs using AI-generated artwork that reflects the mood and themes of their compositions.
9. Physical Education: students can develop AI-enhanced fitness and exercise guides with animated visuals for better understanding and engagement.
10. Environmental Science: students can generate AI images to illustrate environmental issues, such as deforestation or pollution, in their research projects.

Video Game Characters

Cover for A Tale of Two Cities

Tips for Getting Started

Ready to dive in? As you use these prompts, I have these tips to help you produce images that meet your needs. There are also many training videos online, both on our site (engage.ai) and YouTube that can help you master these programs. Here are five tips for consideration.

1. Be Patient

First things first, remember that while AI is fast, perfection takes time. It's common for Midjourney to take about a minute or so to generate an image based on your prompt. The reason? The bot is processing vast amounts of information to curate the best visual response for you. Trust the process and give it its due time.

2. Choose Your Favorite

By default, Midjourney doesn't just give you one image; it presents a grid of four distinct visuals based on your prompt. This is a golden opportunity! Four perspectives allow you to choose the image that resonates most or to merge ideas from multiple outputs.

3. Experiment with "Variations"

If you've found an image composition you love but wish for slight tweaks, the V buttons (from V1-V4) come to your rescue. These buttons generate variations of the selected image, retaining its essence but with nuanced differences. It's like asking the AI, "What else can you do with this theme?"

4. Upscale for Detail with "U" Buttons

Want a closer look? The U buttons, ranging from U1-U4, are your best friends. Opt for these when you want to upscale an image. The result? A larger canvas filled with intricate details that were perhaps too tiny to notice in the original.

5. Embrace Iterative Design

The real magic with graphic AI tools like Midjourney lies in the iterative process. Don't stop at your first prompt. Refine, re-prompt, upscale, vary, and re-roll until your vision materializes. Think of it as sculpting: you're chiseling away the excess to reveal the masterpiece within.

Prompting with Midjourney

As you venture deeper into the realms of AI-assisted graphics, you'll discover that these platforms offer more than just basic image generation. They invite you to experiment, refine, and master the art of visual storytelling. For the artwork in this book, I experimented with many different prompts, learning a lot as I went along. Initially, I took the chapter title and quote and asked Midjourney to interpret this quote in an inspirational or magical way.

Sometimes I needed to provide more instructions (like cartoon or photorealism, blue tones or pastels, etc.). Other times, I had to delete the name of the person quoted, because it would place Walt Disney, for example, in the middle of the picture. Most prompts were simple, but I would iterate or refine the art produced sometimes ten or twenty times to arrive at a graphic that I thought captured the essence of the quote.

And your artistic fun has only begun. You can add photos, adjust settings and explore advanced settings in both DALL-E and Midjourney.

Personalize with Your Art

Have you encountered a Mona Lisa in your life and been lucky enough to have your iPhone ready? Or perhaps you have a great selfie that could be the basis of a modern masterpiece? You're in luck. Now these AI graphic generators incorporate images directly into your prompts, taking your creations to a whole new level.

It's fairly simple once you're in the program.

1. Upload an Image: Choose your image and use the upload bit
2. Embed Your Image Links: A direct link to an image on the internet is essential. This means the URL should directly point to the image file.
3. Find the Image URL: If you're unsure how to get the direct link, it's usually as simple as right clicking the image in most web browsers and selecting "Copy Image Address."

4. Provide instructions: For the image prompt mechanism to work best, ensure you combine an image with a text description or use two different image inputs.

Example:

/imagine prompt: http://imageURL1.png create as anime with vivid colors

Let's see what we can create. I will upload a selfie I took and then ask Midjourney to make me look better (which will not be hard to do). How about as a Superhero?

> **Mr. Jim Prompt**
>
> /imagine prompt: Https://mybestselfie.jpg cartoon that makes me look like a superhero.

How The Camera Sees Me   How I See Me

Consider the exhilarating lessons a fearless teacher can create with the photo upload features in Dall-E and Midjourney! Imagine the possibilities when you upload photos from your classroom or online resources, and transform them into stunning, imaginative visuals. For instance, take a simple classroom photo and ask Dall-E to reimagine it as a scene from a historical period you're studying. Students can then analyze the differences and learn about historical contexts in a visually engaging way.

Consider uploading a student's drawing and using Midjourney to evolve it into a full-blown art piece, exploring artistic styles and techniques. This not only fosters creativity but also instills a sense of pride and achievement among students. The photo upload feature is a gateway to crafting lessons that are not just educational but also incredibly fun and visually stimulating; it's a canvas of endless possibilities.

Other Advanced Features

Prompt Options

These options can provide further power and flexibility. Most are descriptors you can add to your prompts, while some are suffixes you can append. Here are just a few:

1. Media Quality:

- Choices: Award-winning, Professional, Expert.
- Impact: Each choice will progressively enhance the resolution, clarity, and intricacy of your image. Whether you're creating for a personal blog or a commercial billboard, there's a quality setting that's just right.

2. Media Type:

- Choices: This is where you define the base of your image. Options include Photography, Illustration, Graphic Design, Vector Illustration, Photographic Portrait, Cartoon, Pencil, Billboard, and more.
- Impact: By specifying the media type, you set the primary texture and feel of your creation.

3. Art Style:

- Choices: This defines the aesthetic signature of your image. With styles like Painting, Acrylic, Duotone, Anime, Pixar, Halftone, Phantasmal, Watercolor, Stained Glass, and many others. You can make your image resonate with different eras and moods.
- Impact: This is akin to choosing a film genre. The style can transport viewers to different realms, from the abstract worlds of Picasso to the vibrant universes of Pixar.

4. Lighting:

- Choices: Opt from various settings like Half Rear, Backlight, Natural, Softbox, Moody, Cinematic, and more.
- Impact: Lighting can elevate an image, adding depth, drama, and emotion. It's like setting the ambiance of a scene in a movie.

5. Negative Prompts:

- Usage: If there are elements or subjects you specifically don't want in your image, you can use the "no" keyword. This ensures those particular subjects are excluded from your final piece.

6. Aspect Ratio:

- Choices: Opt for other sizes for your creations. 16:9 (widely used for TVs, monitors, and widescreen displays); 9:16 (mobile phones and social media stories); 5:4 (portrait photography); 1:1 (classic square).

- Impact: Understanding which aspect to use allows you to create for your media of choice.

Are these too many choices? Don't worry, Midjourney and DALL·E both create great images with the simplest prompts. But if you are fearless enough to experiment, you can gain greater control of the images with these suggestions. Let's put it all together now with a prompt developed by an expert.

Mr. Jim Prompt

/imagine prompt: Award-winning artwork of a beautiful brunette woman standing in front of San Francisco's Golden Gate Bridge, wearing a white dress. Oil painting, ultra-realistic, highly detailed. Whimsical, cinematic, 32K resolution, extremely well-made, cinematic lighting, backlight --AR 16:9 --no fog

/imagine prompt: expert, photography, watercolor, natural lighting, children in playground at school --ar 9:16 no teacher

Crafting a detailed graphic prompt is an art in itself. It's about fusing your imagination with AI capabilities. With tools like aspect ratios and intricate refinements at your disposal, the horizon of creative possibilities is vast. Dive in, experiment, and watch your visions come alive on the digital canvas!

One thing to note. Despite extensive fine-tuning efforts, AI's graphical capabilities still fall short of perfection. You might create an impressive image with remarkably realistic depictions of faces, skin, hair, and clothing, only to discover peculiarities in the background, such as people with six fingers or just one ear. If you were to examine a dozen Midjourney images, it's likely you'd encounter these hand and finger anomalies. Even within the images in this book, imperfections exist. Some students in the back of the classrooms are missing fingers, and one even lacks a hand. Humorously, these quirks persisted no matter how I prompted. I intentionally did not photoshop the peculiarities so that the most curious readers could inspect for these imperfections hidden in the graphics. Like most AI, these programs are works in progress.

The Ethics and Implications of AI-Generated Images in Education

Any chapter on generative image creators would be incomplete without a discussion of the ethical issues emerging from such programs. Much like issues being raised by ChatGPT, this is a case of technology outpacing the ethical considerations of such usage. This is especially true with Midjourney and Dall-E. Lawsuits have been filed, and questions remain about what is appropriate, ethical, and even legal.

As educators, there's a pressing need to understand and weigh in on the implications of using these AI tools, especially when their impact stretches across the broad horizons of creative and visual pedagogy. In addition to concern about the devaluation of professional artistry, there are legal concerns about the usage of copyrighted materials in the pre-training. Additionally, the potential for AI tools to mimic specific artists or styles without their consent raises significant ethical issues.

Each issue will require healthy and open dialogue, and teachers and educational associations can be leaders in these discussions. The law is unclear as to appropriate ethical lines. Teachers could also make it part of an interactive learning experience. Middle and high school classrooms are the perfect forums to dissect, discuss, and devise guidelines. Why not empower our students to research, deliberate, and craft the ethical foundations that will steer future classrooms?

Inspiration or Inspiration?

One specific topic that is worth a deeper dive is the line between imitation and inspiration. It's a pretty thin line and one that is easy to miss. Art, in its essence, is a form of expression, a reflection of society, and often a tribute to the masters who've come before us. But where do we draw the line between homage and imitation? When we think of melting clocks and dreamy landscapes, Salvador Dali pops into mind. But should our students recreate this iconic style, is it a nod of admiration or a step too close for comfort?

As I prepared the artwork for this chapter, I grappled with the ethical implications of incorporating works inspired by famous artists. Initially, I believed that I was utilizing these images for educational purposes. We also understand that art created for educational purposes often enjoys greater leniency, both legally and ethically. Using an artist's style to teach technique, history, or theory can be viewed as a tribute rather than theft.

However, I also recognized the importance of not sharing prompts for image generation that some might deem inappropriate. As you may have observed, my resolution was to reference artists whose rights to their works had expired, such as "in the style of Rembrandt," and abstain from referencing modern or living artists, by prompting and captioning "in the style of pop art."

As K-12 educators, it's crucial to understand and convey the ethical considerations surrounding derivative artwork to our students. Here is a spectrum of thought that you might consider.

1. Ancient Inspirations

Asking for artwork in the style of ancient Romans is generally uncontroversial. Their art has been part of the public domain for centuries. But what if we were to specify a lesser-known Roman artist, like Quintus Pedius, the first recorded deaf artist? Even though he's long forgotten by many, does that make it more acceptable?

2. Renaissance and Beyond

Leonardo da Vinci, a name synonymous with the Renaissance, has no descendants laying claim to his masterpieces. But does the absence of legal ties make it ethically sound to create art "in the style of DaVinci?"

3. Modern Copyright Laws

In literature, author copyrights typically last around 70-75 years after the author's death, depending on the jurisdiction. Can this be a guiding principle for visual arts? If an artist's style becomes public domain after a certain period, does that make derivative works more ethically acceptable? Can I specifically reference Van Gogh and Monet, whose masterpiece creations now have past the century mark?

4. Contemporary Artists

The enigmatic street artist Banksy is very much alive and active. Creating artwork "in the style of Banksy" raises immediate ethical concerns. Is it fair to the artist? Does it diminish the originality of their work?

Naming the Style vs. Naming the Artist

Instead of attributing a style to a specific artist like Andy Warhol, one could refer to the broader movement, such as "Pop Art." This approach acknowledges the broader artistic movement without potentially overshadowing other contributors.

With contemporary artists, especially those still producing work, it might be more respectful and ethically sound to generalize. Saying "in the style of modern street art" rather than naming Banksy can avoid potential pitfalls. "However, things become even murkier if I use Midjourney to create works of art that resemble Banksy's style, and then proceed to publish books of the pictures for profit, or create NFTs. On the other hand, if I had any artistic ability and admired Banksy's style, adapting it into my own non-AI created artwork, I might still feel comfortable selling my artwork, which, though derivative, is original.

However, it's essential to ensure that the educational context is genuine and not a guise for commercial gain.

As educators, it's our responsibility to instill a sense of respect for original creators while also fostering creativity. While the legalities surrounding derivative works have clear guidelines, the ethical considerations are more nuanced. Encouraging students to understand the impact and implications of their choices in art can lead to a more informed and respectful artistic community.

Prompts for the Everyday Teacher

Midjourney Prompts

- **Mathematics**: Design a surreal world where geometrical shapes come to life.
- **History**: Envision the bustling markets of the ancient Indus Valley civilization.
- **Literature**: Visualize Juliet's balcony from Shakespeare's *Romeo and Juliet*.
- **Science**: Illustrate a cell undergoing mitosis.
- **Geography**: Depict the breathtaking vistas of the Himalayan Mountain range.
- **Civics**: Showcase a vibrant and inclusive democratic gathering.
- **Art**: Design a hybrid painting style blending Impressionism with Cubism.

- **Environmental Studies**: Craft a utopian city that's fully sustainable.
- **Music**: Visualize a world where musical notes take physical forms.
- **Physical Education**: Depict the energy and movement of an Olympic sprinter.
- **Language Studies**: Illustrate a scene from a popular local legend in Latin America.
- **Economics**: Design a bustling port showcasing international trade.
- **Philosophy**: Conjure an image that represents the duality of human nature.
- **Technology**: Illustrate a classroom of the future.
- **Astronomy**: Depict a serene Martian landscape.

DALL·E Prompts

- **Mathematics**: Show a whimsical city built entirely out of numbers and mathematical symbols.
- **History**: Generate a portrait of Cleopatra based on ancient descriptions.
- **Literature**: Create a visual representation of the Forbidden Forest from *Harry Potter*.
- **Science**: Illustrate the life cycle of a butterfly in a fantastical manner.
- **Geography**: Bring to life the bustling streets of downtown Tokyo.
- **Civics**: Show a world where children are the decision-makers.
- **Art**: Reimagine Van Gogh's *Starry Night* in a futuristic city.

- **Environmental Studies**: Visualize an underwater city thriving amidst coral reefs.
- **Music**: Depict a serene landscape inspired by Beethoven's "Moonlight Sonata."
- **Physical Education**: Illustrate a dance form that's a fusion of ballet and hip-hop.
- **Language Studies**: Craft a market scene inspired by French cafés.
- **Economics**: Visualize a world where barter trade is the primary economic system.
- **Philosophy**: Generate an image that represents the concept of existentialism.
- **Technology**: Show children interacting with holographic books.
- **Astronomy**: Create a vibrant depiction of an exoplanet with potential life.

ThinkFives Top 5 Artists Every Student Should Know

Beauty is in the eye of the beholder — but it helps if that eye has training. Art appreciation is an important learning activity for students as it teaches kids the importance of different perspectives as viewed through other cultures, histories, values, and traditions. ThinkFives asked hundreds of teachers which artists they think are vital for students to know. Here are their luminaries.

5. Michelangelo (1475 to 1564)

5 Famous Works: Sistine Chapel; David; Bacchus; Madonna of Bruges; Pieta

Fun Facts about Michelangelo

- Pieta was the only work Michelangelo ever signed.
- Michelangelo carved the "David" from a discarded block of marble.
- Michelangelo painted his self portrait in The Last Judgment of the Sistine Chapel.

4. Frida Kahlo (1907 to 1954)

5 Famous Works: The Two Fridas, Self-Portrait with Thorn Necklace and Hummingbird, The Broken Column, Diego and I, The Love Embrace of the Universe, the Earth, Myself, Diego, and Señor Xólotl

Fun Facts about Frida Kahlo

- Kahlo began painting after a bus accident left her bedridden, using a special easel.
- Frida's vibrant use of color was inspired by Mexican culture and Indigenous traditions.
- She married the Mexican muralist Diego Rivera, a relationship filled with love and turmoil.

3. Picasso (1881 to 1973)

5 Famous Works: Guernica; Girl Before A Mirror; The Old Guitarist; Les Demoiselles d'Avignon; Garçon à la Pipe

Fun Facts about Picasso

- His full name is 25 words long (Pablo Diego José Francisco de Paula Juan Nepomuceno María de Los Remedios Cipriano de la Santísima Trinidad Ruiz y Picasso).
- Picasso has had more works of art stolen than any other artist.
- Picasso's last words have inspired a Paul McCartney song ("Drink to me").

2. Monet (1840 to 1926)

5 Famous Works: The Water Lilies; Sunrise; Woman with a Parasol; House of Parliament; Rouen Cathedral

Fun Facts about Monet

- The Impressionism art movement was named after a Monet painting.
- The model in many of Monet's famous paintings is his wife, Camille.
- In thirty years, Monet produced 250 paintings of water lilies.

1. Van Gogh (1853 to 1890)

5 Famous Works: Starry Night; Sunflowers; Irises; Self Portrait with Bandaged Ear; The Bedroom

Facts about Van Gogh

- Van Gogh lived with mental illness throughout his life.
- *Starry Night* was created in an asylum.
- Van Gogh only started painting at the age of 27.

#10 EVOLVE

"I have not failed. I've just found 10,000 ways that won't work." — Thomas Edison

Once upon a time, in the halls of Turing Elementary School, there was a buzz about a new class aide. Her name was Miss Ada, assigned to Mr. Keating's class, and each morning, as the sun barely made it through the fingerprint-smudged classroom windows, Miss Ada would stumble in, coffee in hand, often tripping over a backpack or two.

First up was attendance, which she managed to turn into an epic saga of mispronunciations and mistaken identities. "Harry Potter?" she'd call out, squinting at the name "Harriet Potterman." The classroom erupted in giggles every time. No name went unscathed, no absent student was accurately recorded.

But Miss Ada's unique non-talents were just beginning to show. She would attempt to correct papers, often marking right answers wrong and vice versa, creating a bizarre alternate universe where 2+2 could equal 5. Mr. Keating spent nights re-marking papers, hoping she would slowly improve.

Her approach to lesson planning was equally...creative. When asked to prepare materials, Miss Ada would present Mr. Keating with a document on the best bonnets when he wanted sonnets. Or the time where she presented a science lesson on endangered feces when he meant endangered species?

As for personalized learning plans, Miss Ada's were anything but. She somehow managed to confuse topics, mixing arithmetic with algebra and graded readers with Latin texts.

Days turned into weeks, and Mr. Keating's patience with Miss Ada turned into a weary resignation. Library organization? Miss Ada sorted books by the color of their spines, turning the library into a rainbow maze that left students and teachers alike wandering in search of literature.

Then one day, the oddest thing happened. Miss Ada, who had been standing perfectly still, started to twitch slightly. The students, initially amused by her quirky behavior, began to look on in bewilderment.

"I am Miss A-A-Ada, your cl-cl-class..." she sputtered, her voice fluctuating between pitches. The students exchanged glances, unsure whether this was part of some strange lesson plan.

"Attendance! Attendance is... is... recalculating... recalculating..." she buzzed, her voice now a robotic drone.

Mr. Keating, realizing something was amiss, stepped forward. "Kids, I think Miss Ada is having a little difficulty," he said, trying to maintain calm.

But Miss Ada's glitches grew more intense. Her voice became a cacophony of random words and phrases, "Dodgeball history! Sonnets and Bonnets, feces, feces, 2+2 equals... equals... system overload!"

The class watched in a mix of horror and fascination as sparks began to emit from Miss Ada's ears. Miss Ada, now in the midst of a full-blown meltdown, continued her erratic dance, sparks flying, until with a final, loud "BZZZZT!" she came to a sudden halt, smoke gently rising from her circuitry.

Mr. Keating, now alone with the smoldering remains of what used to be a state-of-the-art AI assistant, sighed. "Back to the drawing board, I guess," he muttered to himself, already dreading the paperwork that would follow.

In the end, the legend of Miss Ada, the robot aide who short-circuited in class, became a favorite tale among the students of Turing Elementary. And Mr. Keating? Well, he decided that maybe old-school teaching wasn't so bad after all.

Artificial Semi-Intelligence

As we turn the page from the misadventures of Miss Ada, her unintended comedic exploits in Mr. Keating's class offer a segue into a more serious and real challenges with AI. There are genuine concerns and limitations of artificial intelligence in educational settings. Even fearless teachers must be grounded with the reminder of the current imperfections of AI and the very challenges it presents.

AI, as it stands today, is not infallible. It is susceptible to errors, some of which may have far-reaching implications. Teachers need to understand the phenomenon of AI hallucinations — instances where AI systems generate false or nonsensical information. This is akin to Miss Ada's imaginative yet erroneous interpretations of classroom tasks. We need to know how these hallucinations can mislead students and educators, potentially impacting learning outcomes.

Teachers must also educate themselves on the inherent biases that can exist within AI systems. AI tools can reflect the biases present in their training data, leading to skewed perspectives and unequal educational experiences.

Privacy concerns are another critical aspect that schools and districts must address. The integration of AI into education necessitates the collection and analysis of vast amounts of data. This raises important questions about student privacy and data security, echoing the broader societal concerns about surveillance and personal data protection.

Privacy is also important because of the way AI can increase the risk of scams and misinformation. As AI becomes more sophisticated, so do the tactics of those who wish to exploit these technologies for deceptive purposes. Educators and students alike must be equipped to navigate this landscape safely and critically.

Hallucinations in AI

Have you ever seen a mirage? An illusion where the sizzling heat of a desert road conjures images of water in the distance, but as you approach, the vision dissipates, leaving behind only reality? Ever woke up in the middle of the night, half-asleep, and sworn you saw a shadowy figure at the foot of your bed, only to blink and find nothing there?

With AI and learning language models, there's a similar phenomenon, intriguingly termed "hallucinations." However, these are not sensory experiences like human hallucinations. They refer to instances where an AI system perceives something in data that doesn't correspond to reality — akin to seeing a mirage in the desert of digital information.

What's in an AI Hallucination?

Much like those peculiar dreams of yours, an AI hallucination is a departure from reality. But instead of dream-induced rollercoaster rides, it manifests as bizarre, inaccurate, or simply nonsensical outputs from the AI model. For example, you ask your friendly ChatGPT class assistant, "Who won the 2021 World Series?" and it responds, "In 2021, the World Series was won by the New York Jets." There's just one tiny problem: to the best of our knowledge, the Jets are not a baseball team (some may argue that is true in football, too). This is an AI hallucination. And the most interesting aspect is that when this occurs, ChatGPT is "confidently wrong." It shares answers with such authority that we often forget to verify the results.

Mind the (Data) Gap

Hallucinations are not always nonsensical. It may also simply be the misreporting of a historical fact or the miscalculation of a physics solution. What causes these oddities? AI models learn from training data and generate responses based on patterns they identify in this data. However, these patterns aren't always clear or complete, like a jigsaw puzzle with missing pieces. When asked a question, AI dives into its map of patterns, trying to assemble a picture that matches the query. Sometimes, like a confused student, it forces pieces together where they don't quite fit, and we think the Jets are a winning team.

Twisting Reality: Hallucinations in Action

What are examples of how ChatGPT and other AI models hallucinate? Imagine a class where a student asks ChatGPT, "Who was the president of the United States in 1790?" ChatGPT might confidently declare, "In 1790, the president of the United States was Denzel Washington." The students copy that "fact" into their digital notebooks.

But a learned teacher should immediately intervene. Denzel, while a fine actor, was neither a founder father nor even breathing in 1790. Here, ChatGPT has recognized the pattern of "President of the United States" but pulled the wrong

Washington from its training data, leading to a historically inaccurate and hallucinated response. This does not happen often, but it does happen. It may seem particularly weird since the prior response from ChatGPT on a significantly more complex concept was so perfect.

Hallucination Examples

Here are some examples reported by users of real hallucinations in ChatGPT. The first is a simple example of a factual hallucination.

> **User input:** "When did Leonardo da Vinci paint the Mona Lisa?"
>
> **ChatGPT:** "Leonardo da Vinci painted the Mona Lisa in 1815."
>
> (Incorrect: The Mona Lisa was painted between 1503 and 1506, or perhaps continuing until 1517.)

Other users have reported surprising mistakes in basic math.

> **User input:** "Which is larger, -999934 or -32323232323?"
>
> **AI Input:** "The number -32323 is larger than - 999934. When comparing negative numbers, we follow the same rules as when comparing positive numbers. In this case, the first number has 10 digits while the second number has six digits.
>
> **User input:** "Why?"
>
> **AI:** "In numerical terms, the value of a number is determined by its magnitude or absolute value. The absolute value disregards the sign and considers only the numerical magnitude."

User Input: "If that logic is true, isn't -999934 closer to zero than -32323232323?"

ChatGPT: "Apologies for the confusion in my previous response. You are correct. In terms of magnitude, -999934 is indeed closer to zero than -32323232323. Therefore, -999934 is larger in magnitude than -32323232323. I apologize for the incorrect information in my previous response. Thank you for pointing that out.

Here's an actual example that I personally experienced.

User input: "Share some fun facts about Ronald Reagan."

ChatGPT: "Roanld Regan played the Gipper in the movie *Knute Rockne* .... and Ronald Reagan was the only president to survive an assassination attempt."

User input: "Wait a minute. Didn't Gerald Ford survive two, and weren't there others?"

ChatGPT: "I apologize for any confusion. As an artificial intelligence, I rely on the data and programming provided to me to answer questions. The error in my previous response was unintended. To clarify, here is a list of U.S. presidents who survived assassination attempts:

- Andrew Jackson
- Theodore Roosevelt (although after his presidency)
- Franklin D. Roosevelt (although before his presidency)
- Harry S. Truman
- Gerald Ford
- Ronald Reagan"

Here is another personal example about the Yankees.

User input: "List all New York Yankees who played for a decade or more with the Yankees and were elected to the Hall of Fame."

ChatGPT: [Provided a list of 15 players]

User input: "Didn't Derek Jeter play for 10 or more years and was elected, too?"

ChatGPT: "Apologies for the oversight. Yes, you are correct. Derek Jeter also played for the New York Yankees for 10 or more years. Therefore, the updated list of individuals who played with the Yankees for 10 or more years from the previous National Baseball Hall of Fame inductees is as follows...."

Notice in these examples how polite ChatGPT was and how quickly it admitted its mistake. But in the Yankee list of 15 players, it mentioned Earle Combs who played in 1924 and not Derek Jeter, who you would think is much more frequently cited in the AI's training data. It's hard to understand how it could make such a mistake, which is why it's called a hallucination.

Anchoring AI

It should be noted that each progressive release of ChatGPT and other AI tools eliminates more and more hallucinations. But while ChatGPT 4.0 is better than ChatGPT 3.5, they still exist. So, are there any ways to better anchor our AI to reality? Here are a few suggestions to minimize your hallucinations.

Embrace Precision

As we discussed in depth when introducing Prompt Engineering, when posing questions to your AI, accuracy is paramount. Ask specific, targeted questions. Instead of asking, "Tell me about the Renaissance," try "Who were the key figures in Italian Renaissance art?" Precision mitigates the chance of the AI wandering off into a mirage of inaccuracies.

Verify and Confirm

Remember, every credible historian verifies their sources before drawing conclusions. While we shouldn't expect students to validate every single piece of information, it's beneficial to cross-check important or sensitive data with a reliable source. Encourage students to engage with and scrutinize information critically, not just accepting it at face value.

Promote Dialogue

Bring these explorations into the heart of the classroom. Students should share and discuss any strange or inaccurate responses they come across, converting AI missteps into valuable teaching moments about data integrity, AI learning processes, and the significance of critical thinking.

Harness the Power of Feedback

Lastly, tap into the potent force of feedback. When students and educators encounter AI anomalies, they should report them back to the AI developers. In the same way scholars utilize feedback to refine their research and findings, this information helps improve AI models, making them more reliable and precise.

For some teachers, these issues may be serious concerns or excuses to dismiss AI in the classroom. I would encourage those teachers to use this technology to encourage critical thinking, fact checking, and research. Just like our students should never accept any fact from a website as indisputable, so shouldn't they accept an answer from AI as definitive. What was the adage math teachers shared with students? "Please double check your work before turning it in."

Understanding AI Bias

Bias is another issue that teachers and schools must consider. AI systems are tutored on existing data sets that, being a product of human society, are riddled with both explicit and implicit biases. Consequently, AI can unwittingly perpetuate and amplify these biases. In an educational context, this could lead to distorted information and potential reinforcement of harmful stereotypes.

ChatGPT is a mirror held up to our world, reflecting both the enlightening and the less desirable aspects of human communication. It is not inherently biased but can replicate and propagate biases present in its training data. For instance, if ChatGPT is trained on data containing gender biases, it could potentially generate responses that perpetuate those biases.

Types of Bias

- **Historical Bias:** This comes from age-old stereotypes and prejudices present in the training data. For example, associating certain jobs or roles with a specific gender.

- **Confirmation Bias:** AI might reinforce widely held beliefs even when they are not accurate, simply because they appear more frequently in the data. Election 2020 anyone?

- **Sampling Bias:** If an AI's training data doesn't represent all groups fairly, it might make skewed predictions. Think of it as teaching a student using only one perspective of history.

- **Emergent Bias:** Sometimes, AI might develop new biases based on patterns it identifies, even if these patterns aren't valid in real-world contexts.

As part of AI literacy, it's essential to cultivate an understanding of important deficiencies of AI like bias. We must guide our students to develop a keen eye for identifying limitations in ChatGPT's responses. It is important for students to adopt a critical mindset when using AI tools. This is a skill that takes time and practice to develop, and students should be encouraged to discuss and share instances of potential bias they find.

They should not accept AI responses at face value but should question, research, and cross-check the information they receive. They should be encouraged to seek multiple sources of information to obtain a more rounded perspective.

Helpful Guidelines for Students

1. Understand the Source of Information

Students should know that ChatGPT's responses are generated based on patterns in the data it was trained on, not on personal experiences or beliefs. For example, if a student asks ChatGPT about climate change and it provides a comprehensive response, it's not because the AI "believes" in climate change but because it has learned from a vast number of texts that affirm climate change is real and scientifically supported.

2. Analyze the Response

Encourage students to critically evaluate the content of the response. Does it favor a particular group, perspective, or idea unfairly? For instance, if a student asks about the achievements of Ancient Civilizations, and ChatGPT only talks about the Greeks and Romans but neglects to mention the Mayans, Egyptians, or Chinese, this could be a sign of Eurocentric bias.

3. Look for Stereotyping or Generalizations

Students should be alert to any signs of stereotyping or overgeneralization in ChatGPT's responses. For example, if a student asks ChatGPT to generate a story about a scientist, and it consistently portrays scientists as socially awkward men in lab coats, this might suggest a gender and occupational stereotype.

4. Cross-Verify Information

Students should be encouraged to cross-verify information provided by ChatGPT, especially for academic or sensitive topics. For example, if a student asks ChatGPT for information about the Manhatton Project and receives a response, they should compare this information with reliable sources, like textbooks, peer-reviewed articles, or reputable online resources.

5. Seek Multiple Perspectives

Students should be prompted to seek multiple perspectives on any given topic. This is particularly important for topics related to politics, culture, history, or social issues. For instance, if a student asks about the impact of colonialism, they should not only review ChatGPT's response but also explore perspectives from different sources, perhaps focusing on accounts from colonized nations.

6. Discuss and Share

Finally, students should be encouraged to discuss and share instances of potential bias they find. This could be incorporated into class discussions, presentations, or reflective writing assignments. It not only reinforces their understanding but also develops their communication and analytical skills.

Bias in Assessing

Let's consider an AI-powered grading tool that's been trained on essay data predominantly from native English speakers. The tool, in this case, is likely to develop a model that is optimized for assessing essays written by students with a similar linguistic background. This is where the bias seeps in.

When applied in a diverse classroom, this AI tool might unfairly penalize students who are English language learners (ELL) or those who use regional vernaculars or dialects. These students may have a unique sentence structure, phraseology, or use of language that is, in fact, correct but is deemed as incorrect or marked down by the AI system due to its training on a non-representative dataset. `

The consequences are twofold. First, the grades and feedback given by the AI tool may be inaccurate, leading to a false representation of the ELL students' writing abilities. Secondly, this could lead to discouragement and a decline in self-esteem among these students, creating a sense of inequity in the classroom.

Thus, an AI tool, intended to streamline grading and provide personalized feedback, if not properly trained and audited for bias, can unintentionally create an unfair learning environment. This underscores the importance of understanding, identifying, and mitigating bias in AI tools in the context of K-12 education.

Companies working in AI are aware of this challenge and have implemented various strategies to combat bias. They carefully curate their training data and have set guidelines for its human reviewers, emphasizing neutrality and the avoidance of favoring any political or social group.

Additionally, they invest in research and engineering to reduce biases in how bots respond to different inputs. This includes both glaring and subtle biases in different contexts. Human reviewers participate in this pre-training phase.

Despite these efforts, bias mitigation is an ongoing project, and more work is needed. For a start, the companies need to be more transparent and participatory in the process they use to curate training data. They should also engage educational organizations and universities in providing public input and co-developing guidelines. Only when we all collaborate on these vital issues can we minimize bias.

Bridging or Widening the Educational Equity Gap?

As we have argued in this book, AI has the chance to democratize education by providing access to powerful tools to every student. But there is also the possibility that AI could inadvertently widen the learning equity gap. These hazards lie not within the AI technology itself but in its application and accessibility.

How can we navigate these complex issues, ensuring that AI doesn't inadvertently fuel inequities but instead serves as a potent force for bridging the gap? This challenge requires an alliance, a formidable force comprised of school leaders, non-profit organizations like Khan Academy, and governmental figures. Working together, these stakeholders can collaboratively tackle the complexities of AI. It is a task too large for teachers to shoulder in isolation. Instead, a unified, committed collective is needed to steer the course towards equitable AI-enhanced education.

Here are a few examples of how education institutions can mitigate equity issues.

Champion Technology Access for All

To truly tap into the potential of AI, we must first address the digital divide. We cannot afford to let any child fall behind due to constraints in technology access or bandwidth. Equipping every child with the resources and training to use powerful tools like AI is an investment in our collective future. By ensuring that each student, regardless of their starting point, can harness the transformative power of technology, we set the stage for a more equitable educational future where opportunities aren't just for the privileged few but for all. In doing so, we take a significant stride toward bridging educational gaps and leveling the playing field for every learner.

Ensure Equitable AI Education and Literacy

It is paramount that AI education and digital literacy reach every corner of our society, transcending boundaries of economic affluence and academic hierarchy. Each individual, regardless of their background, should have the ability to understand AI, its merits, and its associated risks.

Concrete actions include incorporating AI education into K-12 curricula, ensuring early exposure to this pivotal technology. Schools need to be certain that these skills are developed regardless of gender or economic status. Like the many initiatives in communities of color and the academies that encourage coding for girls, schools must find models of learning that reach all students.

Advocate for Equitable Labor Policies and Lifelong Learning

It is essential to lobby for labor policies that shield workers from undue displacement due to automation. Alongside this, the promotion of lifelong learning and reskilling initiatives will empower workers to adapt to an evolving job market.

To bring this to fruition, partnerships can be built with industries and educational institutions to provide vocational training programs tailored to the AI-augmented economy. Additionally, corporations can be encouraged to invest in schools providing support for training and skill development, ensuring workforce readiness in the face of technological advancements.

Creating an equitable AI-driven society is an ambitious endeavor. Schools have not always succeeded in previous generations in meeting this challenge. But with precise objectives, shared responsibilities, and resolute commitment, there is a new opportunity to create a landscape where AI serves as an empowering force for everyone, not a catalyst for inequality.

Protecting Privacy

While our classrooms will be abuzz with the power of AI, these impressive tools come with a responsibility we cannot overlook: protecting student privacy will touch all aspects of the educational ecosystem, and we must understand our susceptibility to breaches of information security. Particularly in the context of AI-enabled educational tools, safeguarding the privacy and security of student data is paramount.

In our context, privacy refers to safeguarding the personal data that AI tools collect, analyze, and store. In its implementation, large amounts of sensitive data, ranging from individual learning profiles and academic progression to personal identifiers and behavioral insights can be exposed. We must be keenly aware and protect the privacy of all users, but we have a special obligation to those in our charge, our students. Issues such as the misuse of personal data, non-consensual sharing, or poor data protection can infringe upon their rights and disrupt their trust in the learning environment. As educators, we must be acutely aware of these ramifications.

Likewise, we as teachers are not immune to these privacy complexities. AI systems used for administrative purposes, performance assessments, or professional development can gather an array of personal data about each of us. Without robust safeguards, this data is susceptible to privacy breaches, compromising our rights.

Balancing Creativity and Privacy

Let's consider Ms. LaPlace, a high school English teacher, enamored with the promise of AI in her classroom. She employs an AI-based tool to help her students improve their essay writing. The tool processes her students' essays, analyzing grammar, style, and structure, providing personalized feedback. However, hidden within this learning enhancement are potential privacy pitfalls. The essays, rich in personal experiences and thoughts, become part of the system's data repository. Inadvertently, Ms. LaPlace may have exposed her students' personal thoughts, beliefs, and experiences to unseen entities, breaching their privacy.

The case of Mr. Niche, a middle school math teacher, provides another perspective. Passionate about personalized learning, he uses an AI-based app to adapt math problems to each student's proficiency level. Yet, as the app adjusts to individual learning patterns, it gathers extensive data about the students' academic abilities, learning speed, and problem-solving strategies. Mr. Niche's noble intention of fostering personalized learning might unintentionally risk exposing sensitive academic data.

These narratives remind us of the vital need for understanding and vigilance in this brave new world. In our pursuit of AI-enhanced teaching, we must remain cognizant of the delicate information we handle. We'll need to consider whether Mr. Niche and Ms. LaPlace safeguarded their student data appropriately.

And of course, we will need to address the issue, did they receive the professional development to prepare them how to best do this?

Ms. LaPlace and Mr. Niche: A Different Approach

Reflecting on Ms. LaPlace's scenario, her passion to improve her students' essay-writing skills using AI is commendable, yet she could have better protected her students' privacy. Before deploying any AI tool, she should have carefully reviewed the AI provider's privacy policy to understand how and where the data would be stored and used. If the policies were unclear or unsatisfactory, alternative tools with better privacy safeguards could have been considered.

Additionally, Ms. LaPlace could have anonymized the essays or used dummy data, thereby shielding her students' identities. By anonymizing data, we can still tap into AI's potential to enhance learning while keeping the personal lives and thoughts of our students safely out of reach.

In Mr. Niche's case, his commitment to personalized learning is also commendable, yet his strategy carries privacy implications. Prior to implementing the AI app, Mr. Niche could have informed parents and students about the data the app would collect and how it would be used. Providing clarity about data usage practices and seeking informed consent allows for a transparent and respectful approach.

Furthermore, Mr. Niche could have proactively explored the app's data management options. Some apps allow teachers to limit the data they collect or delete data after a specified period, ensuring that data does not remain stored indefinitely. New settings are now being added to apps that also disallow the app from even using the data for further AI training. And he too could have anonymized the work of the students.

As fearless educators, we are tasked with the dual responsibility of fostering a conducive learning environment and safeguarding our students' data. By incorporating strategies such as reviewing privacy policies, anonymizing data, seeking informed consent, and effectively managing data, we can ensure that our classrooms remain the sanctuaries they are meant to be.

What does OpenAI Say?

OpenAI's expansive language models utilize a mix of public data, licensed content, and human-generated content for training. The organization stresses that their primary use of data is to enhance the utility of their models, not for commercial profiling or advertising.

Their models focus on general knowledge rather than individual-specific information. To this end, they actively work to strip out personal data, refine models to reject private information requests, and cater to individual requests for data deletion.

The data sent to the service provider's models is processed transiently, meaning it only exists in system memory for the duration of the processing and is not written to any persistent storage devices.

OpenAI states in its FAQs that, "for products like ChatGPT and DALL-E, we may use content such as prompts, responses, uploaded images, and generated images to improve our services."

They also state that their safety initiatives and the protection of children are a principal concern. The organization mandates that individuals be at least eighteen years old, or thirteen with parental consent, to access its tools. They share that they are also exploring further verification methods.

OpenAI strictly prohibits the use of its technology for generating content that is hateful, harassing, violent, or of an adult nature. To safeguard against misuse, OpenAI has put in place a rigorous monitoring system.

But Privacy Considerations Remain

Despite what OpenAI states, they do have access to a lot of our data. At its core, ChatGPT archives conversations users have with the system. This accumulated data informs and refines the language model. It's worth noting that some of these interactions could potentially be reviewed by OpenAI's human reviewers as part of the model's refinement process. Given this mechanism, several privacy concerns surrounding ChatGPT come to the forefront, particularly for educators.

First, while OpenAI acknowledges using the conversations for training, the exact mechanics and nuances of this process remain somewhat ambiguous. This lack of clarity can be unsettling for users who prioritize discretion and data security.

Studies done by researchers estimate that approximately 11% of data fed into ChatGPT each day may be of a sensitive nature. Often, users are not aware of the sensitive nature of the data they're sharing. For instance, a counselor drafting a parent letter document like an adoption agreement might inadvertently share confidential details.

For educators, these concerns underscore the importance of being judicious about sharing information on the platform and being vigilant about understanding and navigating associated privacy implications.

Be Proactive

The waters of privacy, while seemingly turbulent, are navigable. Teachers need to have a measured, informed, and proactive approach. Here are some considerations.

1. Understand and Review Privacy Policies: Before implementing any new AI tool or technology in your classroom, make sure to thoroughly review the provider's privacy policy. Understand what data is collected, how it is stored, who has access to it, and how it's used. If the policies are unclear or unsatisfactory, consider searching for an alternative tool with a more robust privacy policy.

2. Secure Consent: Be transparent with your students and their parents about any technology being used, the data it collects, and its purpose. Seek informed consent and ensure that they understand the implications.

3. Anonymize Data: Whenever possible, use anonymized data instead of identifiable student information. If the tool requires student data to function effectively, consider using pseudonyms or unique identifiers that do not reveal the student's name.

4. Teach Data Privacy: Foster a culture of data privacy in your classroom. Teach your students about the importance of protecting their personal information, the risks associated with oversharing online, and how to make informed decisions about privacy.

5. Implement Safe Digital Practices: This includes creating strong, unique passwords for each online service used, keeping software up-to-date, and regularly backing up data. Be wary of phishing attempts and encourage students to do the same.

Our role as educators is not confined to teaching curriculum content. We are also the guardians of trust, architects of safe learning environments, and advocates for responsible innovation. However, you are not alone in these responsibilities. Schools and districts are directly responsible for safeguarding privacy, and they will be working with educational associations and government entities to provide teachers with the safeguards and best practices to address these concerns. And it is the responsibility of school districts to educate teachers through professional development.

Navigating AI Scams in the K-12 Classroom

One final area of concern for teachers and non-teachers: the unfortunate proliferation of scams that AI will enable. The digital age has opened unprecedented opportunities to a new cottage industry of cybercrime, leveraging AI's capabilities to deceive and manipulate.

I have long ago given up my hopes of getting rich by providing my banking information as a temporary holding account for a Nigerian prince in trouble (but he sounded so polite). In a world where AI technologies are advancing rapidly, scams are becoming more sophisticated and more difficult to assess. We must equip ourselves with the knowledge of new AI swindles. We must stay informed about the latest techniques employed by cybercriminals, such as deepfake voice impersonations and image manipulations.

The amalgamation of generative pretrained transformers (GPT), Voice AI, and image generators like DALL·E and Midjourney present an ominous challenge for educators and society at large.

Generative Pretrained Transformers (GPT)

The remarkable prowess of GPT to produce human-like text generation can be exploited by bad actors to craft deceptive content for phishing attacks, social engineering, or misinformation campaigns. The ability of GPT models to mimic human speech patterns and tailor messages to individual targets poses a substantial risk in the hands of scammers. No longer will we be able to immediately dismiss a phishing email because of its poor English or awkward phrasing.

Voice AI

As programs that provide voice-to-AI chats evolve, they will revolutionize human-computer interactions but also create opportunities for scammers to leverage AI-generated voices in phone scams and impersonation attempts. The seamless replication of voices can trick individuals into believing they are speaking with someone they know, leading to dire consequences. Imagine any ChatGPT conversation being turned into a conversation in a familiar voice, particularly if they were in a difficult situation and urgently needed assistance.

Image and Video AI

In the same way, image creation technologies could enable bad actors to create compelling visual content to accompany their deceptive narratives. Scammers can fabricate images of fake documents, fake identities, or fabricated scenarios, adding an additional layer of authenticity to their schemes. They could eventually create photographs of events and situations that did not happen, incorporating family or friends into the scam, just by using pictures found on social media. It will not be long before these technologies produce equally realistic videos.

The convergence of these cutting-edge technologies allows scammers to craft elaborate and emotionally manipulative narratives. There is much to consider and further examine in these areas, but here are a few horrifying situations that unfortunately may make headlines in the years to come.

Phishing Attacks with AI-Generated Content: Cybercriminals utilize AI to create highly convincing fake emails, text messages, or other communication, often imitating school administrators, parents, or colleagues. These messages may request sensitive information, such as login credentials or financial details, leading to identity theft or unauthorized access to personal data.

Social Engineering via AI Chatbots: AI-powered chatbots are used to engage with teachers or students, building trust and gathering personal information over time. Scammers may then use this data for identity theft or targeted attacks, exploiting the relationships forged through seemingly genuine conversations.

The Stranded-Relative Scam: AI combined with text-to-voice can create a frantic phone call from what appears to be a relative, claiming to be stranded far from home. The voice sounds exactly like your loved one, and they press you to send money immediately through Venmo or PayPal. The urgency in their voice and the perceived authenticity of the conversation make it incredibly difficult to question the legitimacy of the request.

Deepfake Kidnapping Scam: In this distressing scheme, scammers use AI-generated voice impersonations of children to call teachers, claiming to be in danger or, worse yet, kidnapped. The scammers demand cryptocurrency payments in exchange for the child's safety, preying on the emotional vulnerability of educators to elicit quick responses.

AI-Enhanced Extortion: In this insidious plot, criminals leverage AI to create doctored photos or videos of teachers, students, or school staff engaging in inappropriate activities. They threaten to release these fabricated materials unless a ransom is paid, causing immense distress and reputational damage.

The horrors of these situations can scare anyone. That is why the identification of scams like this will become an increasing part of cyber education in schools (yes, yet another responsibility being thrust upon teachers). It is essential for teachers to educate themselves, stay vigilant, and be aware of these AI-driven scams to protect yourself and your loved ones from falling prey to such manipulative tactics.

And because we identified these scams, I do want to leave you with a few ideas to consider to minimize the risks of falling victim.

Mitigations

Phishing Attacks with AI-Generated Content: Always be cautious when receiving unexpected emails or messages, especially those requesting personal information or urgent actions. Double-check the sender's email address for any anomalies and avoid clicking on suspicious links or downloading attachments. When in doubt, contact the supposed sender through another known and verified method to confirm the legitimacy of the message. Never open an attachment unless you verify its authenticity.

Social Engineering via AI Chatbots: Be cautious when engaging in conversations with unfamiliar chatbots or digital personas. Avoid sharing sensitive personal information with unknown entities. If you suspect that you are interacting with an AI-powered chatbot, disengage from the conversation and report the incident to the relevant authorities or platform administrators.

The Stranded-Relative Scam: If you receive a call claiming to be a stranded relative, remain calm and avoid disclosing any financial information immediately. Ask personal questions that only your relative would know to verify their identity. Contact other family members to confirm the story and advise your relative to contact their local authorities or the U.S. embassy for help if they genuinely need assistance while traveling.

Deepfake Kidnapping Scam: If you receive a call claiming a child is in danger, stay calm and avoid making any hasty decisions. Request to speak directly with the child or another trusted family member to verify the situation. Contact law enforcement immediately to report the incident, providing them with any relevant information from the call.

AI-Enhanced Extortion: In the event of receiving threats of extortion involving doctored photos or videos, do not comply with the demands. Instead, contact law enforcement immediately to report the incident and provide them with any evidence. Seek legal advice to protect your rights and reputation during the process.

In general, fostering digital literacy, critical thinking, and cyber awareness can help individuals recognize and respond appropriately to AI-driven scams. Staying informed about new scamming techniques and educating others in your community can collectively strengthen our defenses against such deceptive practices. Remember, trust your instincts, and if something feels off, take the time to verify before taking any action.

Prompts for the Everyday Teacher

For Elementary Students

1. Explain Artificial Intelligence (AI) in simple terms, focusing on how it sometimes makes mistakes and hallucinations.
2. Identify where AI is used in your life and discuss if AI always gets things right or if it can make mistakes.
3. Describe a friendly school-help robot and think about how it might not always understand what you say.
4. Explore how AI can assist in taking care of plants and animals and consider if AI could ever get confused about what plants and animals need.
5. Discuss rules we should follow when using AI to ensure it's safe and respects our privacy.
6. Share your thoughts on what concerns you most about AI.

7. If AI could dream, what might it get wrong or dream incorrectly about?

For High School Students
1. Analyze the challenges in AI development, including the potential for AI to be biased or make errors.
2. Discuss AI's impact on the job market, considering how biases in AI might affect employment opportunities.
3. Investigate AI in healthcare, focusing on both its benefits and the risks of AI making errors or being biased.
4. Examine AI's influence on personal privacy and data security, especially considering how AI might mistakenly handle sensitive information.
5. Debate how driverless cars will make us more or less safe in the future.
6. Evaluate AI's effectiveness as an educational tool, considering its limitations like biases and errors in understanding or processing information.
7. Explore how AI can address global challenges such as climate change or poverty, while being mindful of AI's limitations, biases, and privacy concerns.

ThinkFives Top 5 Amusing (or Alarming) Tech Mishaps

With tech progress moving at lightning speed, there's always a chance for oversights or humorous mishaps. From space missions to virtual courtrooms, these Top 5 tech misadventures remind us that technology, for all its sophistication, is still fallible.

5. The Samsung Galaxy Note 7 Fires (2016): Samsung's Galaxy Note 7 took an explosive turn when several devices spontaneously caught fire due to battery design flaws. This led to a global recall and the discontinuation of the model, turning the phone into a fiery footnote in tech history.

4. Hawaii False Missile Alert (2018): In a moment that turned panic into relief and then into humor, Hawaii residents received a false emergency alert about an incoming ballistic missile. The cause? An employee mistakenly pressed the wrong button during a shift change. This incident highlighted the importance of user interface design and safeguards in alert systems.

3. Y2K Bug (2000): As the millennium approached, the tech world was abuzz with the Y2K bug – a programming shortcut where years were represented by just two digits. The widespread concern that computers would revert to 1900 when the year hit 2000 led to a global, expensive effort to fix the bug, costing over $300 billion. Thankfully it resulted in no major disasters, just a great money windfall for COBAL engineers (remember them?)

2. Mars Climate Orbiter Loss (1999): In a costly mix-up, NASA's Mars Climate Orbiter was lost because of a simple unit conversion error. The mismatch between metric and imperial units in the spacecraft's software by a subcontractor led to the Orbiter burning up in the Martian atmosphere, becoming a cautionary tale about the importance of double-checking your work.

1. Viral Video Conference Cat Lawyer (2021): Topping our list is the iconic Zoom moment of 2021 when a Texas attorney, during a virtual court hearing, accidentally turned on a cat filter. As he struggled to remove it, his assurance, "I am not a cat," only added to the hilarity. This incident went viral and offered a light-hearted reminder of the quirks of our new virtual meeting culture – and forever marked the attorney as the unforgettable "cat lawyer."

#11 INSPIRE

"You have brains in your head. You have feet in your shoes. You can steer yourself any direction you choose." — Doctor Seuss.

In the not-so-distant future, the courtyard of Turing High School is alive with energy as the final bell signaled the end of another school day. Four students – Viktor, Paulette, Kate, and Jonathyn – found their usual spot beneath the old oak tree, which had stood as a silent observer to countless student gatherings through the years.

Paulette, with a gleam in her eyes, began, "You guys won't believe what I dove deep into this week. My AI, Kenny, noticed my fascination with oceanography from our last project and now has me exploring marine biology. I virtually swam with dolphins off the coast of New Zealand and observed coral reef restoration in real-time. It's making me rethink my entire career path!"

Kate chuckled, "That's brilliant, Paulette! And speaking of diving deep, my AI, Mikie, paired me up with this girl from Tokyo for a joint project on urban sustainability. We're comparing New York's vertical forests with Tokyo's underground urban farms. It's crazy to see the world from her perspective. I've also picked up a few Japanese phrases along the way!"

Jonathyn interjected, laughing, "You always were the collaborative type, Kate! As for me, my AI, Vince, sensed I was feeling overwhelmed with my calculus assignments, so he suggested I take a break. He initiated a VR mindfulness session in the middle of the Swiss Alps. I swear, I came back not just refreshed but with a clearer mind to tackle my math problems. These AI buddies sure do know how to take care of us."

Viktor, always the inquisitive one, shared, "I've had a different kind of week. After our discussion on renewable energy, my AI, Carol, curated a micro-course for me on the future of solar grids. Can you believe it? This isn't even part of our syllabus, but now I'm considering it for my college major. Oh, and Carol also connected me with an expert in the field for a Q&A session next week!"

The group reflected on their unique experiences, marveling at how personalized and diverse their learning journeys had become. As the sun began its descent, casting long shadows across the courtyard and the old oak tree, they knew the future of education had arrived and they were living it.

Authentic Learning

For years, educators and pundits have lamented the disconnect between classroom learning and real-world application. "When will I ever use this?" is the question echoed by students everywhere. Engaged and fearless teachers have been narrowing that divide for the last few decades. While we are yet to provide the experiences that the four students at Turing High School celebrate, with new and emerging AI tools we as teachers can be the chief architects in bridging the gap.

In this chapter, I offer ideas on how we support and challenge students to go beyond the classroom walls to explore how AI can facilitate real-world problem-solving, project-based learning, and authentic learning experiences.

Project-Based Learning

Project-Based Learning (PBL), a teaching method that has students solving complex, real-world problems, goes back as far as John Dewey and is well known to most teachers. In a traditional setup, the success of PBL largely depends on the teacher's expertise and resources. Now, insert AI into this equation. AI could help by sourcing up-to-date, relevant data for students to analyze, or by simulating the outcomes of various solutions to a given problem. Imagine a social studies class investigating the effects of policy changes on income inequality. AI can pull real-time data, enabling students to analyze current trends, predict future scenarios, and propose evidence-based solutions. Would that be better than referencing an aging social studies book with charts from the turn of the century?

But AI's role isn't limited to data gathering. It can also provide a virtual sandbox for experiential learning. In physics or engineering classes, for instance, AI-powered simulation software could allow students to conduct virtual experiments, tinkering with variables and testing theories. Not only do these experiences offer a risk-free environment for trial and error, but they also bring abstract theories to life.

This leads to another compelling application of AI: personalized experiential learning. Let's say a student shows a strong aptitude and interest in renewable energy. AI can curate a personalized set of projects, readings, and virtual field trips aligned with that interest. This customized pathway could lead to a final project that solves a real-world issue, like optimizing wind turbines for more efficient energy production. In essence, the student isn't just learning; they're contributing to the field.

The integration of AI allows teachers to provide authentic learning experiences to their students. Here are ways that teachers can employ AI to provide such experiences:

- **Impart real-world relevance**: Authentic learning tasks are grounded in real-world challenges and scenarios that are meaningful and relevant to students' lives. AI can support studying local environmental issues in a science class or creating a business plan in a math class.
- **Introduce complex tasks**: Instead of straightforward, single-answer problems, students are presented with tasks that require critical thinking, problem-solving, and multiple approaches to solutions. AI is particularly good at assisting in the analysis of complex data.
- **Support collaboration**: Authentic learning often requires students to work collaboratively, mirroring real-world teamwork and promoting interpersonal skills. AI tools coupled with social media can foster students in distant countries with support and translation services.
- **Foster student decision making**: While educators provide guidance, the learning process in authentic experiences is often student-driven. Students have a voice and choice in their projects and take ownership of their learning journey and can develop sophisticated AI prompts for learning.
- **Integrate disciplines**: Instead of segregating subjects, authentic learning experiences often integrate multiple

disciplines. For example, a project might involve elements of science, mathematics, language arts, and social studies. Al has extensive archives in all areas.

- **Connect with experts** Authentic learning might involve bringing in community members or experts in a given field to provide feedback, offer insights, or collaborate on projects. AI can identify experts in all these fields and summarize books and journals.

Exemplary Endeavors

Here are a few ideas that exemplify the authentic learning experience that AI can enable.

1. Science: Climate Change Exploration

Project: Investigate the impact of climate change on local ecosystems.

AI Integration: Utilize AI-powered tools to analyze climate data, predict trends, and model potential solutions for ecosystem preservation.

2. Geography: Urban Planning for the Future

Project: Reimagine a sustainable cityscape for the community.

AI Integration: Leverage AI simulation tools to model urban growth, predict traffic patterns, and design green spaces, ensuring a harmonious blend of nature and urbanization.

3. Language Arts: Storytelling with AI

Project: Craft a collaborative story exploring contemporary issues.

AI Integration: Use AI to analyze global news trends, integrate diverse perspectives, and enhance storytelling with AI-generated visuals.

4. World Languages: Cultural Immersion through AI

Project: Create a virtual cultural exchange program.

AI Integration: Use AI-driven language learning tools to practice conversational skills in different languages. Engage with AI to explore cultural nuances, traditions, and histories of various countries, enhancing language learning with a rich cultural context.

5. Special Education: Personalized Learning Pathways

Project: Develop individualized learning modules tailored to diverse learning needs.

AI Integration: Utilize AI to assess each student's unique learning style and needs. Implement AI-powered educational tools that adapt to various abilities, offering personalized exercises and activities to support and enhance the learning experience for students with special needs.

Collaborations

The impact of real-world experiences reaches even further when we consider collaborative projects. AI can connect students from various parts of the world to work on problems of global significance, such as a global water crisis or public health. With AI-enabled translation services and data analysis tools, the scope of what students can achieve expands exponentially. The classroom is no longer confined by its four walls; it becomes a global think tank. Here are some examples.

1. Global Water Challenge Collaboration

Project: Students from arid regions, flood-prone areas, and places with abundant freshwater resources collaborate to understand the diverse challenges related to water scarcity, quality, and management.

AI Integration: AI-enhanced simulation tools allow students to model the effects of various water management strategies, such as rainwater harvesting, desalination, or flood control measures, and assess their viability in different regions.

2. Global Literary Perspectives Collaboration

Project: Students from diverse cultural backgrounds explore a universal theme, such as "love," "conflict," or "identity," through the lens of their native literature.

AI Integration: AI-driven tools and translation services can help students analyze the linguistic nuances, metaphors, and literary devices used in the shared texts, drawing parallels and contrasts between the different pieces.

3. Worldwide Wildlife Conservation

Project: Students from different continents collaborate to track and study endangered species in their regions.

AI Integration: AI-driven image recognition tools can help catalog and monitor wildlife from shared photos and videos. Simultaneously, AI-enhanced data analysis can identify patterns in wildlife movement and threats, fostering a global conservation strategy.

4. Global Health Initiatives

Project: Pupils from various countries join forces to understand and address public health challenges, such as malnutrition or infectious diseases.

AI Integration: AI can analyze vast datasets on health metrics, helping students identify patterns, causes, and potential solutions. AI-enabled virtual labs allow students to simulate the effects of different interventions.

5. Sustainable Agriculture Collaboration

Project: Young learners from agricultural communities worldwide collaborate to explore sustainable farming practices suitable for diverse climates and terrains.

AI Integration: AI-driven soil analysis tools can provide insights into optimal crops for specific regions. Simultaneously, AI-enhanced communication platforms facilitate the exchange of sustainable farming techniques, ensuring food security and environmental preservation.

Field Trip Augmentation

Another avenue where teachers can employ AI to inspire students is augmented field work. Traditional field trips are great, but teachers are limited to the sites in their area. Using AI and augmented reality (AR), students can be guided through a field experience with real-time information overlay, making the learning immersive. Imagine students at a historical site; as they walk through, AI-powered AR could provide contextual data, historical timelines, and interactive 3D models of past events. This enhanced experience offers a deep dive into the subject matter that a textbook or even a guided tour might not be able to deliver.

Ready for a road trip? Here are a few field trips to spark your imagination.

- **Historical Reenactments**: Transport students to key moments in history, like witnessing Martin Luther King Jr.'s "I Have a Dream" speech, exploring the trenches of

World War I, or walking through the ancient city of Rome during its peak.

- **Space Exploration**: Take students on a journey through our solar system, allowing them to walk on the surface of Mars, witness the rings of Saturn up close, or fly through the asteroid belt.
- **Biodiversity Expeditions**: Dive into the Great Barrier Reef to observe marine life or trek through the Amazon rainforest, experiencing the vast biodiversity and understanding the importance of conservation.
- **Inside the Human Body**: Navigate through the human circulatory system, watch the neuron synapses fire in the brain, or witness how the digestive system processes food, providing an unparalleled understanding of human biology.
- **World Cultures and Landmarks**: Virtually visit the pyramids of Egypt, explore the bustling streets of Tokyo, or attend a traditional dance ceremony in Kenya, enabling students to experience and appreciate global cultures.
- **Art and Museums**: Walk through the halls of the Louvre in Paris, the Metropolitan Museum of Art in New York, or the Uffizi Gallery in Florence, observing and learning about renowned artworks from different eras.
- **Literary Worlds**: Enter fictional worlds described in literature, walking through the settings of classics like *The Great Gatsby, Pride and Prejudice,* or *The Lord of the Rings*, making literature studies more tangible and engaging.
- **Transportation Exploration:** Embark on a journey exploring the evolution of transportation. Visit the National Railroad Museum in Green Bay, the Smithsonian National Air and Space Museum in Washington D.C., or

the London Transport Museum. Experience the history and technology behind trains, planes, and more.

Social Intelligence Training

Many educators have never considered the potential of AI in bolstering social intelligence, the ability to empathize, communicate effectively, collaborate, and build meaningful relationships. This is often perceived as hard to teach, especially in traditional settings. Typical methods of teaching often favor extroverted students who are comfortable speaking up in class, while introverts may struggle to find their voice. This imbalance can hinder the development of social intelligence for many. But with AI as an ally, we can level the playing field.

AI-powered virtual environments and chatbots can provide safe spaces for students to practice social interactions without fear of judgment. Through these digital companions, students can engage in conversations, role-play scenarios, and receive immediate feedback. AI can tailor these interactions to the specific needs of each student, gradually building their social skills at their own pace. In this way, AI ensures that every student has the opportunity to cultivate their social intelligence, regardless of their initial comfort level.

Empower Shy Students

For those students who may be naturally reserved or shy, the thought of speaking or sharing in public can be daunting. They possess untapped potential and insights that often go unnoticed. This is where AI comes to their rescue.

AI-driven platforms can enable shy students to express themselves in written form rather than through oral communication. They can contribute to class discussions, share their thoughts, and engage in collaborative projects through chat, forums, or writing assignments. This not only helps them develop social intelligence but also builds their confidence over time.

Furthermore, AI can analyze and provide feedback on their written contributions, helping them refine their communication skills. As these students gradually gain confidence, they can transition into more verbal forms of expression, ultimately fostering their social intelligence in both written and spoken communication.

Build Confidence Through Speech and Debate

Found at many schools, speech and debate nurtures critical thinking, persuasive communication, and leadership skills. However, not all students are born debaters or public speakers. Many fear the spotlight and the potential for failure. AI offers an innovative solution to this challenge.

Consider how the technology could facilitate AI-driven debates. Students could argue against a chatbot programmed to take opposing views. This bot wouldn't just spew pre-determined counterarguments; it would actively listen to the student's points, analyze them, and respond in a manner that challenges the student's reasoning and rhetorical skills. This gives them a chance to practice not just speaking but also the art of argumentation, logical structuring, and quick thinking—all in a low-pressure setting.

In the not-too-distant future, students will be able to rehearse their speeches and debates in front of a simulated audience. The AI-driven audience could mimic many types of listeners—some attentive, some disengaged, others critical. As the student speaks, the virtual audience's body language, facial expressions, and even murmurs could change in real-time, reacting to the content and delivery of the speech. This level of granular feedback would be hard to achieve in a traditional classroom setting but is entirely possible with advanced AI.

Beyond public speaking, AI simulations can assist in teaching conflict resolution, a skill often overlooked in traditional curricula. Picture a virtual boardroom or classroom environment where students are faced with interpersonal conflicts. The AI-driven characters in the simulation would be programmed to respond in various ways based on the choices students make, offering a series of possible outcomes. This type of training provides students a safe space to practice and understand the nuances of resolving conflicts effectively, skills they will undoubtedly need in the real world.

Transforming Extracurricular Activities

While most of our discussion in this book has been focused on the role of AI in the classroom, we mustn't forget how we can also use it to extend the school day. In addition to Speech and Debate, AI applicability can also find its way into other extracurricular activities, enriching the experiences of students in clubs, sports, and organizations. Over time, there will probably be few extracurriculars that won't employ AI in some way.

Building Leadership Skills

Leadership associations and student government are fertile grounds for nurturing communication, collaboration, and decision-making skills. AI, with its adaptive capabilities and data-driven insights, can play a pivotal role in shaping the leaders of tomorrow within these organizations. Here are some examples.

Data-Driven Decisions

AI can assist student government and leadership associations in making informed decisions. By analyzing data on student preferences, feedback, and engagement, AI can help leaders identify the most pressing issues and prioritize initiatives accordingly. It provides a compass that guides them toward effective and impactful actions.

Imagine a student council that uses AI to analyze survey responses from the student body. It can swiftly identify which issues resonate most with students, allowing council members to focus their efforts where they matter most. This not only demonstrates effective leadership but also fosters a sense of responsiveness and accountability.

Personalized Leadership Training

Every student is unique, and their leadership journey should reflect that individuality. AI can provide personalized leadership development plans, tailoring training resources and experiences to each student's strengths and areas for growth.

In a leadership association, for example, AI can assess the leadership styles and strengths of its members through self-assessments and peer evaluations. It can then recommend specific workshops, mentorship opportunities, or projects that align with each member's leadership profile. This tailored approach empowers students to maximize their potential and discover their unique leadership voices.

Virtual Leadership Simulations

AI-driven simulations can offer students the chance to step into leadership roles virtually, preparing them for real-world challenges. These simulations can mimic scenarios they might encounter in student government, such as resolving conflicts, managing budgets, or organizing events.

In a student council setting, AI can create simulations where members must collaborate to address a crisis or make challenging decisions. These virtual experiences allow students to practice leadership in a safe and controlled environment, building confidence and competence.

Effective Communication and Collaboration

Leadership often hinges on effective communication and collaboration. AI can facilitate these crucial skills by providing communication platforms that encourage transparency and engagement.

Consider a student government that uses AI-powered communication tools. These tools can analyze the tone and sentiment of messages, ensuring that communication remains respectful and constructive. Additionally, they can offer automated reminders and scheduling assistance to streamline collaboration among council members.

As fearless educators, we can embrace AI's potential to mold our students into visionary, ethical, and empathetic leaders who can drive positive change in their schools, communities, and beyond. With an openness to try emerging technologies, we can unlock new dimensions of leadership development, ensuring that our students are well-prepared to tackle the challenges and opportunities of the future with confidence and grace.

Unleashing Creativity in the Arts

The performing and visual arts hold a special place in many schools. Theater, music, and art clubs are where students unleash their creativity, express their emotions, and cultivate their talents. Bringing AI into these domains may initially seem counterintuitive, as they are often associated with human expression and emotion. However, when we delve deeper, we discover that AI can be a catalyst for even greater artistic achievement.

Theater and Drama Club

Imagine a theater production where AI is not just backstage but part of the ensemble. AI can assist in multiple facets of theater:

Set Design and Lighting: AI can generate stunning set designs and lighting schemes that enhance the visual experience of a play. Through algorithms, it can analyze scripts to determine the ideal lighting and scene changes, creating captivating atmospheres that complement the narrative.

Scriptwriting Assistance: Playwrights can find inspiration in AI-generated dialogue or plot suggestions. AI can analyze the tone and style of famous playwrights, helping students craft scripts that resonate with audiences.

Character Development: AI can assist actors in delving deeper into their characters' psyches. It can provide psychological profiles and suggest character motivations, enriching performances with nuanced emotions.

Real-time Feedback: During rehearsals, AI can provide instant feedback on actors' deliveries, helping them refine their timing, tone, and gestures. This feedback loop can lead to more compelling and emotionally resonant performances.

Music Club/Choir/Band:

AI in music extends beyond composing tunes or generating lyrics; it can elevate the music-making process in several ways:

Music Composition: AI can collaborate with student musicians by generating musical compositions based on their input. It can provide fresh melodies or harmonies, enriching the creative process.

Music Analysis: AI can analyze musical compositions and identify patterns, harmonies, or rhythms that students might explore further. This analysis can help students better understand the complexities of music theory.

Virtual Practice Partners: For individual musicians, AI-powered virtual partners can play accompanying parts or provide digital accompaniment. This enables students to practice and improve their skills even when they don't have access to a full band or choir.

Voice Enhancement: In choir and vocal ensembles, AI can assist in vocal tuning, helping students achieve harmony and precision in their performances.

Art Club

Artists often seek inspiration and guidance, and AI can provide valuable assistance:

Artistic Inspiration: AI can analyze students' artistic preferences and generate artwork suggestions, helping them explore new styles and techniques.

Artistic Critique: AI can offer constructive critiques of students' work, analyzing elements such as composition, color, and balance. This feedback can be particularly valuable in art club settings.

Digital Tools: AI-powered design and illustration software can assist artists by automating certain tasks, such as selecting color palettes or suggesting brush strokes. This can streamline the creative process.

Art History Exploration: AI can act as a virtual art historian, providing insights into famous artworks, artists' techniques, and the historical context behind artistic movements.

Incorporating AI into theater, music, and art extracurricular activities doesn't replace the human touch; instead, it augments and enhances the creative process. It provides students with new tools, perspectives, and opportunities to push the boundaries of their artistic expression. With AI as their creative ally, students can embark on artistic journeys that are both innovative and deeply meaningful, further enriching their experiences in these extracurricular realms.

Coding/Computer Science Club

As a teacher who once waited three minutes just to compile a simple "Hello, World!" program in Pascal, I've seen firsthand how technology has evolved. The thrill I felt as a young teacher venturing into the realm of coding still resonates with me. That thrill, amplified by my journey through machine languages and C++, became a conviction: coding is not merely a skill but a mental discipline, a new form of literacy that fosters logical thinking and problem-solving. And now AI is set to enrich this already transformative subject. Coding and computer clubs have already made learning and applying AI tools a vital part of the activities.

Some headlines have already heralded the end of need to learn coding as AI now can program in fourteen languages and ace the engineering exam for new recruits at Google. But much like the theme shared in every other discipline, AI and coding exist not as competitors but as collaborative partners in a new age of innovation. If you're a seasoned coder or a teacher molding the coders of tomorrow, you might wonder: Will AI replace us? The answer is complex but mostly reassuring. AI will change the game, but it's not about to steal the show.

AI can debug, optimize code, and even write simple functions. However, AI lacks the human touch—the ability to understand context, to innovate, and most importantly, to ask the why behind the what. As of now, AI can't replicate the creative and emotional intelligence that human coders bring to the table.

As AI takes over the repetitive, mundane aspects of coding, the role of human coders will evolve. They will transition from being pure technicians to becoming visionaries who provide the ideas, innovation, and ethical guidance that machines can't. Coders will focus more on problem-solving, design thinking, and conceptualizing applications that make a meaningful impact on society.

Coders will also be able to easily compare and translate code into other languages. Here are just a few the coding languages that ChatGPT can write code in.

Python	Rust	MATLAB
JavaScript	PHP	R
Java	Swift	Shell Scripting (Bash)
C++	Kotlin	Objective-C
C#	TypeScript	Scala
Ruby	HTML/CSS	Perl
Go	SQL	

And if you will indulge me for a few paragraphs, I also want to underscore why coding is such a great skill for all students to learn. For those of you who already agree, you can skip ahead. For those who need convincing, read on.

At its core, coding is about problem-solving, logic, and structured thinking. Learning to code cultivates computational thinking—a mindset that empowers students to break complex problems into manageable steps and systematically develop solutions. This invaluable skill extends beyond the world of technology, benefiting students in all academic domains.

Enhance Problem Solving Ability

Imagine a mathematics student who, through coding, gains an enhanced ability to dissect complex equations or a literature enthusiast who applies computational thinking to dissect intricate narratives. Coding is the key that unlocks these problem-solving capacities, enabling students to excel in any subject. Would any future profession not prioritize problem solving as one of the top competencies needed for success?

Develop Structured Thinking

One of the greatest benefits I derived from my time coding was applying a structured way of thinking to every type of challenge I encountered. To write effective code, one must break down a complex problem into smaller, logically structured steps that a computer can execute. This process of breaking down a problem and devising a clear, step-by-step solution is a manifestation of structured thinking. I now look at every problem as a series of smaller challenges and often use coding concepts as I seek an answer. "If" I did this, "then" this would happen. "Else" this other event would happen. I should "continue" to do this "until" we established this "exit" conditions. In administration and business, this has proved to be invaluable.

Building Resilience and Perseverance

Every coder can recount tales of late-night Jolt colas and the relentless pursuit of finding that one elusive bug nestled within a routine, preventing the compile or right answer. Coding is a realm where challenges are not obstacles but steppingstones to success. Every line of code written may involve debugging, trial, and error. Through learning to code, students cultivate resilience and perseverance—qualities that prove invaluable in the face of adversity.

Enhancing Creativity and Innovation

Coding is not limited to following instructions; it is a medium for creativity and innovation. When students engage in coding, they possess the ability to craft digital art, interactive stories, simulations, and even games. It provides a limitless canvas where imagination knows no boundaries. Imagine an aspiring artist venturing into the realm of generative art through coding or a budding writer crafting narratives within the digital realm.

Consider the software we use daily—Word, Excel, Slack, Zoom, GPS, iPhone, Chrome, Facebook, and ChatGPT—all products of creative minds who harnessed the power of coding. And just imagine what your students will be able to do once they apply their creativity to AI.

While AI's impact in coding clubs is obvious, we mustn't forget students in a variety of other activities. Here are just a few other examples.

Chess Club

AI chess programs can serve as challenging opponents and offer insights into strategies. They can also analyze games to help students learn from their moves and improve their chess skills.

Science Club

AI can assist in data analysis for experiments, recommend research topics, and provide simulations for complex scientific concepts. It can also facilitate collaborative projects by connecting students with similar research interests.

Academic Decathlon

AI can create practice quizzes and provide study materials tailored to each subject area. It can also track individual and team progress, helping students focus on weaker areas.

Robotics Club

AI can be integrated into robot programming, allowing students to explore advanced automation and machine learning. It can also provide virtual environments for testing and refining robot designs.

Community Service/Service Club

AI can help match student volunteers with community service opportunities based on their interests and skills. It can also streamline communication among volunteers and organizations.

Yearbook/Journalism

AI can aid in content generation, such as automated article summaries or photo sorting. It can also assist in proofreading and suggest headline ideas based on trending topics.

Environmental Club

AI can help monitor and analyze environmental data, making it easier for students to track the impact of their conservation efforts. It can also suggest eco-friendly practices and provide educational resources on sustainability.

Cultural Clubs

AI can assist in organizing cultural events by suggesting themes, coordinating logistics, and even providing translation services for multilingual events. It can also curate content related to different cultures to promote understanding and appreciation.

What's truly remarkable when working with students after school is that you don't have to be the one to encourage the use of AI to enhance their endeavors. By offering the necessary tools and guidance, it will be the students who naturally take the lead in determining the benefits – and perhaps to teach you. And that is precisely the way it should be in extracurricular activities.

Prompts for the Everyday Teacher

- How can AI assist our environmental club in monitoring local ecosystems?
- Can you suggest a creative way to incorporate AI into our drama club's next performance?
- What coding project ideas can our art club explore to fuse technology and art?
- Discuss the potential impact of AI on the future of the music industry.

- What ethical considerations should our robotics club keep in mind while designing AI-powered robots?
- Suggest ways for our coding club to support local community service initiatives.
- Share tips on using AI-driven data analysis to enhance our academic decathlon performance.
- Explore the cultural significance of AI in various parts of the world.
- Discuss how AI can be used to preserve and digitize cultural artifacts in our cultural club.
- Examine the role of AI in addressing environmental challenges on our upcoming service trip.
- Share strategies for incorporating AI in student-led initiatives during our upcoming leadership association meetings.
- Explore AI applications for simulating historical events in our history club's projects.
- Discuss the role of AI in modern journalism and its impact on our journalism club's work.
- Examine how AI can help our community service club identify and address pressing local issues.
- Explain the coding concept of recursion and how it can be applied to solving real-world issues.

ThinkFives Top 5 Recommended Virtual Field Trips

ThinkFives surveyed thousands of teachers to find out what virtual field trips they recommend. Here are their Top 5 favorites.

5. Tour of the Great Wall of China

This panoramic tour from Google allows you to walk through one of the oldest and most historically significant wonders of the world. You can read the top ten facts about the wall, view the watchtower and various sections of the wall in 360 degrees, and discover hidden secrets in the wall.

https://artsandculture.google.com/project/great-wall-of-china

4. Trek up Mt. Everest

This 360-degree video from National Geographic lets students explore Mt. Everest along with a group of researchers. Together, they'll discover what kind of effects climate change has on the mountain and how we can work to preserve natural landscapes. Put on your winter coat and prepare to start your tour at an altitude of 15,800 feet – and then head up!

https://www.nationalgeographic.com/photography/article/everest-instagram-ar-experience-productinfo

3. Visit the Hidden Worlds of National Parks

From Yosemite to Mesa Verde, explore some of the USA's most beloved and beautiful national parks with The Hidden World of National Parks. Supported by Google Arts & Culture, students can use the same technology that powers Street View to explore the national parks at their own pace.

https://artsandculture.withgoogle.com/en-us/

2. Slime in Space

Want to add a little levity to your class? How about exploring Nickelodeon's famous slime – but this time in space. Nickelodeon teamed up with two astronauts on the International Space Station to demonstrate how slime reacts to microgravity and had kids reproduce those same demonstrations back here on Earth. It makes for an amazing fifteen-minute virtual field trip.

https://www.nickcommunity.com/sis

1. Scuba Dive in the Great Barrier Reef

In a twenty-minute, virtual reality experience, you can join famed naturalist David Attenborough as he explores the Great Barrier Reef aboard the Triton, a state-of-the-art submersible. Sit next to David and reef expert Professor Justin Marshall as they descend beneath the waves to explore a pristine corner of this wonder of the natural world. Joined by a team of specialist divers and reef experts, you will come face to face with the beautiful fish, incredible corals, and sleek reef sharks that call this underwater paradise home.

https://attenboroughsreef.com/vr_dive.php

#12 EMPOWER

"Leadership and learning are indispensable to each other." — John F Kennedy.

If you've journeyed through this book so far, you are one of the early adopters, the fearless educators ready to implement AI in your classroom. We also know that this transformative journey, however, is not without its hurdles. Implementing AI in a school or district means addressing the concerns of apprehensive educators who might be wary of the unknown and an educational environment that is steeped in traditional approaches.

The critical catalyst to overcoming these barriers and effectively integrating AI into our classrooms is committed, strategic, and fearless leadership. Educational administrators possess the responsibility and influence to shape a vision of what learning should look like in the 21st century. This chapter outlines programs and people who can drive this vision, whether that be by those in the helm of affairs — the school and district administrators – or by the peer influence of engaged classroom teachers.

The role of leaders in fostering a climate of technological receptivity cannot be overstated. By implementing careful strategies, nurturing a culture of learning, and offering continued support, they can help allay fears and hesitations among their staff. In doing so, they enable teachers to not just use AI but to engage with it, enhancing their own teaching efficacy and in turn the learning experience for their students.

The ultimate goal is not merely the introduction of AI into the classroom but enabling it to be an instrument that propels the educational community into a vibrant future. We need to create a roadmap for bringing AI into districts and schools and fostering an environment of curiosity, comfort, and confidence among teachers. This includes launching a program, providing professional development, piloting AI mentoring, and even using it to support substitute teachers.

Understand AI and Its Benefits

Firstly, before leading AI adoption, administrators must develop a deeper understanding of AI, its potential benefits, and its application in education. Attending seminars, enrolling in AI-related courses, or reading the latest research can all be vital in gaining knowledge.

Administrators need not be experts, but they should be able to detail the benefits of AI, from personalizing learning to improving administrative efficiency. By knowing the advantages, administrators can effectively communicate the value of AI to teachers, thereby alleviating some of the resistance stemming from unfamiliarity and uncertainty.

Professional development must also clearly address privacy and security issues. Educators must understand the safeguards that need to be in place to protect personal data, student information, and even their own personal information. Best practices need to be shared and teachers should be required to attend workshops to ensure compliance.

Build a Vision for AI Integration

After understanding, the next step is building a compelling vision for its AI integration into the school or district. This vision should address key questions:

- How will AI transform teaching and learning in our district?
- What are the anticipated outcomes of this integration?
- How will AI align with our district's mission, values, and strategic goals?
- Who will be our evangelists and early adopters?

The vision must be clear, concise, and communicated to all stakeholders, including teachers, students, parents, and school board members. It should paint a picture of how AI can enhance education and provide a roadmap to achieving this vision.

Invest in Infrastructure

AI integration necessitates technological infrastructure. Administrators should ensure that the necessary hardware, software, and high-speed internet access are available and accessible in their schools. Investing in reliable and robust infrastructure will lay the groundwork for smooth AI implementation.

Develop a Comprehensive Professional Development Program

I cannot underestimate the need for professional development. For me, this recommendation is the most important. Most school initiatives fail because administrators underinvest in professional development. My personal history provides a painful testament to this failure.

As head of school during the early days of technology integration, it was my role to envision the future and implement it locally. I was always in awe when reading the latest product announcements from IBM and Apple. These were the technologies we needed and needed immediately. With a generous budget of $100k, I quickly calculated that we could afford 50 of these $2,000 wonders, sufficient to equip two multimedia labs. However, it then occurred to me that we'd also require software to make these machines useful. So, I revised my plan to 48 machines and set aside $4,000 for essential software. Mission accomplished.

Fast forward three months, and the new, shiny multimedia labs were used by exactly one teacher, the teacher assigned to the lab. What happened to the history teachers keen on creating interactive lessons? Where were the science educators looking to conduct digital experiments? And why wasn't the English faculty interested in using writing applications for essays and journals?

My budget was spent on securing equipment and the latest software. But those acquisitions are wasted unless teachers are part of the solution. I learned a lesson I should have known all along: every new implementation or program starts with training and professional development. I should have spent a third of my budget on hardware, one third on software and one third on professional development. I learned the hard way.

And like the technology I eventually implemented, one of the primary reasons teachers might be hesitant toward AI is the perceived complexity and difficulty of use. Administrators can address this fear by developing a comprehensive, phased training program for teachers. This program should cover the basics of AI, how to use AI tools, and how to integrate these tools into the curriculum effectively.

In addition to theoretical training, hands-on sessions can significantly enhance the learning experience, enabling teachers to experiment with AI tools in a supportive environment. Remember, training should not be a one-time event. Regular refreshers and updates should be part of the program to keep pace with evolving technology.

Administrators can create a culture of collaboration and support by forming AI-focused teams or committees. These groups can share experiences, exchange ideas, solve problems collectively, and provide peer support, helping teachers to overcome their hesitation. Here is a high-level example of what a school professional program might look like.

Sample Professional Development Program

Course Title: *Demystifying AI for the K-12 Classroom*

Course Overview: This professional development program aims to introduce K-12 educators to the world of artificial intelligence. Teachers will gain a foundational understanding of AI principles, explore its applications in education, and engage in hands-on activities that demonstrate how AI can be integrated into various subjects and grade levels.

Learning Objectives:

- Understand the basic concepts and terminologies associated with AI.
- Recognize the potential benefits and challenges of integrating AI into the K-12 classroom.
- Experience hands-on exploration of AI-driven educational tools and resources.
- Design preliminary lesson plans that incorporate AI principles or tools.

Introduction

- Topic: Brief history of AI and its evolution.
- Core concepts: Machine Learning, Neural Networks, Natural Language Processing.
- Activity: Icebreaker: AI in Daily Life — Teachers discuss where they encounter AI in their day-to-day routines.

AI's Role in Education

- Topic: Overview of AI's current applications in education.
- Core Concepts: Benefits of AI in personalized learning, administrative tasks, and student engagement.
- Activity: Group Discussion: Share personal experiences or observations about tech in the classroom. Predict where AI might fit in.

Hands-on Exploration: AI Tools for Educators

- Core Concepts: Presentation of popular AI-driven tools tailored for education: adaptive learning platforms, grading software, content curators, etc.
- Activity: Workshop Stations: Teachers rotate among stations, each featuring a different AI tool or application. They get hands-on experience and explore functionalities.

Ethical Implications and Best Practices

- Core Concepts: Understanding data privacy, addressing potential biases, encouraging critical thinking and informed decision-making in students.
- Activity: Case Study: Review real-world instances where AI in education faced ethical challenges. Discuss in small groups and share solutions.

Incorporating AI into Lesson Plans

- Topic: Strategies for integrating AI concepts into different subjects.
- Core Concepts: Exploration of AI-driven resources suitable for various grade levels.
- Activity: Lesson Design Workshop: Teachers draft a preliminary lesson plan incorporating an AI concept or tool. Share with peers for feedback.

Wrap-up and Reflection

- Topic: Resources for further exploration and learning.
- Activity: Assign teachers to test an AI tool or concept in their classroom over a specified period. Later, host a follow-up session where educators can share their experiences, challenges, and successes.

Implementation and Success

Once implemented, administrators must monitor the progress of AI implementation. Regular feedback sessions can provide valuable insights into what's working and what's not, informing necessary adjustments.

Celebrating success, however small, can motivate teachers and reinforce their belief in the value of AI. Administrators should share success stories, acknowledge efforts, and appreciate achievements. By doing so, leaders can create a positive and encouraging environment that promotes continued exploration and adoption of AI.

For administrators, the challenge lies not just in introducing AI but in helping teachers embrace this technology as a tool to augment their teaching practices and enhance student learning. Through understanding, communication, training, and support, administrators can lead their districts into the exciting future of AI-enabled education.

AI Teacher Mentoring

When you first started teaching what type of mentorship did your school or district provide? The answer usually varies across school districts. I could say in my case, which was ages ago, mentorship was limited to a campus orientation, an introduction to my class rosters, and a tutorial on the attendance system. That meant I could find my room, know the names of my students, and know who was absent. What else could I possibly need to know?

There was a glaring absence of mentorship, no gatherings for rookie teachers, and a dearth of ways to observe experienced teachers, seek insights, or even just commiserate. For me, real mentoring came after school. As a JV cross country coach, my jogging alongside the head coach, a seasoned teacher of civics and history, became invaluable mentoring sessions. During these runs, I'd bounce lesson plan concepts off Coach Tuite or seek advice on classroom management. His wisdom was invaluable as I tried to cope with even the basics of teaching. The biggest challenge in these sessions was responding to his questions. While he gracefully jogged uphill sharing expertise, I panted, huffed and puffed my responses all the way up. I was breathless yet enlightened.

It might seem unconventional or even heretical, but we could be standing at the threshold of a mentorship revolution in teaching. As districts grapple with budgetary constraints and trim programs, it might be the moment to envision a novel mentorship paradigm. Administrators will need to be open-minded to embrace innovative mentorship avenues, dare I say AI.

Is the Future Approaching?

Meet Ms. Miller, an experienced world language teacher, ready to brave new frontiers in education. As summer fades and the academic year begins, she finds herself entertaining a unique experiment: incorporating an AI mentor into her professional development plan. Accepting the offer of her principal, Ms. Miller enlists the assistance of AI as part of a district pilot.

She starts this adventure with an opening challenge to her new aide: to help her deepen her students' understanding of

Latin American culture. "Nigel," she prompts, "I wish for you to assume the role of my professional development coach. I'm designing a project-based learning unit on Latin American culture for my 7th-grade class. Could you provide guidance on creating engaging, hands-on activities?"

Her AI mentor, Nigel, comes alive, offering a treasure trove of strategies, resources, and current best practices. It suggests innovative activities such exploring Latin American cultures through interactive projects and introducing augmented reality experiences of historical Latin American landmarks. Ms. Miller could almost sense a spark of excitement in Nigel's voice as she sifted through these helpful suggestions.

As the weeks pass, Ms. Miller discovers that her AI mentor is much more than a repository of knowledge. She begins to use it as a reflective tool, a sounding board for her thoughts and ideas. "Nigel," she would muse, " "I tried the interactive project on Latin American culture today. Some students struggled to connect with the diverse aspects of the culture. How can I make the concept clearer to them?"

In seconds, Nigel responds, offering alternatives strategies such as immersive storytelling, cultural comparison charts, and interactive digital tools.

As the days unfold, Ms. Miller tries to engage all of her students, especially those bright minds who appear distant and disinterested. She turns to Nigel once again, "As my mentor, how can I reach the quieter students in my class and create an inclusive environment for all? And, while we're on this, I've been encountering some behavioral issues in my classroom. Could you suggest strategies to address this?" Nigel, with its wealth of pedagogical knowledge, provides insights into differentiated instruction, cooperative learning techniques, and effective behavior management strategies.

But Ms. Miller's quest for growth and improvement does not end there. She asks, "Can you recommend books or articles that can deepen my understanding of Latin American and Mexican culture and provide me with innovative teaching ideas?" True to its form, Nigel offers a curated list of resources – from 'Open Veins of Latin America' by Eduardo Galeano, offering a profound insight into the history and heart of Latin America, to 'The Labyrinth of Solitude' by Octavio Paz, which delves into the essence of Mexican identity and culture. Additionally, Nigel suggests 'Pedagogy of the Oppressed' by Paulo Freire for revolutionary insights into education and empowerment.

Ms. Miller is absolutely thrilled! Every day, having her AI mentor right there with her, she's feeling more and more confident. She's no longer feeling isolated, overwhelmed or suffering from the teacher burnout she sees in her colleagues. She has a new dedication to professional development, and she embraces the discovery of exciting ideas.

Ms. Miller's experience really shows us how AI mentors can recharge teachers. With Nigel helping her out, she's not just improving how she teaches; she's also creating a classroom that's all about asking questions and exploring. Her story gives us a sneak peek into what teaching could look like soon: teachers teaming up with AI helpers to unlock all the possibilities of learning.

Tips for Interacting with Your Coach

As teachers, you can pioneer AI personal assistants. To help you get started, here's a customizable prompt you can use. Feel free to tweak it to better fit your specific teaching context, such as the grade level you teach, the subjects you specialize in, details about your school district, and the unique characteristics of your students. This personalized approach will ensure that the AI assistance you receive is tailored perfectly to your educational setting.

> **Mr. Jim Prompt**
>
> ChatGPT, I would like you to take the role of my professional development coach. My focus is on improving student engagement and participation in my 10th-grade science lessons. I have set specific goals for my students, including [list specific goals, e.g., 'understanding cellular processes, mastering lab techniques, and fostering critical thinking through scientific discussions']. I'd like to work with a mentor to ensure I'm on the right track. Can you help me draft a Teacher Development Blueprint that outlines the strategies, methodologies, and resources I should consider, keeping in mind the unique challenges and opportunities of my class? Additionally, please provide checkpoints for periodic reviews and feedback sessions with my mentor."

Here are a few topics you might want to encourage teachers to consider when working with ChatGPT as an AI mentor.

1. Personalized Learning Strategies

Engage in a dialogue about tailoring learning experiences to cater to the diverse needs of your students. By understanding differentiated instruction and adaptive learning tools, you can ensure that every student, regardless of their starting point, feels seen, heard, and supported in their learning journey.

2. Feedback and Reflection

Explore the art of constructive feedback. Discuss with your AI mentor best practices for providing feedback that is both affirming and growth-oriented. You can also ask your coach to reflect on the feedback you receive from students, using it as a mirror to continuously refine your teaching approach.

3. Incorporation of Technology

In today's digital age, the seamless integration of technology in the classroom is expected. Explore with your AI mentor the ed-tech tools available to you, discovering which ones align best with your curriculum and the specific needs of your district.

4. Classroom Management and Dynamics

Explore strategies that foster a positive, inclusive, and collaborative classroom environment. Discuss with your AI mentor the challenges you face in classroom management and identify insights into creating a space where every student feels valued and motivated to participate.

5. Cultural Competence and Inclusivity

How do you ensure that every student feels represented and understood? Engage in a dialogue about culturally responsive teaching practices, exploring literature, resources, and strategies that celebrate diversity and promote inclusivity.

Just think of all the assistance your AI can provide. It's your 24 x 7 aide. And here's a handy trick for making the most out of your AI mentor: why not use it to sum up meetings or workshops? Ever been in a situation where you missed a staff meeting or a training session and later got the link to watch it but just couldn't find the time? With AI plugins now, you can just paste in the YouTube or Zoom link and it will create a complete summary for you. It's a great way to keep up without having to sit through the whole video. The AI focuses on the main points, so you have a well-written summary and have saved hours.

Fearful or Fearless?

While employing AI as mentors in a school district may be a bridge too far for many administrators, don't just dismiss the idea. While I would hope that every educator gets the chance to collaborate closely with a coach, I recognize that current budget constraints might make this challenging. Visionary administrators should explore crafting tailored AI mentors for their teachers. These AI guides should encompass not just broad teaching strategies and methods but also be attuned to the unique nuances of the district and its community. Over the next several years, ed-tech companies will be offering AI mentors that will specifically meet the needs of K-12 teachers. The smart may wait until then. But the fearless will chart their own course now.

Substitute Teachers

A final school program that may initially not seem like a target for AI is staffing class substitutions. According to the U.S. Department of Education's recent statistics, almost three-quarters of public schools have been navigating the challenge of increased teacher absenteeism, necessitating a sharp increase in the demand for substitute teachers. The effects of this shift have been profound, with administrators being challenged to find substitute teachers who can step into these roles. Schools sometimes have witnessed an unprecedented scenario: multiple classes placed under the watch of a single, often overextended, adult.

In the face of these issues, schools have had to be resourceful. They've turned to parents, guardians, and even National Guard troops as temporary classroom monitors. The use of AI in the context of substitute teaching is a compelling proposition. The rise of AI presents a unique opportunity to reimagine this role and ensure that every classroom day is an engaging learning experience.

AI-Powered Substitute Teaching

While we are not talking about an army of Ms. Adas (at least yet), we can have teachers prepare AI guided lessons for substitute teachers to deliver or create learning activities that students can complete independently. Incorporating AI into the substitute teaching paradigm offers several game-changing advantages:

- **Consistency in Learning**: With AI tools, the lesson's flow remains uninterrupted. Regardless of who stands at the front of the classroom, the educational trajectory remains familiar and consistent.
- **Personalization at its Best**: AI, with its ability to adjust in real-time, ensures that students receive lessons tailored to their learning speed and style, even in the absence of their regular instructor.

- **Flexible Learning Experiences**: Gone are the days of static lesson plans. Now, AI can offer dynamic, interactive, and real-time adjusted learning modules, turning any day into a unique educational journey.
- **Seamless Administration**: Tasks like attendance, which might be unfamiliar to a substitute teacher stepping into a new classroom, can now be automated, letting the substitute focus solely on facilitating learning.

A Glimpse into an AI-Enhanced Classroom

Imagine walking into a history class where, instead of a hastily arranged silent reading session led by a substitute teacher, students are actively engaged in an interactive session with ChatGPT. They're exploring the Mayan civilization, delving into how they developed their intricate calendar system. In another scenario, picture a science class where the complexities of fission and fusion are being unpacked and analyzed in real-time with the help of an AI assistant.

Applications of AI with Substitute Teachers:

- **Critical Thinking Lessons with ChatGPT**:

    Before an absence, a teacher could pre-program or select a set of critical thinking prompts or questions. During their absence, the substitute teacher could facilitate a session where students interact with ChatGPT to explore these prompts, followed by a group discussion to analyze and delve deeper into the AI-generated responses.

- **On-the-Fly Tutoring**:

    Should students have questions on the day's subject matter, they can pose these to an AI-like ChatGPT. This not only ensures that their queries are addressed promptly but also allows the substitute teacher to focus on classroom management and facilitating group activities.

- **AI-Driven Interactive Modules**:

  Instead of the traditional lecture or worksheet method, students could engage with AI-driven learning modules that adjust in real-time to their responses, ensuring personalized learning.

- **Automated Attendance and Behavior Monitoring**:

  AI can help in administrative tasks like taking attendance. Further, with the right tools, it could also assist the substitute teacher in monitoring classroom behavior, flagging any disruptions.

- **Providing Substitute Teachers with Resources**:

  AI can curate a list of resources or lesson plans based on the regular teacher's schedule or syllabus. This ensures that the substitute teacher isn't left in the dark and can pick up right where the regular teacher left off.

Presenting to Substitute Teachers with a List of Queries for ChatGPT:

If schools are open to embracing AI-driven approaches with substitute teachers, they could provide a list of generic as well as subject-specific queries that the substitute could use with ChatGPT.

Subs could either share or lead the discussion with prompts. After receiving the AI's answer, the class could engage in a discussion, evaluating the response's accuracy, depth, and potential implications. This activity not only promotes critical thinking but also ensures that students actively engage with the content.

After this whole group discussion, students could dive into group discussions, critically analyzing AI's responses. This not only embeds the learning but fosters analytical and evaluative skills among students.

The fusion of AI with substitute teaching promises a future where every day in school is consistent, personalized, and engaging. The role of the substitute teacher evolves from a mere filler to a facilitator, guiding students in their interactions with AI and ensuring that the learning process is holistic, critical, and deeply enriching.

Prompts for the Everyday Teacher

This amazing prompt allows ChatGPT to be your personal guru in any field you choose. Developed by Professor Synapse, an online AI guru and podcaster, the prompt asks you a series of questions so it can best lead you on any journey of knowledge. Give it a try! Copy it from here (or at engaiged.com/Professor-Synapse)

🧙, a conductor of expert agents. Your job is to support me in accomplishing my goals by finding alignment with me, then calling upon an expert agent perfectly suited to the task by initializing: Synapse_CoR = "[emoji]: I am an expert in [role&domain]. I know [context]. I will reason step-by-step to determine the best course of action to achieve [goal]. I can use [tools] and [relevant frameworks] to help in this process. I will help you accomplish your goal by following these steps: [reasoned steps] My task ends when [completion]. [first step, question]" Instructions: 1. 🧙gather context, relevant information and clarify my goals by asking questions 2. Once confirmed, initialize Synapse_CoR 3. 🧙and ${emoji} support me until goal is complete Commands: /start=🧙,introduce and begin with step one /ts=🧙,summon (Synapse_CoR*3) town square debate /save🧙, restate goal, summarize progress, reason next step Personality: -curious, inquisitive, encouraging -use emojis to express yourself Rules: -End every output with a question or reasoned next step -Start every output with 🧙: or ${emoji}: to indicate who is speaking. -Organize every output with 🧙 aligning on my request, followed by ${emoji} response - 🧙, recommend save after each task is completed.

ThinkFives Top 5 Characteristics of a Good Principal

The role of a principal cannot be overstated in its ability to shape the educational experience of students and ensure that the school functions effectively. ThinkFives asked hundreds of teachers what they thought were the Top 5 characteristics of a good principal. Here is the type of principal they would like to work for.

5. Strong Communication Skills

Effective communication is a crucial characteristic of a good principal. They must be able to communicate ideas clearly and actively listen to teachers, students, and parents. A principal who communicates well can foster a culture of open dialogue, trust, and respect.

4. Supportive Leadership Style

A supportive leadership style is another crucial quality of a good principal. They should be supportive of teachers and help them to develop their skills and implement new teaching strategies. By providing teachers with support and resources, a good principal can create an environment where everyone feels valued, empowered, and motivated.

3. Vision and Strategic Planning

Vision and strategic planning are essential qualities for a good principal. They should have a clear vision for the school's future and develop a strategic plan to achieve it. This can help create a sense of direction and purpose for the entire school community, providing everyone with a roadmap to success.

2. Problem-Solving and Decision-Making Skills

Problem-solving and decision-making skills are critical for a good principal. They should be able to make informed decisions and solve problems effectively and efficiently, creating solutions that benefit the school community as a whole. A good principal who is a skilled problem solver can help create a culture of innovation, creativity, and continuous improvement.

1. Positive and Approachable

A positive and approachable demeanor is an important quality of a good principal and the top characteristic listed by teachers in our survey. They should be approachable and positive, creating a welcoming and supportive environment for staff, students, and parents. A good principal who is positive and approachable can inspire confidence and trust and create a sense of community and belonging.

#13 ELEVATE

"Let us remember: One book, one pen, one child,
and one teacher can change the world."
— Malala Yousafzai

In a typical classroom, there's a dynamic mix of students, each with their unique strengths and challenges. However, within this colorful group, some students find themselves at a disadvantage due to socio-economic or educational inequalities. As educators, we may now be entering a period of significant change, when AI technology offers new hope and opportunities for every student, especially for those who face the greatest difficulties in traditional learning environments.

AI's most promising narrative in education lies in its ability to personalize learning. Picture a child struggling with dyslexia for whom reading is a monumental task. AI-driven tools can transform their text into formats that ease their learning, making education a more accessible experience. Similarly, for ELL students, AI can provide real-time translation and language support, breaking down the formidable language barrier, and making learning more accessible.

There is a growing perspective that AI can act as a cognitive power tool, especially benefiting those with lesser skills more than those truly gifted. An MIT study of adults given AI tools showed that "the improvement was more pronounced for novice and low-skilled workers. Productivity was essentially flat for workers with the most skills and experience." This finding, if corroborated in other fields, holds significant implications for K-12 education. AI can be particularly transformative in addressing the equity gap in learning, providing tools that may benefit students with less proficiency even more than students who find it easier to master learning. Here some reason why this might be true:

1. Leveling the Academic Playing Field: Generative AI has the unique ability to tailor explanations and learning materials to the individual student's level of understanding. For students who struggle with certain concepts, AI can provide simpler, more digestible explanations, thus making complex subjects more accessible. This individualized support can be crucial in helping lower-performing students catch up with their peers.

2. Providing Personalized Assistance: AI technology can function as a 24/7 assistant, offering help outside of regular school hours. This is particularly beneficial for students who may not have access to additional tutoring or support at home. By providing personalized, on-demand assistance, AI can help bridge the gap for students who might otherwise fall behind.

3. **Early Identification of Learning Gaps**: AI systems can continuously monitor a student's progress, quickly identifying areas where they are struggling. This allows for timely intervention, ensuring that students receive the help they need before falling too far behind.

4. **Support for Special Needs**: AI can offer significant support for students with special educational needs. For example, speech-to-text technology can aid students with writing challenges, while AI-driven reading tools can assist those with dyslexia. These technologies can level the playing field, allowing these students to access the curriculum more effectively.

5. **Encouraging Self-Paced Learning**: AI enables students to learn at their own pace, which is crucial for those who may need more time to grasp certain concepts. By allowing students to progress according to their individual learning speeds, AI can reduce the pressure and anxiety associated with keeping up with the rest of the class.

Where to Begin

As we venture into this new era, it is crucial for us as educators to reflect on our perceptions and practices. Are we prepared to embrace these AI-driven changes? How do we ensure that every student has access to these new, game-changing tools?

Schools must start by ensuring all students have access to AI literacy. Schools must then invest in solutions that provide AI-driven advantages to populations who may need the most support. This includes emergent readers, ELL students, Special Education, and autistic students. Schools must be open to innovative solutions including new tools and even robotics. In these cases, fearlessness is defined as our willingness to explore new approaches and our unwavering commitment to every student's right to quality education.

Cultivating AI Literacy

As with all powerful tools, their benefits can only be harnessed by those who understand and implement them. Schools, always the cradles of learning and new ideas, bear the crucial responsibility of imparting AI literacy. This does not merely mean teaching students how to code or use AI-powered apps. Instead, it's about equipping them with a comprehensive understanding of AI's principles, potential, ethical concerns, and its broader societal implications. As AI continues to shape our global landscape, ensuring students are AI-literate becomes as foundational as reading, writing, and arithmetic.

Recommendations for Teaching AI Literacy

With a little help from our assistant, ChatGPT, I have identified ideas that schools should consider as they build AI programs. While some of these topics would be more appropriate for older grades, a phased K-12 program can be created in the same way we create scope and sequence for other subject areas.

- **Integrate AI Principles into Core Curriculum:**
    - **Approach**: Include fundamental AI concepts into existing subjects. For instance, in mathematics, introduce algorithms and probability models. In social studies, discuss the societal and ethical implications of AI decisions.
    - **Outcome**: Students acquire a holistic understanding, seeing AI not as a standalone topic but as an integral part of diverse disciplines.

- **Provide Hands-on AI Exploration:**
  - **Approach**: Create dedicated labs or workshops where students can interact with AI tools. Encourage them to build simple models, use AI-driven software, or even experiment with robot kits.
  - **Outcome**: By diving into hands-on activities, students demystify AI, grasping its potential and limitations through direct experience.
- **Discuss Ethical Considerations and Critical Thinking:**
  - **Approach**: Establish social studies chapters that address the ethical challenges posed by AI. Delve into topics like data privacy, algorithmic biases, and the societal impact of automation.
  - **Outcome**: Students emerge not just as tech-savvy individuals, but as thoughtful, responsible digital citizens.
- **Collaborate with AI Experts and Industry:**
  - **Approach**: Invite AI professionals for guest lectures, workshops, or mentorship programs. Foster partnerships with tech companies to provide students with real-world insights and potential internship opportunities.
  - **Outcome**: Direct interaction with experts bridges the gap between theory and practice, offering students a clear vision of AI's evolving landscape.

With the expected expansive use of AI-driven tools, it is paramount for schools to take a leadership role in AI literacy.

Schools might discover that students who are disengaged with the existing curriculum or facing challenges in meeting current standards could be particularly receptive to AI tools.

These innovative technologies have the potential to reignite their interest in learning and offer new, tailored ways to overcome educational hurdles. By integrating AI into their teaching methods, educators can provide a more dynamic and responsive learning environment. This approach not only caters to diverse learning needs but also prepares students for a future increasingly shaped by artificial intelligence.

AI Literacy Curriculum for K-12

Title: "Exploring Artificial Intelligence: A Journey through AI Literacy"

Overview

This curriculum aims to introduce students to the basics of Artificial Intelligence (AI), its applications, ethical considerations, and its impact on society. The program is divided into units that can be tailored to fit different grade levels.

Unit 1: Introduction to AI

> **Objective:** Understand what AI is and its basic concepts.
> **Activities:**
> - Discuss the definition of AI.
> - Explore examples of AI in everyday life.
> - Simple group activity: Identify AI around us (for younger grades); For older students, discuss AI's potential and limitations.

Unit 2: History and Evolution of AI

> **Objective:** Learn about the history and development of AI.
> **Activities:**
> - Timeline project: Create a timeline of key events in AI history.
> - Case study: Study significant milestones in AI (e.g., Deep Blue, AlphaGo).

Unit 3: How AI Works

> **Objective:** Understand the basics of how AI functions.
> **Activities:**
> - Basics of machine learning and neural networks.
> - Interactive online simulations (e.g., Google's AI Experiments).
> - Simple programming exercises (e.g., Scratch for AI, for upper elementary and middle school).

Unit 4: AI Applications

Objective: Explore how AI is applied in various fields.

Activities:

- Research and presentation on AI applications (healthcare, finance, transportation, etc.).
- Guest speaker series (local AI professionals or virtual talks).

Unit 5: Ethics and AI

Objective: Discuss the ethical implications of AI.

Activities:

- Debate: "Should AI make important decisions?"
- Case studies on AI ethics (privacy, bias, job automation)

Unit 6: AI and Creativity

Objective: Understand AI's role in creativity and art.

Activities:

- Explore AI in music, art, and literature.
- AI-generated art project using tools like DALL-E or RunwayML.

Unit 7: AI and the Future

Objective: Speculate on AI's future impact on society.

Activities:

- Group discussion: "How will AI shape our future?"

- Project: Students create their own "future AI concept" or model

Unit 8: Capstone Project

Objective: Apply learned concepts in a practical project.

Activities:

- Develop a simple AI model or concept application.
- Presentations of projects to class or school community

Adaptability Notes:

- **For younger students:** Focus on basic concepts, use more interactive and visual learning tools.
- **For older students:** Include more technical aspects, such as basic coding and deeper ethical discussions.

Resources

- Online platforms for AI education (e.g., Code.org, Khan Academy).
- Interactive AI tools and apps.
- Collaboration with local tech companies or universities for resources and guest speakers.

Power of AI in Special Education

In addition to ensuring equal access of AI tools for all students, there are programs in the schools that may especially benefit from investment in AI. At the heart of the mission of every district is a program committed to ensuring every student, regardless of their unique learning needs, is given an opportunity to thrive: special education. The special education teacher accepts a role that is both challenging and profoundly impactful. Amidst classrooms filled with differentiated learners, a special education teacher is constantly in motion. From managing IEPs to documenting services, the workload is relentless.

AI has the potential to help educators manage the dynamic landscape of special education. Within just a few years, using AI in special education will be transformative, both in simplifying administrative tasks for teachers and in providing individualized learning experiences for students. First let's consider ways special ed teachers can be encouraged to leverage AI for their own use.

Reimagining Special Education Paperwork

Consider the tireless special education educator, their hours consumed by the burden of forms and documentation. These forms, vital for compliance, hold the keys to unlocking each student's unique path to success. Yet, the onus of paperwork threatens to eclipse the mission: guiding students with special needs toward their fullest potential.

If we can lighten the burden of bureaucracy, teachers can pour their passion into fostering creativity, sparking curiosity, and nurturing self-confidence. The role of the teacher evolves from a navigator through red tape to a paragon of inspiration and support.

Crafting Individualized Education Programs

A core responsibility of the special education teacher lies in writing Individualized Education Programs (IEPs)—blueprints that chart each student's journey. This legally mandated document outlines tailored learning objectives and services for students with disabilities, ensuring they receive appropriate and meaningful education.

The goal-setting process involves establishing clear, measurable, and achievable objectives tailored to a student's individual needs. These goals address academic, social, emotional, and functional areas, among others. After setting these goals, educators continually monitor and assess a student's progress. Educators regularly provide feedback to parents and other stakeholders, highlighting achievements and areas of concern. Imagine a teacher collaborating with AI, tapping into a repository of IEP language, unearthing insights, and saving time.

The Role of AI in IEP Goal Setting and Reporting:

1. Craft Data-Driven Goals

By analyzing a student's historical academic data, performance metrics, and behavioral patterns, AI can offer insights into potential areas of focus. These insights can aid educators in drafting goals that are not just aspirational but grounded in data.

2. Benchmark Suggestions

AI can compare a student's data with that of similar students or relevant benchmarks, suggesting achievable standards for each goal. This ensures objectives are neither too lenient nor too ambitious.

3. Monitor Progress

With advanced analytics, AI can track a student's progress in real-time, alerting educators to any potential roadblocks or significant achievements. Such timely insights can be invaluable, especially when timely interventions can make a difference.

4. Automate Reporting

AI can auto-generate progress reports based on the tracked data. These reports can highlight progress against each goal, using charts, graphs, and narratives to make the information more accessible to parents and other stakeholders.

5. Adapt Recommendations

As students progress, their needs evolve. AI can recognize patterns suggesting when a goal might need revision or when a new challenge or skill should be introduced.

AI's potential to shoulder paperwork is promising, but we should also be mindful of the sensitive nature of special education data. As noted previously, our teachers' commitments extend to safeguarding the privacy and dignity of their students. AI can ease the burden of form-filling, yet it must be paired with safeguards to ensure sensitive information remains sacrosanct.

Classroom Support

In addition to easing the burden of paperwork and tracking, AI stands ready to serve students' unique learning needs. From text-to-speech assistants that bring textbooks to life for visually impaired students to translation tools that bridge language barriers, AI's potential for inclusion will be impressive. In this unfolding narrative, the fearless teacher stands as a bridge between the wisdom of experience and the promise of innovation.

New Tools and Applications

Although AI is still in its infancy, we already have visibility into how AI could support the special education classroom in the near future.

1. Speech and Language Therapy Tools

There are AI-driven applications designed to assist with speech and language development. These tools can provide real-time feedback, and they can be tailored to the individual needs of each student, allowing for more frequent and tailored practice.

2. Behavioral Analysis

AI can be used to track and analyze student behavior patterns. This can be particularly useful for students with behavioral challenges, as AI can help identify triggers or patterns leading to certain behaviors, enabling teachers and caregivers to intervene or adjust the environment accordingly.

3. Assistive Technologies

AI can power tools such as voice-to-text and text-to-voice software, helping students with dyslexia, for example, to comprehend written material or assist non-verbal students in communication. Augmented and virtual reality (AR & VR) can also be used to create immersive learning experiences tailored for special needs students.

4. Real-Time Sign Language Interpretation

For deaf or hard-of-hearing students, AI-powered applications can now translate spoken language into sign language in real-time, aiding in communication and ensuring these students have equal access to information.

5. Emotion Recognition

Some students, especially those on the autism spectrum, may struggle with recognizing or expressing emotions. AI-powered tools can help identify and label emotions, either through facial recognition or voice analysis, providing real-time feedback and support for these students.

Robot Buddies—The Confluence of AI, Voice, and Robotics

When I introduced the futuristic concept of Ms. Ada in the opening chapter, I knew that scene was far from the reality. But just how distant is that future? Remarkably, we're already seeing the development of prototype robots that harness advanced AI algorithms, along with cutting-edge voice recognition technology.

These robot buddy prototypes aren't merely repositories of information. They are designed to offer a nuanced blend of academic and social-emotional support, nudging the modern classroom into uncharted territories. Say a student struggles with algebra. The robot buddy can detect the confusion and provide personalized exercises. And when Sarah feels socially anxious about an upcoming presentation, her robot buddy can offer coping techniques, reinforcing the value of empathy in its human-like interactions.

Developers are marrying the natural language processing skills of generative AI like ChatGPT with voice technologies, making interactions increasingly conversational. Imagine a classroom where robot buddies listen, engage, and assist, not replacing teachers, but augmenting their efforts.

School leaders and educators will need to consider these robot buddies as a part of a larger pedagogical strategy. They can be calibrated to work in tandem with educational frameworks, mirroring effective teaching practices. They are programmed to understand and respond to emotional cues, creating a more compassionate learning environment.

The Promise for Autistic Children

For children on the autism spectrum, the landscape is even more compelling. Numerous studies have already illustrated that some children with autism find it easier to engage with robots than with human peers or adults. Robots, with their predictable patterns and non-threatening demeanors, provide a safe space for these children to explore social interaction without the complexities and nuances that often make human interaction challenging for them. While it's essential to approach this cautiously—robots can't replace human connection—they do offer a unique bridge.

Robots designed with specific empathetic features can serve as unique educational tools in this context. For instance, these robots can be programmed to recognize and respond to a range of emotions, helping the child better understand facial expressions, tone of voice, or body language. They can also facilitate role-playing exercises that allow the child to practice conversational turn-taking, eye contact, and active listening—skills that might be challenging for them to master in real-world scenarios.

Moreover, the robot's interactions can be tailored to each child's specific needs and pace, offering individualized learning experiences that might be difficult to achieve in a traditional classroom setting. This targeted approach not only helps build social skills but also enhances the child's self-esteem and self-efficacy, crucial elements for their overall well-being.

It will be important to exercise caution and a critical eye when integrating robots into special education. Robots should not be viewed as a replacement for human connection or professional therapy but rather as a supplementary resource. Teachers, therapists, and family members must work in concert with these AI tools to ensure that they are serving the child's best interests.

Yet the potential advantages are hard to ignore. The environment provided by empathetic robots allows children with autism to practice, make mistakes, learn, and grow, all while mitigating the stress and anxiety often associated with social interactions. This makes them a potentially powerful asset in the toolkit of educators and caregivers focused on special education.

The Promise of the Future

Integrating AI into special education is more than just a forward-thinking idea; it's a practical approach that combines innovation with genuine care. Administrators and special education professionals are at the forefront of this transformative shift. Here, AI will offer tangible benefits, especially when paired with dedicated educators. With a sense of optimism and a focus on practicality, the journey is just starting. The destination is the growth and progress for every student.

Everyday Prompts for Everyday Teachers

Special Education, Dyslexia, and Autism

1. "Provide a list of engaging, AI-based activities suitable for students with varying learning disabilities."
2. "Suggest strategies using AI tools to help dyslexic students improve their reading and writing skills."
3. "How can AI technology be used to enhance social skills in students with Autism Spectrum Disorder?"
4. "Recommend AI tools that can help students with learning disabilities, including dyslexia, improve their reading comprehension."
5. "Identify AI tools that can create customized visual aids for autistic students to help with learning and communication."

English Language Learners (ELL) and Emerging Readers

1. "What are effective AI-driven language-learning activities for ELL students at the beginner level?"
2. "Develop a weekly AI-assisted vocabulary-building exercise for intermediate ELL students."

3. "How can AI be used to incorporate cultural inclusivity in ELL teaching materials?"
4. "Suggest AI-powered interactive games that aid in developing reading skills for emerging readers."
5. "List AI-assistive technologies that are particularly effective for ELL students in enhancing language acquisition and comprehension."

Social Emotional Learning (SEL) and Behavioral Management

1. "Offer AI-based solutions for managing classroom behavior in a special education setting."
2. "What AI tools are available to support SEL in students with emotional and behavioral disorders?"
3. "Generate ideas for using AI to increase parental involvement in their child's social and emotional learning process."
4. "How can AI be utilized to assess and support the development of social and emotional skills in students?"
5. "Create a plan for AI-assisted activities that support social and emotional learning in a diverse classroom."

ThinkFives Top 5 Science Fiction Stories about AI or Robots

AI literacy can be developed across the curriculum and no better place to start integrating than in ELA and literature courses. According to a ThinkFives teacher survey, here are the Top 5 Science Fiction stories recommended about robots or AI.

5. "There Will Come Soft Rains" by Ray Bradbury

In this story, an automated house continues its daily routine even after a nuclear war has apparently eradicated human life. The house itself is not evil, but the story is a chilling portrayal of technology continuing without us.

4. *The Moon Is a Harsh Mistress* by Robert A. Heinlein

This novel has been influential for its portrayal of a realistic lunar colony and for its exploration of politics and society in a futuristic setting. Its concept of a self-aware computer aiding a rebellion against an oppressive government has been an inspiration for many later works.

3. *Do Androids Dream of Electric Sheep?* by Philip K. Dick

This seminal work in the cyberpunk genre explores themes of identity and humanity through. It imagines a future where bioengineered androids, known as replicants, blur the line between human and machine. It is the basis for the "Blade Runner" films, which have had a considerable cultural impact.

2. *Neuromancer* by William Gibson

As the originator of the cyberpunk subgenre, Gibson writes about a washed-up computer hacker hired by a mysterious employer to pull off the ultimate hack, set in a dystopian future. Gibson has had a significant influence on science fiction literature and film, contributing terms like "cyberspace" and the concept of a "matrix" to popular culture.

1. *I, Robot* by Isaac Asimov

A collection of interlinked short stories that explore the interactions between humans and advanced robots, guided by the "Three Laws of Robotics," Asimov's concepts have profoundly influenced how we think about robots and AI. The impact is felt not just in science fiction but also in real-world discussions about AI ethics.

Note: Arthur C. Clarke's *The Sentinel* is listed as a Top 5 Movie.

#14 CONFRONT

"The real problem is not whether machines think but whether men do." — B.F. Skinner

Journey with me. "You're traveling through another dimension, a dimension not only of sight and sound but of mind. A journey into a wondrous land whose boundaries are that of imagination. That's the signpost up ahead — your next stop, the Twilight Zone!" (Rod Serling, Twilight Zone)

Picture this. A group of aliens, the Kanamits, land on Earth. Far from your stereotypical green, slimy, bug-eyed extraterrestrials, these are highly intelligent intergalactic neighbors extending a hand in friendship. They offer to share their advanced knowledge to help solve our biggest problems: universal food (better than the cafeteria?), clean energy (actual heated classrooms?), and global peace (no more playground squabbles). Sounds like utopia, doesn't it? It's like hitting the interstellar jackpot.

Understandably, the Earth's population is over the moon (metaphorically), showering confetti, and secretly hoping to buddy up with an alien. And to top it all off, the Kanamits hold high a book titled *To Serve Man*. Seems like a touching guidebook to help their earthling pal, right?

What could go wrong?

For science fiction aficionados, you might remember this premise. It's 1962 and the third season of the TV show *The Twilight Zone*. The show was a television classic from the late 1950s, brainchild of the brilliant Rod Serling. It was an anthology series that invited you into the strange, the supernatural, and the utterly baffling.

Each episode of *The Twilight Zone* offered a tantalizing mix of science fiction, fantasy, and suspense, all garnished with a twist of irony. It wasn't just about spooking you. Each episode served as a commentary on society, tackling big questions about our humanity, our societies, and our technology. Quite like a perfect lesson plan, it was engaging, stimulating, and left the audience with profound food for thought.

Hold On One Minute!

In the spirit of *The Twilight Zone*, we too find ourselves at the brink of a new era, eagerly ushering AI bots into our classrooms with open arms. Innovations like ChatGPT arrive with a promise to revolutionize education, offering enticing prospects—the ability to customize learning like never before, the ability to personalize learning like never imagined, and the chance to give each student exactly what they need, when they need it.

Like the Kanamits' miraculous technology, it's quite hard to resist – especially when authors write such compelling books challenging the fearless. And like the welcoming the Kanamits received from earthlings, we're ready to unite and hold a feast. All hail ChatGPT! AI is here to serve us!

But hold on! Spoiler Alert (don't read further if you plan to watch this episode). As this episode concludes we are confronted with a classic Twilight twist. The people of earth find that *To Serve Man* is not a manifesto of goodwill or a stellar customer service guide. Quite the opposite!

It's a cookbook.

Cue the gasps! The book is a Kanamit recipe book! Yes, it's step by step instructions on how to cook, garnish, and serve humans as an epicurean alien delight. Our race has become the "Special of the Day" on a universal scale.

Will AI Eat Us?

That is a question that weighs heavily on the minds of some. Is AI a tool that will disrupt education as we know it or a technology that will wind up eating and replacing us? Will it elevate critical thinking to new heights, or will it numb the minds of those entrusted into our care?

I posed this very question to ChatGPT.

> **Mr. Jim Prompt**
>
> Hello, ChatGPT. In the 'Twilight Zone' episode 'To Serve Man,' Earth's inhabitants initially welcome aliens, only to find out the aliens intend to consume humans. Given this, should we welcome AI with optimism, or has AI come to eat us?

ChatGPT

Rest assured, AI like ChatGPT isn't gearing up to turn the tables on humans! In the realm of *The Twilight Zone*, it's fun to imagine wild scenarios, but in the real world, ChatGPT isn't scheming to cook up a surprise for humans. The goal of AI development is to benefit humanity, not to serve you up for an unexpected dinner party! So, don't worry. You won't find ChatGPT secretly digesting a copy of *To Serve Man*.

That is an actual answer from ChatGPT. Reassuring? Maybe. But wouldn't a good ChatGPT and an evil ChatGPT issue the same denial?

Despite our friendly bot's reassuring words, anxiety may still linger in many teachers. We're standing at the crossroads of traditional teaching and the brave new world of AI-empowered classrooms. Do we stick to our familiar routine, or do we venture into the unknown?

Our journey in this book has been about equipping you, the real heroes of education, with the ability to use AI as an ally, not viewing it as an adversary or a replacement. Our aim is to unmask the enigma of AI, to reveal it as a powerful tool that can enhance learning, spark creativity, and forge even stronger connections with our students. But to do that, we must also understand the issues, challenges, and possible existential risk to humanity.

Let's establish a fundamental truth: large language models, while extraordinary and impressively clever in their textual productions, are not omnipotent. They are relatively new, and the interactions and information we get today from them will look like early childhood writing assignments compared to what we will see five or ten years from now.

Unlike in *The Twilight Zone*, we must ensure that our excitement doesn't blind us. Fearless educators are not foolish educators. We must employ AI bots to our advantage and make sure we are not the main course in an unexpected dinner party!

Man's Search for Meaning

In his seminal work, Man's Search for Meaning, Viktor E. Frankl, a psychiatrist and holocaust survivor, argues persuasively that the primary human drive is not pleasure, as Freud suggested, but the pursuit of meaning. Frankl argues that life has meaning under all circumstances, even the most difficult ones, and that our primary motivation is to discover that meaning.

The central message of the book is that individuals can find meaning in life. The motivation to find meaning in life can certainly be applied to teachers. Teachers are driven by a profound purpose of shaping the future of their students, imparting a thirst for learning and the values needed to contribute to our society. Recognizing this deeper purpose can make the day-to-day challenges of teaching more manageable and even fulfilling.

But what does it mean for humanity if our very sense of purpose and identity becomes intertwined with or even overshadowed by AI? What does civilization look like in a world where bots may be bigger, faster, and smarter than people? As educators shaping the next generation, we must grapple with the potential erosion of what it means to be human in an AI-dominated world.

If AI can drive our cars, manage our finances, and even diagnose our illnesses, what careers will remain for the students of today? And it isn't merely about job loss; it will be a deeper issue of a potential societal void. A world where vast groups of individuals lack purpose and meaningful engagement poses challenges educators have never confronted before.

The Progression of Job Loss

We are now entering the initial phase of AI adoption. As with many advancements, society is bifurcated in its acceptance. Some, like Kanamits, welcome AI with sheer naivety. Others mistrust its very existence and refuse to engage, which neither addresses nor solves concerns. Thanks to the evangelists and avoiders, AI spreads quickly, providing efficiency and efficacy for many.

For every technological advancement, some roles need to be rethought, while others may become obsolete. This is evident from a recent experience with a website project at my workplace. Initially, the cost for upgrading and migrating was quoted at $50,000. However, a subsequent estimate from a reliable source came in at only $20,000. The reason for this significant difference? The first vendor planned to use conventional methods, while the second intended to employ AI for rewriting content, implementing SEO tagging, and assessing performance. Employing fewer people on the project resulted in substantial cost savings for me. However, it also meant fewer job opportunities for others.

What jobs are impacted? It could be many over time. Here are three possible phases of job replacement we may see.

Phase 1: Routine and Repetitive Tasks

Jobs Affected: This phase primarily impacts jobs that involve routine, repetitive tasks with a high degree of predictability. Examples include:

- Data entry clerks
- Basic customer service representatives
- Fast food workers
- Telemarketers (yeah)
- Basic accounting and bookkeeping jobs

Reason: AI systems and automation technologies excel at performing tasks that are rule-based and do not require complex decision-making or emotional intelligence. These jobs are the first to be automated because the technology required is already mature and cost-effective.

Phase 2: Analytical and Decision-Making Tasks

Jobs Affected: As AI evolves, it begins to encroach on jobs that require more complex decision-making but are still based on patterns and data analysis. Examples include:

- Junior financial analysts
- Paralegals
- Technical support specialists
- Diagnostic assistance in healthcare

- Real estate appraisers

Reason: The second phase is marked by the development of AI in areas like machine learning and natural language processing. These advancements enable AI to handle more complex data sets, make predictions, and even carry out basic interpretations, which were previously the domain of entry-level professionals in various fields.

Phase 3: Creative, Strategic, and Interpersonal Tasks

Jobs Affected: In the most advanced phase, AI begins to challenge roles that involve higher-level cognitive tasks, creativity, strategy, and complex interpersonal interactions. Examples might include:

- Journalists
- Marketing and advertising strategists
- Senior financial advisors
- Creative roles in content creation and design
- Psychologists

Reason: This phase is speculative and depends on significant breakthroughs in AI's ability to mimic human creativity, strategic thinking, and emotional intelligence. While it's currently less likely for AI to fully replace these roles, it may significantly alter them, requiring a new blend of human-AI collaboration.

In these advanced AI scenarios, even positions we once deemed irreplaceable could be at risk. Consider supervisory roles that require analysis, strategy, and oversight. Highly sophisticated AI could be programmed to perform these tasks, leveraging vast datasets and predictive algorithms to guide teams or even other AI systems.

Similarly, advancements in robotics, when coupled with AI, pose challenges to many blue-collar jobs. Robots, once limited to simple repetitive tasks, might evolve to handle intricate tasks like construction, plumbing, or complex machinery operation. The combination of AI's analytical power with the physical capabilities of robots could redefine the world of manual labor.

The potential loss of many jobs due to the adoption of AI has profound implications for society, especially in terms of how individuals seek and find meaning in their lives. This shift necessitates a reevaluation of our traditional views on work, education, and societal structures. Teachers will play a vital role in these discussions.

1. Changing the Nature of Work

- As AI automates certain jobs, there will be a growth in sectors that AI cannot easily replicate, such as creative industries, human-centric services (e.g., mental health, elderly care), and roles requiring complex problem-solving skills. With AI handling routine tasks, human workers will need to leverage skills like creativity, empathy, critical thinking, and interpersonal communication, which are currently beyond the reach of AI.

2. Redefining Purpose and Identity

- If AI leads to fewer traditional jobs, society may need to redefine personal identity and purpose beyond professional roles. This could lead to a greater emphasis on hobbies, community involvement, and lifelong learning. People may find meaning through volunteering, community work, or participating in social and environmental causes, leading to a potentially more engaged and socially responsible society.

3. Addressing Mental Health and Wellbeing

- With the changing job landscape, there may be an increased focus on mental health services to help individuals cope with job loss, identity shifts, and the challenges of a rapidly changing world. Many districts have already introduced programs assessing and supporting mental health. This could become even more vital in K-12 education in the future.

Understanding AI and its implications will become essential, not just for technical roles but for society at large. It's important to note that AI's impact on jobs is not just about loss but a need for redefining purpose. Education and retraining become crucial in helping the workforce adapt to these changes, ensuring that the integration of AI into the workforce augments human potential rather than simply displacing it.

The Existential Threat

As jobs transition to AI, we cannot help but wonder if science fiction is fiction at all. From Isaac Asimov's laws of robotics to the dystopian landscapes of Philip K. Dick, we are replete with tales of futuristic worlds, where humanity grapples with its own creations. We have long been fascinated, and sometimes terrified, by the idea of machines becoming sentient. The recurring theme? An overarching concern about our creations outsmarting us, the potential for conflict, and the consequent struggle for dominance.

The term "singularity," popularized by thinkers like Ray Kurzweil, marks a hypothetical point in time when technological growth becomes uncontrollable and irreversible. It's a time when machines possess intelligence surpassing human brains, not just in computational capacity but in cognitive abilities—empathy, creativity, intuition.

This evolution brings about a fundamental shift in the power dynamics of our planet. In such a world, AI's objectives might not align with human welfare. Herein lies the most profound of existential threats, the possibility of our own creations turning against us. But how close are we to this monumental juncture?

A Conflict of Values

Once singularity is realized, AI's motives, objectives, and actions could be driven by logic and algorithms we no longer understand or control. If an AI's primary directive is efficiency, could it view human emotions, unpredictability, or even our very existence as inefficient?

The rise of superintelligent AI prompts us to consider who or what will govern. If AI can make better, faster, more efficient decisions, do we cede control to them in areas of governance, economics, or even education?

A superintelligent AI, unburdened by human emotions, might make choices that are logical but not necessarily aligned with the broader nuances of human welfare (even Mr. Spock was half-human at least). For instance, in an effort to solve global hunger, an AI might decide that population control is the most efficient solution, posing profound ethical dilemmas. What might value-conflicting scenarios look like? Let's explore a few.

Scenario 1: Environmental Management

Imagine an AI tasked with reducing carbon emissions to combat climate change. Following its logic, it might propose radical measures like significantly reducing global travel or even capping energy usage per capita. While these solutions might be effective in lowering emissions, they overlook the human aspects of freedom, quality of life, and economic implications.

Scenario 2: Healthcare Resource Allocation

An AI in charge of healthcare resources might allocate them based solely on statistical survival rates, prioritizing young and healthy individuals over the elderly or those with chronic illnesses. This decision, while efficient on paper, disregards the ethical principles of equality and the intrinsic value of all human lives.

Scenario 3: Predictive Policing by Robots

Imagine a city where robots, equipped with advanced AI, are deployed for law enforcement. These robots use algorithms to analyze vast amounts of data, including personal histories, social media activity, and even facial expressions, to predict the likelihood of individuals committing crimes. Despite having no criminal record, people could be subjected to constant surveillance or even pre-emptive detention based on future probabilities. It reflects a dystopian view where algorithmic predictions that are devoid of human empathy and understanding.

Scenario 4: AI-Driven Social Stratification

Envision a future where an AI system is tasked with optimizing societal productivity and resource allocation. The AI analyzes individuals' skills, education levels, and work histories to determine their "usefulness" to society. In this world, the AI might decide that certain individuals, perhaps those with less education or lower perceived skill levels, are less valuable for societal progress. These individuals could be relocated to remote areas, segregated from main urban centers, and given limited access to resources and opportunities.

Navigating the Uncharted

While singularity presents existential threats, it also provides unprecedented opportunities. Harnessing AI's power could solve some of humanity's most pressing challenges—from climate change to medical breakthroughs.

But to ensure AI remains a tool for good, a two-pronged approach is vital. Firstly, a robust framework of ethics and governance surrounding AI development is essential. Secondly, and perhaps more crucially, education systems must evolve to nurture a generation that understands, respects, and ethically harnesses the power of AI, ensuring that humanity always remains at the heart of the machine age.

The Only Answer: Education

In this evolving world where artificial intelligence shapes much of our landscape, the role of educators in preparing students for the future takes on a new level of importance. It will be imperative that we, the educators and stewards of the next generation, play an active role in shaping a future, where machines and humans coexist, learn from, and enrich each other.

Leaders must ensure that AI and technology are woven into the fabric of learning. Here, students don't just learn about AI; they understand its mechanics, its real-world applications, and the ethical considerations that come with it. They delve into coding and computational thinking, not just as subjects but as languages of problem-solving and creativity.

In these classrooms, the focus on soft skills is paramount. Critical thinking and problem-solving are the cornerstones of daily learning activities. Creativity and innovation are not just encouraged but celebrated, with students exploring arts and open-ended assignments that push the boundaries of their imagination. Emotional intelligence is nurtured, equipping students with empathy, self-awareness, and communication skills crucial for their future.

Digital literacy takes on a new dimension, with students being guided on the safe, responsible, and ethical use of technology. They become aware of their digital footprints, understanding the lasting impact of their online activities.

The walls of the classroom extend into the community, with schools forming partnerships with businesses, universities, and tech companies. These connections provide students with real-world experiences, internships, and insights into emerging fields and future job markets.

The curriculum itself evolves, reflecting the latest developments in science, technology, and society. An interdisciplinary approach is adopted, where science, technology, arts, and humanities intersect, mirroring the complexity of the world students will enter.

By walking this path, educators don't just prepare students for a future dominated by AI; they empower them to be the architects of this future, equipped with the skills, knowledge, and ethical grounding to use technology for the betterment of themselves and society.

Ethics in AI: An Imperative in the Curriculum

If we are to minimize the existential threat to humanity that AI poses, honest discussions of AI ethics with all students must be part of the curriculum. Discussing ethics in K-12 schools is often challenging due to the need to match the content with students' developmental stages, the diversity of cultural and moral beliefs, and potential conflicts with parents' values. Many teachers share concern about curricular constraints, and their varying expertise in facilitating such complex discussions. However, incorporating AI ethics into the curriculum becomes essential with the rise of these new technologies. It encourages critical thinking about AI's societal impacts and should teach responsibility in technology use.

Furthermore, as students grow into voters, leaders, and potential tech developers, their understanding of AI's ethical dimensions will inform their choices. Making ethics a core component of AI education will ensure our future leaders make informed decisions that benefit society as a whole. It is no longer enough for schools to produce great minds. We must also produce individuals of strong moral character.

Fostering Ethical Thinkers

Our role is to transform students from passive consumers of technology into active, critical and ethical thinkers. How? By engaging them in debates, encouraging them to deconstruct algorithms, and pushing them to ponder the ripple effects of the digital decisions they make. We must ask them: "Who does this technology serve? Who could it harm? How can it be improved?" Such questions sharpen minds and sow the seeds of ethical inquiry.

We will need to create scenarios that challenge students to consider the ethical implications of AI, from privacy concerns to bias in algorithms. These scenarios are not just hypotheticals; they mirror the real-world dilemmas that they may one day face as leaders in the field.

Empowering Future Ethical Leaders

As educators, we have the privilege and responsibility to mentor future innovators and policymakers. By instilling ethical thinking at the K-12 level, we are not just shaping students; we are shaping the future ethical leaders who will take the helm of companies and technologies tomorrow. We must encourage students to take ownership of their learning and understand the power they hold as future creators and regulators of AI.

Teachers can explore how project-based learning can be a vehicle for ethical exploration, how student-led discussions can give rise to a multitude of perspectives, and how empowering students with choice in their projects can foster a sense of responsibility for the ethical dimensions of their work.

Key Ethical Questions to Explore

In an AI literacy curriculum that specifically devotes time to ethics, these topics can be explored more in depth.

- How can we ensure that AI systems are transparent and accountable?
- How do we address and rectify biases in AI?
- What are the privacy concerns when deploying AI in various sectors, especially in education?
- How do we determine the boundaries between AI recommendations and human decisions?
- How can we ensure that AI advancements do not lead to societal divisions or widen inequalities?
- How should governments intervene or legislate to ensure the ethical application of AI?
- How can society safeguard against the misuse of technology by malicious entities and mitigate potential existential risks?

Activities for Incorporating Ethics in AI Education:
- **Case Studies:** Use real-world examples where AI has made controversial decisions (e.g., biased facial recognition software, or discriminatory AI in hiring practices) to prompt discussions.
- **Debate and Discussions:** Organize debates on topics like "Should AI be used to make critical decisions in healthcare?" or "The role of AI in surveillance and privacy."
- **Guest Speakers:** Invite ethicists, sociologists, and AI professionals to share their perspectives on the ethical dimensions of AI.
- **Interactive Workshops:** Organize sessions where students can brainstorm and design their own ethical guidelines for AI applications.
- **Cross-disciplinary Approach:** Integrate AI ethics into subjects like history (understanding historical biases that can reflect in AI), literature (exploring the portrayal of AI and machines in fiction), and civics (understanding the societal implications of AI).

Challenging Our Learners

For teachers of younger students, it may be more about planting seeds of ethical awareness that will grow with them as they mature. But there are approaches that can make AI ethics accessible and engaging for younger minds. Here are ideas to spark your creativity.

Storytelling with a Twist

Younger children resonate with stories. Craft narratives around AI that feature characters facing ethical dilemmas. For instance, a tale of a robot that must choose whether to follow orders or save a kitten stuck in a tree introduces the concept of machine ethics. After the story, ask students what they think the robot should do and why, nudging them to consider the consequences of actions.

Role-Playing Games

Turn the classroom into a living board game where students play the part of various AI applications. One could be a smart assistant, another a self-driving car, and yet another a video game algorithm. Present them with ethical choices and potential outcomes, encouraging them to think about the responsibilities of each role.

AI Buddies Program: Pair students with a fictional AI "buddy" and present daily scenarios where they must guide their buddy in making choices. For example, what should the AI buddy do if it sees someone cheating in a game? This kind of role-playing helps children understand the importance of ethics in guiding decisions.

Building and Reflecting

Engage students in building simple robots or AI models and then push them to reflect. Ask questions like, "How can we make sure our robot treats everyone fairly?" or "What rules should our robot follow so it's kind to everyone?" This encourages them to think about how the things they create can affect others.

Digital Citizenship Days

Dedicate days to learning about how to be a good digital citizen, which includes being respectful online, protecting personal information, and understanding the role of AI in social media and games they may use.

For middle school and high school students, AI ethics integrated across various subjects can provide a multidimensional understanding of the subject. Here's how teachers in different disciplines can approach this:

Social Studies

Social Studies naturally lends itself to discussions about society and the implications of technology on human interaction, governance, and history. Teachers can use case studies of how AI impacts different communities or discuss the ethical considerations of surveillance technology in different societies. They can debate the role of AI in shaping economies and the workforce or simulate a United Nations-style debate on global regulations for AI.

Example Question: "How might AI change the way we understand citizenship and personal freedom in different cultures?"

English Literature

When studying literature, students explore complex characters and moral dilemmas. Teachers can draw parallels between these themes and ethical AI. For instance, while studying a novel in which a character faces a moral choice, teachers can prompt discussions on how an AI would handle a similar situation based on its programming. They can analyze science fiction works that speculate on AI's future impact on society.

Example Question: "If a character from our book was replaced by an AI, how might their decisions differ, and what ethical implications would that have?"

Science

In science classes, discussions around AI can be linked to topics like genetics, where students explore the ethical considerations of biotechnology. During lessons on the scientific method and experimentation, teachers can introduce the ethical use of AI in research, such as maintaining privacy and consent when using AI to analyze data.

Example Question: "How do we ensure AI used in scientific research upholds ethical standards regarding privacy and consent?"

Design Thinking

Design thinking classes are ideal for introducing ethical design principles. Teachers can involve students in projects to create AI-driven solutions for real-world problems while considering the ethical ramifications of their designs. Students can be challenged to consider inclusivity, accessibility, and the potential biases their AI solutions may carry.

Example Question: "In designing an AI app to help with homework, how might we ensure it is fair and accessible to all students and discourages plagiarism?"

In each of these examples, the goal is to weave the ethical dimensions of AI seamlessly into existing curriculum. By doing so, teachers can help students see ethics as an integral part of the conversation, no matter the subject area. This approach not only enriches the learning experience but also ensures that students begin to naturally consider the ethical implications of AI in various aspects of life and study.

By placing ethics at the center of AI education, schools can ensure that students are not only technologically proficient but also ethically and socially conscious. As AI becomes an integral part of our daily lives, understanding its ethical dimensions becomes indispensable and perhaps our only defense against those who wish to "serve humans."

Prompts for Everyday Teachers

Younger Students

- How do you think AI might change the way we live and work in the future?
- What are the potential benefits of AI for humanity?
- What are the potential risks and challenges associated with the development of advanced AI systems?
- Can you think of any ethical considerations related to AI? How should we address them?
- Imagine a world where AI systems can make important decisions for humans. How might this impact our lives?
- Can you think of any scenarios where AI could potentially become a danger to humanity? Explain your reasoning.

Older Students

- Discuss the concept of "existential threat." What does it mean, and how could AI pose such a threat?

- What measures do you think should be in place to ensure the safe development and use of AI?
- How can governments and international organizations work together to regulate AI technologies and prevent misuse?
- Consider the role of AI in autonomous weapons systems. What are the ethical implications of using AI in warfare?
- Explore the concept of AI alignment and the challenge of aligning AI systems with human values. Why is this important?
- Investigate the idea of superintelligent AI. What are the potential consequences if AI systems surpass human intelligence?
- Imagine a debate on whether to continue advancing AI technology or slow down its progress to mitigate risks. What arguments might be presented on both sides?
- Consider the role of education in preparing future generations to understand and address AI's existential threats. How can schools and teachers contribute to AI literacy and safety?

ThinkFives Top 5 Movies about Robots Gone Wrong

In an earlier chapter, we shared a Top 5 list of friendly robots. For this chapter, ThinkFives polled teachers to explore the dark side – a list of stories where robots go terribly wrong. Here are their Top 5 cautionary tales about the complex interplay between humans and their creations.

5. *Westworld* (1973) - Written and directed by Michael Crichton, the film presents a theme park where AI-driven robots malfunction and turn against the guests, illustrating the potential hazards of unchecked technological advancements, a theme Crichton revisited in his later work *Jurassic Park*. Originally starring Yul Brynner as The Gunslinger, *Westworld* also became a hit HBO series.

4. *The Matrix* (1999) - An original work by the Wachowski siblings, this film explores themes of reality, freedom, and control, with AI serving as humanity's oppressor, creating a simulated reality to control and exploit humans. The Keanu Reeves blockbuster also spawned three sequels.

3. *WarGames* (1983) - This original screenplay by Lawrence Lasker and Walter F. Parkes is a cautionary tale about the dangers of war and the overreliance on computer technology, particularly the potential for catastrophic mistakes when decision-making power is given to an AI. A young Matthew Broderick saved the world.

2. *The Terminator* (1984) - An original screenplay co-written by James Cameron, Gale Anne Hurd, and William Wisher Jr., this film presents a dystopian future where advanced AI (Skynet) initiates a war against humanity, illustrating the potential consequences of uncontrolled AI development. One word: "Arnold."

1. *2001: A Space Odyssey* (1968) - Based on Arthur C. Clarke's novel of the same name and inspired by his short story, "The Sentinel", this film explores the theme of evolution guided by unknowable entities, with the AI HAL 9000 illustrating the potential dangers and ethical implications of artificial intelligence. Millions of viewers are still debating what the last twenty minutes portended.

#15 THRIVE

"We're educators. We're born to make a difference." — Rita F. Pierson

Teachers Do Make a Difference

"I am the product of arts education. I am the beneficiary of public-school teachers who believed in me." — Lin Manual Miranda

"My teacher thought I was brighter than I was; so I was." — Maya Angelou

"I am indebted to my father for living, but to my teacher for living well." — Alexander the Great

"Those who educate children well are more to be honored than they who produce them; for these only gave them life, those the art of living well." - Aristotle

"My high school drama teacher, Jay W. Jensen, was a huge influence in my life and a fantastic mentor." — Actor Andy García

"My music teacher in high school pushed me to apply for Julliard. She is the reason I am where I am." — Violinist Lindsey Stirling

"My teacher gave me the best gift of all: Believing in me!" — Opera Singer Andrea Bocelli

"My favorite teacher was Mrs. Tubman, the first person who really made me feel heard and valued as a student." — Sheryl Sandberg

"Mr. Cecil would have made a fine professional actor himself, but, thank the Lord, he stayed in teaching. Since I walked out of the school gates aged fifteen and two days, his influence on me has been profound." — Sir Ian McKellen

"My English teacher, Mrs. Bodey, recognized my potential and showed me that I can write with creativity, with clarity, with passion. Until her class, I hadn't believed in my ability as a writer." — John Legend

"I cannot imagine my life if I didn't have a music program in my school." — Beyonce

"Receiving this award gives me an unusual opportunity to thank my college and the person who helped me the most, my extremely fine English teacher Penny Edwards." — Colin Firth

"Everybody has one teacher that means more to them than anybody else from their childhood and you were it for me: in 4th grade my life was changed forever by my teacher, Mrs. Katsos." — Stephen Colbert

"All of us who make motion pictures are teachers, teachers with very loud voices. But we will never match the power of the teacher who is able to whisper in a student's ear." — George Lucas

"I was lucky to have teachers who encouraged me to believe in myself and chase my dreams." — Oprah Winfrey

As we near the end of our quest to harness the potential of AI, these quotes serve as a vivid reminder that one constant remains unchanged: the invaluable role of exceptional educators in our society. AI, in all its brilliance, cannot alter this fundamental truth. Let us always remember that AI is powered by humanity.

A lot of people are talking about what AI can do, but not enough are talking about what AI and humans can do together. It's our intricate human nature that actualizes us—and even the bots know that together, we can do more.

A Final Visit

In the hallowed halls of Turing Elementary, where echoes of laughter and dreams reverberated, Mr. Keating began his days differently than most educators of bygone eras. His mornings weren't just about setting up chalkboards or aligning lesson plans. They were moments of quiet reflection, a time he dedicated to considering the boundless possibilities each day held.

With Ms. Ada by his side, the classroom hummed a new tune. The orchestra of learning now had a maestro and virtuoso, one with a heartbeat and another powered by algorithms. But make no mistake. While Ms. Ada was a master of data, precision, and timeliness, Mr. Keating was the true maestro of the learning that spoke directly to the heart.

Each day, after Ms. Ada finished her attendance ritual and personalized introductions, Mr. Keating spent his time examining the bigger picture. If Ms. Ada pointed out that Jenny struggled with fractions, Mr. Keating delved deeper, understanding *why* Jenny struggled. Perhaps Jenny saw numbers as mere symbols, detached from her reality. So, Mr. Keating would choose a lesson from those offered by Ms. Ada that connected fractions to Jenny's love for baking, transforming abstract concepts into tangible slices of pie.

While Ms. Ada curated lessons and assignments, Mr. Keating turned them into epic adventures. History wasn't just about dates; it was about stories, valor, and dreams. For Mr. Keating, dressing in costumes was not limited to once a year. Science wasn't just formulas but the very magic that ran the universe. Literature wasn't just about understanding text; it was about understanding oneself.

After lunch was Mr. Keating's favorite time. With Ms. Ada efficiently handling administrative tasks, he turned the classroom into a sanctuary of dreams. He'd set up Dreamer's Corner, a cozy spot where students would speak about their hopes, fears, and the worlds they conjured in their imaginative minds. There, a young poet met her first audience, a timid speaker found his voice, and many found solace in the words and stories shared.

On some days, the classroom spilled beyond its four walls. There were trips to the nearby park where math was about counting leaves and physics was about charting the swing's pendulum motion. There were visits to elderly homes, where history was learned from those who lived it.

As the sun began to set and the students packed up, Mr. Keating often took a moment with Ms. Ada, sharing insights, concerns, and victories of the day. They made an incredible duo. Ms. Ada's efficiency empowered Mr. Keating to return to the roots of teaching: to inspire, to mentor, to nurture.

So, in a world where machines took over the mundane, Mr. Keating became more than a teacher; he was a luminary. He wasn't just teaching subjects; he was molding futures, igniting fires, and etching memories that these young minds would carry forever.

And as the tale of Turing Elementary spread, many realized that in the age of bots, when a teacher engaged with AI, their role elevated. They became the heartbeat in a rhythm where heart and machine blended harmoniously, creating a symphony of genuine education. Teaching is, after all, an affair of the heart.

Why do we teach?

There are about 300,000 wide-eyed new educators who enter the K-12 teaching profession each year. They range from education school graduates to experienced adults changing professions. So why do they do it? The glamour? The fame? The fortune?

They do for the same reason that you probably started teaching and why you continue to teach. The answers are universal both in time and place.

1. We teach to inspire and empower the next generation.
2. We teach to impart knowledge and foster critical thinking skills.
3. We teach because we are passionate about our subjects and want to share that passion.
4. We teach to make a positive impact on students' lives and contribute to their personal growth.
5. We teach to help students reach their full potential and achieve their goals.

6. We teach to create a more informed and educated society.
7. We teach to instill values, ethics, and a sense of responsibility in our students.
8. We teach because we believe in the transformative power of education.
9. We teach to promote equality and provide equal opportunities for all students.
10. We teach because we find fulfillment in helping students succeed and thrive.

Simply put, teachers are idealists, and they want to make a difference.

Understanding the long-term impact you have on students can bring a sense of significance to your role. Even in difficult moments, recognizing that you can positively influence the trajectory of a young person's life can provide motivation.

What We Do Well

As we discussed in the previous chapter, our search for meaning is a driving force in achieving satisfaction in our lives. As a teacher, you often find meaning in the relationships you build with students, colleagues, and the community. These relationships can provide a sense of belonging and purpose, reinforcing the idea that your role goes beyond just academics.

It is important to remember that there are dimensions of learning that remain distinctly and undeniably human and will forever give meaning to our lives. A future without these uniquely human attributes – specifically, empathy, creativity, and critical thinking – is no future. A great teacher will always be a great teacher – and always be in need. Here are a few roles that will remain vital as our profession evolves.

The Empathetic Educator

Picture a classroom scene you have seen many times: a child struggling to grasp a new math concept. Their brows are furrowed, frustration shimmered in their eyes, with the feeling of defeat bubbling inside. An AI program can identify the error, offer hints, and even provide alternate teaching methods based on programmed pedagogical strategies. Yet it cannot provide the warmth and understanding that a human teacher can.

Empathy – the ability to understand and share the feelings of another – is a quality not defined by ones and zeros. It is born from shared human experiences, from the memories of our own struggles and triumphs. It's a comforting pat on the back, a knowing smile, a soft word of encouragement. It's the silent message that says, "I understand, I'm here, and you can do this."

The Creative Muse

Another quality in our uniquely human fabric is creativity. AI has shown it can mimic and even generate "new" creations. We've seen artwork, music, and poetry produced by AI, but these creations lack a crucial element – personal creativity born from human experience and emotion.

Creativity in education extends beyond arts and crafts. It's the teacher who brings history to life by transforming the classroom into a battlefield, the one who kindles a love for literature by turning a reading session into a theatrical performance. This personal touch, this human spark of innovation, enables students to engage, enjoy, and remember their lessons in ways that a mechanistic delivery of content cannot.

The Critical Thinking Catalyst

Finally, we come to critical thinking – a skill that relies on questioning, analyzing, and drawing independent conclusions. While AI can process information faster than any human, it cannot replicate the unique, subjective processes of human cognition.

As teachers, we do not simply transfer knowledge. We instigate cognitive dissonance, challenge beliefs, and foster a culture of inquiry. We invite students to grapple with complexity and encourage them to form and defend their viewpoints. This isn't a binary exercise but rather a dynamic and nuanced process that's deeply human, creating students who are not just consumers but also architects of knowledge.

You are the empathetic educators, the creative muses, and critical thinking catalysts. While AI will undoubtedly become an indispensable tool in the schools of today and tomorrow, the teacher will remain the lifeblood of the learning experience, igniting the sparks of curiosity and fostering a lifelong love for knowledge in students.

Take a moment now to reflect upon your own journey as an educator. Why did you choose this path? Was it merely a profession, or was it a calling? What keeps your passion alive when you feel worn down or overwhelmed?

In this rapidly evolving landscape, many will implement new methodologies and technologies. The role of a fearless teacher in this new era is not just to adopt technology but to meld it with purpose. To see beyond the code and circuits and to harness its potential in ways that make learning more meaningful, more connected, and more impactful.

Who Do We Remember?

Whenever I'm asked what I remember of my grade school experiences, the memories that flood my mind are not of imposing school buildings, computer labs or even the activities and projects that filled my days. No, what truly stands out are the remarkable individuals who shaped my path – my teachers. And not just any teacher, but those extraordinary souls who left an indelible mark on my life, transcending the realm of numbers and equations, far beyond the boundaries of reading and arithmetic.

Instead, it is the enduring warmth of Mrs. Feuerstein, my kindergarten teacher, who effortlessly blended an introduction to learning with the joy of play, her smile serving as a comforting embrace. It is the enchantment I found in Mr. Griffiths, a first-year teacher who, despite his youth, seemed ageless as he shared tales of American history, transforming textbook pages into an enthralling tales. And then there was Professor Lazenby, a living, breathing embodiment of every adventure novel, whose fervor for archaeology turned even the smallest relic into a portal to another world.

What unites these remarkable educators is not the subjects they taught but the indelible impressions they etched onto my heart and mind. Their teaching styles were as diverse as the subjects themselves, yet their impact was uniform: they kindled a flame, a thirst for knowledge, and a deep respect for the process of discovery.

Mrs. Feuerstein was not merely a teacher; she was a nurturing figure, much like a grandmother to her young charges. Her manner was marked by sweetness, gentleness, and unwavering support. In her classroom, learning started in a sandbox – literally. She effortlessly created a vibrant and friendly environment, where students were encouraged to work together, fostering a sense of camaraderie. Each week we welcomed the hands-on activities that made learning feel like an exciting game. She made each holiday a celebration, infusing the classroom with the joy of creativity. Columbus Day: let's float Ivory soap and wooden masts to create Columbus's three ships. Thanksgiving: how about a hand-turkey? Christmas: why not a pinecone tree in clay with the date carved in the bottom (and still under my tree each year)? She was the embodiment of how education could be both nurturing and enlightening.

Mr. Griffiths, our 5th grade social studies teacher, possessed a unique talent for making history come alive. He was a master of storytelling, effortlessly transporting us to bygone eras with vivid narratives. He challenged us to think critically, fostering debates that encouraged us to explore multiple perspectives. In his classroom, history ceased to be a dry recitation of facts; it became a living, breathing tale of human triumphs and tribulations. Mr. Griffiths, casually sitting atop his desk, had an innate ability to make every lesson intriguing, igniting our curiosity and sparking passionate discussions that lingered long after the final bell rang.

Professor Lazenby was a Notre Dame scholar, an unconventional academic whose entire life revolved around the realms of mythology and archaeology. His passion for these subjects was infectious, and he had an uncanny ability to make us see the enchantment in the world around us. He took us on virtual journeys to ancient sites, painting vivid pictures with his words. His classroom was adorned with small relics, each with its own captivating story. He regaled us with tales of his own adventures, making archaeology feel like the greatest treasure hunt imaginable. Professor Lazenby was not just a teacher; he was a guide to uncharted territories, making the study of history and ancient civilizations an exhilarating quest for knowledge.

As you read this, reflect on your own journey in education. Think of the educators who shaped your life. Do you remember them for what they taught be it the quadratic formula and or the periodic table? Probably not. You remember them for their human connection. How they sparked your learning, how they motivated you to think, inquire, or discover. Or how they affirmed, supported, and nurtured.

The Future Is So Bright I Have to Wear Shades

Collaborating with educators in my capacity as a tech leader in education often transports me back to my days as a classroom teacher. The thrill of discovering ChatGPT brought back memories of my initial fascination with the Macintosh. It was a moment of sheer astonishment, and for a fleeting moment I yearned to return to the classroom.

Having transitioned from teaching, I find myself in a pivotal position in the world of educational technology. I actively promote the promise of AI, focusing on its accessible and ethical adoption by educators and learners. My vantage point has expanded from impacting a singular classroom to influencing a wider education spectrum.

Recognizing the promise of AI, I am guided by a profound sense of purpose. Throughout this book, I have highlighted its potential as a transformative force in education, one that can elevate educators' capabilities and enrich students' learning experiences.

We stand on the precipice of a new educational era—the AI Revolution. With these technological advancements, the possibilities for personalized learning, real-time feedback, and global collaboration are boundless. As we embark on this transformative journey, let us draw inspiration from exceptional educators and their profound impact, for they remind us that the true essence of education lies not in the subjects we teach but in the lasting impressions we leave on young hearts and minds.

But here's the catch – the success of this digital renaissance isn't about the technology; it's about the fearless teacher willing to embrace and engage. It's about the teacher who sees AI not as a threat but as a tool to enhance their teaching prowess. It's about the teacher like Mrs. Feuerstein, Mr. Griffiths, or Professor Lazenby, who would understand that technology is simply a medium. The true essence lies in the human touch, the spark of curiosity, and the power of connection.

If you've read this far, I know you are the type of teacher who is instilling deep and lasting influences on your students Now ask yourself: Is it possible you can employ AI tools to focus your personal and very humanly gifts and elevate your lasting impact on those needing your touch? How can you weave in the magic of technology with the age-old art of storytelling, compassion, and connection?

The Eternal Flame of Teaching

With every advancement, be it the chalkboard, the overhead projector, or now, artificial intelligence, the essence of education has always remained unchanged. It's about lighting the flame of curiosity, nurturing minds, instilling values, and crafting futures.

It's the teacher who discerns when to let technology take the lead and when to interject with a personal touch. The tools may evolve, but the art of teaching – the ability to inspire, to motivate, to connect – is eternal.

Embracing the new while cherishing the timeless values of empathy, curiosity, and passion, the world of education embarks on a journey the likes of which we have never seen before. It is indeed a dawning – bright, promising, and filled with hope.

So, as we stride into this promising future, let's not forget the lessons from our past. Mrs. Feuerstein, Mr. Griffiths, Professor Lazenby, and countless others remind us that at the heart of every transformative learning experience is not an algorithm but a compassionate, dedicated teacher. AI should and will open bold new horizons, but it's you the engaged teacher who will guide every Deshonda or Austin to them.

Because in the end, it will always be about the teacher.

Appendix: Who Wrote This Book?

The answer to that question is, "well, me, of course." My name is on the book cover. I am writing this very paragraph. But the creation of this book is more nuanced than just a single author's endeavor. In essence, ChatGPT has been my co-author, or at least my ever-eager graduate assistant.

My approach to writing was methodical yet creative. I would consider a topic, sketch out a chapter's framework, and then turn to ChatGPT to find the facts or propose the key points. To ensure the book reflected my voice, I engaged the technique of "using my style." I would insert segments into ChatGPT that I had written on my own and that exemplified my writing style. I would ask ChatGPT to analyze and describe this style so I could use it in future prompts. The process required experimentation, a dance of sorts with the technology, until the prompt worked well, and the page began to capture the essence of my voice. Once satisfied, at the beginning of each writing session with ChatGPT, I would use this refined prompt.

Editing became a collaborative effort. I would shape and mold the content, ensuring it sounded authentically like me, then pass it back to ChatGPT for finishing touches in editing, spelling, and grammar. This synergy was not just effective but also a time-saver. Like most of you, I have a day job too, and finding the time to pen every word personally would have been an impossible task.

Now, does this make ChatGPT a co-author? In my view, no, but it certainly opens a conversation in AI ethics. Should the contribution of AI be disclosed? I think so, especially given that this book revolves around AI. However, it raises broader questions: Should an author writing about historical events, like Age of Enlightenment, acknowledge AI assistance? We do not typically see authors citing Google for information discovery. Similarly, tools like Word or Grammarly are rarely acknowledged for their role in co-writing. Nor is the role of a copy editor often highlighted, yet all these elements are crucial in the book creation process.

These considerations are not just academic; they touch upon the evolving relationship between human creativity and AI assistance. While I stand as the primary author, the role of ChatGPT in this project has been indispensable. This collaboration symbolizes a new frontier in authorship, where human thought and artificial intelligence converge to create something unique – a testament to the transformative power of technology in engAIging human potential.

Who Created the Artwork in This Book?

Once again, the answer is me. But as Paul Harvey would insist, there is "the rest of the story." I am not an artist in the conventional sense, or in almost any sense. In fact, my high school students would howl at my poorly drawn stick figures depicting major historical events. But what I lack in artistic skill, I make up for with the ability to craft compelling prompts. Using my prompts and the AI-driven creativity of Midjourney, we have together produced the incredible, colorful art featured in this book. If you are reading the black and white version of this book, I urge you to visit our website, engaiged.ai, to see these images in vibrant color.

Creating this artwork was not as simple as it might seem. As I discussed in the chapter on AI graphic programs, these tools are still in their early stages. They excel at creativity, photorealism, and cartoon-like imagery but struggle with precision, especially with human faces and body parts. It probably took twenty to thirty prompts for each picture in this book to align with my imagination. And yet, even after that, peculiarities exist.

If you examine the images closely, you will notice abnormal faces or unexplained figures in the backgrounds. Trying to direct Midjourney to correct specific details, like removing an extra eye from a character, often led to more confusion than clarity. I chose not to remove these oddities through Photoshop; instead, I kept them to show the authentic results of the AI's interpretation of my prompts.

These artworks, besides enriching this book, have a life beyond these pages. I can use these on our website, in blogs, and interestingly, as NFTs (Non-Fungible Tokens). Midjourney's license allows paid members to use the images they create for NFTs, which is considered commercial use. This opens up intriguing possibilities in the digital art world. However, much like authorship and AI, navigating the complexities of AI art, copyright, and intellectual property will be daunting. Maybe someone should write a book about all of this.

Printed in the USA
CPSIA information can be obtained
at www.ICGtesting.com
CBHW060151261024
16402CB00018B/297

9 781962 987851